Wheeler has killed. A dozen times he's killed. He didn't get to choose his victims. He didn't know how they were picked. As his former masters go on trial for conspiracy to murder, Wheeler is watching. All he needs to do is protect his new identity and stay out of the crosshairs of Det.-Sgt. Roger Hickey, who is determined to find the one who got away.

But even the best-laid plans can go awry.

Clueless
Copyright © 2019 V.V. Drummond
ISBN: 978-1-4874-2648-4
Cover art by Martine Jardin

Published by eXtasy Books Inc or
Devine Destinies, an imprint of eXtasy Books Inc

Look for us online at:
www.eXtasybooks.com or www.devinedestinies.com

CLUELESS

BY

V.V. DRUMMOND

DEDICATION

The author is grateful to John Hill, for his excellent advice about legal and courtroom procedure, and to Jon Bradbury, for his attentive editing.

CHAPTER ONE

Looking across the peaceful valley of olive trees and vineyards, Wheeler asked himself again what did he really know about Malvolio. That he was devilishly good at Italian skittle pool, he knew that. They'd played *cinque birilli* often enough at that bar in Toronto's Little Italy between jobs, Malvolio sometimes letting him challenge but always making sure he saved something clever to put the game away, like a *masse* shot on the castle.

The only other thing he knew was that the man had always been particular about Castelventrano olives, even placing orders in the old days for direct shipments from home. And that was what had brought Wheeler here on nothing more than a hunch, to the Belice river valley in the province of Trepani in western Sicily. The Castelventrano olive was most famously grown here.

Wheeler had put his odds of finding Malvolio on that slim evidence at maybe a hundred to one, a needle in an Italian haystack. But his exile was coming to an end and he knew he had a question that only Malvolio could answer.

How do I get away with murder?

The warm air smelled faintly of almonds and fennel but what held Wheeler's attention were the legions of gnarled olive trees standing sentinel on the far hill, arrayed in haphazard rows, their thick trunks frozen in bizarre twisted shapes as if they'd been storm-tossed for centuries and suddenly commanded to stop. His Sicilian driver referred to them as Saracens, inherited from the Arab rule in Sicily in the ninth

1

century, meaning these ones were probably hundreds of years old and still productive. In a few weeks nets would be spread at their feet and the olives picked by hand. The trees reminded him of Malvolio, the venerable, worldly-wise warrior who had taught him so much. He, on the other hand, was more like the young green vines staked in neat rows in other fields in the valley, their grapes not yet bearing any vintage.

"Salaparuta," the driver said, pointing to the collection of buildings they could see across.

Wheeler thought perhaps he had lucked out, his hunting instincts paying off against the long odds. In a few minutes he would know for sure, over there in that little village.

Even though they'd once been student and teacher, Wheeler had never known Malvolio's real name. Mafiosi, he knew, usually retired to their birth towns but a man like Malvolio, a killer with a past, would not want to use his mob name here. Wheeler had flown in from Rome nonetheless and within two days had found a bar in Castelventrano where old men played skittle pool.

He told two of them in halting Italian that he was looking for someone their age who spoke good English, a big man but light on his feet. "You would know him by the way he plays with a special left-handed spin, the kind that gives him advantages with the *battente* when snookered."

"This man," the one who looked like he had old knife scars on his face asked. "Tell us why you want to see him?"

"A friend from the old days," Wheeler said. "Toronto."

Scarface gave him a long, hard look. He conferred silently with his friend, who gave Wheeler an even colder glance. They made him wait for his answer.

"There is such a man, named Colletti. Lives near Salaparuta, where he tends his olives and keeps a stall in the market behind the church on Sundays."

Church bells were ringing across the valley, signalling the end of Sunday mass. Salaparuta had been destroyed in an earthquake in 1968 but was rebuilt half-way down the hill, so all the sharp-angled new buildings now gleamed like implants on the lower jaw of Salaparuta while the upper featured just the decayed stumps of the old, medieval structures too badly damaged to be worth restoring. Many in the town of 1,800 probably knew of the earthquake only by what they could discern in the devastation it left behind, up there on the heights, where the biggest stump was a crumbling, abandoned castle, still sitting watch over the valley.

Will Malvolio know I am coming? Did those men in the bar send word that someone from away was looking for him?

"I suppose you wouldn't go looking for Mafiosi in this valley, would you?" Wheeler asked jokingly as his driver turned the Fiat down a wounded road.

The man stared back at him in the mirror. "No, my friend. Sicilians are clannish and territorial, and they look after their own. *Stranieri* looking for them are especially marked, since they might have old grudges to settle."

Wheeler knew he had no choice. While it was dangerous looking up *soldatos* like Malvolio in Sicily, it was not as dangerous as what awaited him back in Toronto—those detectives who must be on his trail, or the woman he made the deal with who knew him that other way.

The market was crowded, with many people still in their church finery. Stalls teemed with grappa, olives, zucchini the size of a child's arm, pasta, grains, and artichokes still attached to their long stalks. Wheeler strolled once around the small square, then once the other way, but he did not find an olive stand presided over by Malvolio. He stopped at a food vendor and waited in line for what seemed like the most popular choice for breakfast, something that looked and tasted like veal, deep fried and infused with risotto balls. He ate it with his fingers off a paper plate, standing up like everyone else.

He thought how improbable it was that Malvolio could be found here. For years, he'd been chief enforcer of the Mafia in Toronto and Buffalo, a grim and efficient killer with an iron-clad *modus operandi*. He'd turn up for work in two-thousand-dollar suits and always seemed to be immaculately groomed and impeccably mannered. Only those flinty eyes and ice-cold demeanor gave away his sinister purpose, that look he must have reserved for his victims as he placed the barrel of a pistol against their temple.

Wheeler had been running errands for the loan sharks and Malvolio had taken a liking to him, used him to procure and run his guns across the border. Wheeler learned the assassin's rules along the way. One of them was how not to get caught, but he'd been unlucky at the border that once. By the time he got out of prison, Malvolio was retired. He wondered if the old man had any inkling that his protege had put his assassin's skills to such use.

Perhaps, Wheeler thought, he was being watched, not by the churchgoers or plainly clothed locals milling among the stalls but by harder eyes. If Malvolio was here, if he wasn't at a stall but somewhere in the shadows watching for him, he might be accompanied by men of a more menacing nature.

Right then, he felt a hand rest gently on his shoulder.

"Ah, so it's you, *Cavalletta*. Do you find that you enjoy our *arancina*, then?"

He didn't turn around. His attention was fixed on two men, one at 10 o'clock, the other at 2 o'clock, who seemed to be interested in him, too. But their attention only lasted for an instant. Perhaps Malvolio gave them the clear, because they quickly disengaged and became two more shoppers.

"Greetings, *Insegnante*," he replied then, half turning to his old friend. "You were expecting maybe someone else from your past?"

The old man snorted and enveloped him in a gruff hug, crushing him to his chest. Malvolio smelled faintly of brine and wore a dark Sicilian peasant's cap with a scarf loose around his neck. The craggy face was familiar but older, deeply lined and etched by the sun and now split in an uncharacteristic grin. It had been five years since they'd seen each other and he wondered which was the real Malvolio — this jovial, bandy-legged peasant or that dapper, icy-eyed assassin. *Insegnante.* He had always called Malvolio *teacher*, out of deep respect for the man who had passed on his tradecraft. To Malvolio, he had always been *Cavalletta,* the Grasshopper, from that old *Kung Fu* show.

Malvolio squeezed his shoulder again, affectionately, signalling that he approved of the firmness he felt there. "*Cazzo!* You have grown into such a man!" Wheeler smiled but he knew his gym muscles were no match for the thick arms and shoulders of the older man, who must have built them harvesting olives from centuries-old trees and back-breaking farm work on the craggy and unforgiving slopes of Mount Etna. Always a calculating and precise man, Malvolio, well into his sixties now, had managed to save enough of his life so he could harden his hands in the soil here, much like his ancestors had done for centuries. Wheeler, more than thirty years younger, felt that his future was much less certain.

On the drive back to Castelventrano, he told Malvolio the story he probably wanted to hear first — how he had decided to detour here to search for him. It was a good story. Rome had been his last stop on the way home to Toronto, and to pass the time he'd taken a day-long guided tour of the Vatican. In St. Peter's Basilica, he'd been drawn to the magnificent statuary of Bernini, and in particular to the niche that contained the sculptor's tribute to his mentor, Pope Urban VIII. Below the bronze figure of the pope was a white female figure of justice holding a sword, and Wheeler of course had associated that with the medallions of Lady Justice that Mandamus had made him leave at the scenes of his crimes, that had nearly been his undoing.

But there was more about the monument that fascinated him. Bernini used a skeleton to represent death for the first time on that statue, a grim reminder that all humans, even a pope who had been born into privilege as Maffeo Barberini, were destined to die.

That was when he knew he had to try to find his old mentor.

Malvolio took in the story with relaxed good humour. "So," he said finally, as he waved left at a crossroads for the driver to follow the sign for Castelventrano, "*figlio di troia,* you came to find me because you were suddenly struck with the idea that you will die someday . . . and you think I can tell you how to prepare for it?"

Wheeler laughed. "Nothing so grand as that, *Insegnante,*" he said. "Some other kinds of advice perhaps. Tell me. Where are we going?"

Malvolio said he lived near Montevago, a few miles into the hills on the other side of Castelvantrano, but that they'd stop for lunch in Castelventrano.

"Italians sometimes call that statue you saw the *memento mori* monument, you know," Malvolio said after they'd driven a few kilometres in silence. "It can mean many things."

Of course, there were features of Urban's monument that carried other messages, much as the parables of Homer often wrapped the truth in enigmas. The carved stylized bees, for instance, that playfully adorned the sword of Justice. Bernini also carved them across the magnificent canopy covering the nearby tomb of St. Peter, and elsewhere in the vast basilica — even outside, in various squares and fountains of Rome.

Those flourishes, inspired by the industrious bees on the Barberini family coat of arms, could make you forget that Urban's rule was marked by rampant nepotism. Cynics likened those bees to the relatives of the pope who flew in swarms from Florence to Rome to suck the honey out of the church, unpious men who Urban made prefects and cardinals. That pope, for all his attention to art and beauty, was also infamous for making Galileo recant.

Wheeler thought how he should approach this. "When I went to prison for your gun," he asked, "did you wonder what happened to me?"

"Of course. But you understand that I couldn't come. And I was gone before you got out."

Wheeler looked at him. "No, I didn't mean that. I meant . . ." He paused. "All that you taught me, *Insegnante*, did you not think I might use it?"

Malvolio looked at him with a more serious and fixed expression now. They were entering the outskirts of Castelventrano, a town of 30,000 with a maze of one-way streets designed as carefully as a labyrinth to funnel traffic to its centre.

"Ah," Malvolio said. "Then that's a much bigger subject, *Cavalletta,* and one that should probably be considered discreetly and most definitely after lunch."

They parked and Malvolio led him to a table in the grandly named *Trattoria di Sant Arcangelo*, which was actually a simple place with a dozen tables and no printed menu. The waiter, who Malvolio introduced as Massimo, the son of the owner, listed the dishes of the day and Malvolio ordered in rapid Italian. Soon the small table was filled with plates containing eggplant in tomato sauce, sheep cheese and bruschetta and, of course, Malvolio's favourite, his green, nutty, buttery Castelventrano olives which he said should be eaten with the local black bread.

"You will be interested in this place," Malvolio said, pointing to the stairs. "A somewhat famous Mafia *capo* once got popped up there. Back in the nineteen forties, I think. A bad but careless man, wanted for the murder of several *carabinieri*, he was cornered here when it used to be a brothel. Being Italian, you understand, the police allowed him to finish whatever he was doing. Then they rushed in and cut him down. *Morto*. Massimo and I could show you the holes still in the plaster!"

The appetizers were followed by ravioli with artichokes for Malvolio and, for Wheeler, at Malvolio's suggestion, the special of the day, omelette with ricotta and breaded cutlet. It was delicious and far more authentic than what he'd been served at his hotel.

Over the meal, Malvolio explained that Castelventrano was a farming town, not so much a tourist town, so they could talk about anything so long as they talked in English. The town, he said, had a history of Mafia chieftains who had managed to elude the law. The current one, Matteo Messina Denaro, was a mythical figure who'd been a fugitive for 25 years. He was responsible for killing at least 50 people, making him one of the most-wanted criminals in the world. Supposedly Denaro was the hand-picked successor of legendary Mafia boss Bernardo Provenzano, who'd also been a fugitive for more than 30 years and who was said to have named Denaro in one of his *pizzini*. Malvolio explained that *pizzini* are small slips of paper wrapped in sticky tape that Mafia leaders traditionally use to communicate among themselves to avoid telephone conversations.

"Denaro, you understand, is almost never talked about in Castelventrano," Malvolio said in a conspiratorial whisper. "But he wields unquestioned power behind the scenes and relishes his nickname, Diabolik, which he took from an uncatchable Italian comic book hero. His most famous saying is,

I filled a cemetery all by myself."

"Tell me," Wheeler asked. "Does he live humbly or does he, shall we say, enjoy the fruits of his power?"

"Why do you suppose I know him?" Malvolio asked. "I am retired, *Cavalletta.*" He gave a sly wink. "But yes, I am told that he does not live like a monk."

"This Denaro," Wheeler said. "Surely he must know about you, perhaps from time to time think that you could be useful to him with your experience."

Malvolio shook his head. "The Mafia has changed here. It's changed everywhere. What I was good at is no longer in demand. Denaro and his people would rather intimidate someone in their debt, such as by threatening family members. A dead debtor, you see, is not a good debtor. He can never pay you back. And priorities have changed. Instead of collecting protection money, Denaro's people invest in things like shopping centres and food distribution companies, those wind farms we saw driving here, agriculture. They earn their money where it can be laundered for them, *Cavalletta.* They have learned much about capitalism."

Malvolio signalled with a wave of his hand that Massimo should add the bill for lunch to his tab and gathered up his things. "Come, now I will show you the little farm I left, all those years ago, so I could come to Toronto to kill people for a living."

When they got there, to a modest tiled-roofed cottage on a bald hill just outside Montevago, Wheeler met the woman who'd stayed behind in Sicily to look after the farm for all those years, the tiny, round, smiling Vittoria Colletti, who greeted him sweetly and showed off a cluster of rich grapes she'd just harvested from the vines behind their place. Malvolio's wife did not speak English so the tour of their house was punctuated with eager nods of approval and smiles, especially when she showed him the one bedroom, where she had presumably slept alone for those 20 years her husband was away.

After that, it was Malvolio showing him around his land, three hectares teeming with 500 olive trees and arcades of dangling grapevines. The grapes were sent away for crushing into a decent Chardonnay but they harvested the olives themselves, picking them early, Malvolio said, because healthy young olives keep all their vitamins inside and make the best oil. Interspersed with the olives were small orchards of avocados, oranges, figs and lemons as well as assorted herbs and organic vegetables.

The secret of olives, said Malvolio, lies in the curing. "It's like fermentation," he said. "Only you convert the olive's natural sugars into lactic acid. Bite into a just-picked olive, it's bitter. When properly cured with brine, the harsh-tasting phenols get leached out and you have the classic meaty Castelventrano taste. *Delizioso!*"

Later, when they'd settled into chairs on the front porch and sipped wine served by Vittoria, Malvolio asked, "So, *Cavalletta*, I suppose it is time. What is it you came so far to ask me?"

Wheeler hadn't noticed a computer in the house and he doubted Malvolio had any other channels for recent news from Toronto.

"I don't suppose you've heard of something called Mandamus," he asked.

Malvolio shook his head.

"It was a secret society of lawyers in Toronto, some really top lawyers actually, who were apparently concerned that the justice system wasn't working very well. Bad people were walking free. Or if they were caught and convicted, they served short terms and lapsed back into crime. Mandamus saw criminal justice as a revolving door and they decided to do something about it, something extreme, to send a message.

Mandamus, in case you don't know, is a legal term and their motto was *Vengeance is Mine,* and that's how I came into the picture. They obviously needed someone like me."

"So, the vengeance was actually yours then, *Cavalletta.*"

"I killed people for them, yes. People they decided needed to die."

Malvolio took another sip of wine and swished it around in his mouth thoughtfully. "And so, how much of that did you do? And how did they find you?"

Wheeler did what anyone would do, he answered the easier question.

"I learned how much later," he said. "A retired judge drew the lawyers into Mandamus. He happened to be the judge who'd sentenced me, who had asked me again and again who the gun was for and who had hired me to run it across the border. Of course, I never said a word. I guess when I got out, he tracked me, and I was out for maybe a week when I got the call. Not from him, of course, from someone else. At first, they made it sound as if it might be just for one job, and the money was good. What else was I going to do, fresh out of prison?"

"And?" Malvolio asked. "How often did you work for them?"

"A dozen times," he said. "Or rather eleven at their direction. The twelfth was for me to get away."

"This is over then?" Malvolio asked after a long pause. Wheeler wondered how many people Malvolio had killed. *Might the student have approached his master?* But he saw no sign of a reaction that way.

"They were all arrested. It made huge news three months ago. You wouldn't believe who some of those lawyers were, *Insegnante.* Powerful, highly respected, rich people. The scandal was epic."

"And you, *Cavalletta,* I suppose you are now on the run?"

He shook his head. "I don't think so. The judge is dead. His successor, one of the lawyers, also knew me." He made a slashing gesture across his throat. "He was my number twelve. The arrests of the others, they came a few days later. It's not clear how they were found out but there were hints that at least one of the insiders must have been careless."

"But someone was dealing with you, directing you . . ."

Again, Wheeler smiled. "Only that lawyer I had to kill."

"No one else?"

"No, no one else." But he said it a little too quickly, and Malvolio fixed him with a long, level stare.

"For certain, or so far as you know?"

He shrugged. "Yes, as far as I know."

Malvolio raised an eyebrow.

Wheeler then told him that his three-month exile had taken him to Thailand and Australia and Turkey and Italy and if anyone had any inkling about his identity, he'd certainly have been stopped by now.

Malvolio nodded his agreement. "But you are going back. Why exactly?"

Wheeler explained that the money he'd allotted for his getaway was running out and he had to find some work back home, perhaps under an assumed identity. He was travelling under his real name, not Wheeler, which was the name Malvolio had given him, and his real name had a prison record attached to it that would get in the way. Did Malvolio have any advice?

"So, you're asking me what you should do now, *Cavalletta*. But it seems you have already decided."

Wheeler nodded, then smiled, waving his hand at the groves of olives. "Let's just say I'm looking for life lessons from a notorious *capodecina* who, against all odds, was successful in avoiding detection and now is living out his old age in peace and quiet."

"Understand this. You are unwise to go back," Malvolio

said.

Wheeler shrugged. "Perhaps I could find some work with our old associates. Perhaps you could give me a recommendation."

"*Affatto!*" Malvolio said. "The Calabrians have taken over everything! They've just about pushed the Sicilians out of Toronto."

The Calabrian N'drangheta, he explained, operated around the world but their richest and most powerful arm was believed to be the Siderno group in Toronto—seven families who came from Reggio Calabria on the southern mainland of Italy across the Strait of Massina from Sicily. They're into drugs and gambling and wash the illegal money by investing in bars and restaurants.

"Toronto is not like it was when Sicilians controlled it," Malvolio said. "Organized crime, like everything else, has gone multicultural. There are Chinese Triads and Jamaican gangs, Hell's Angels and Satan's Choice, all taking their share. The old people, those who might remember you, are all retired like me. Retired and living in Woodbridge, *Cavalletta*."

"Ah, then you're saying we can't make a marriage," Wheeler said solemnly, deliberately using mob-speak for *no possibility of an arrangement.*

"What was that song? Mama put my guns in the ground, I can't shoot them anymore?" Malvolio was quoting the lines from the old Guns 'n Roses hit that they used to joke about back in the day. He supposed Malvolio wanted to tell him that, if he was stupid enough to go back to Toronto, he'd better be smart enough to find some other line of work.

"They'll be looking for the gun, my friend. Don't let them find the gun."

Part of his reason for going back, Wheeler knew, was so he could be in a position to follow the police investigation and what was bound to come out eventually at the trial of the

Mandamus lawyers. The investigation to find the missing trigger man would of course be ongoing, and sooner or later that might include a review of Mr. Justice Samuel Leishman's cases, particularly anything to do with gun crimes. His name would come up in that, Wheeler expected, and police would want to question him. If they found he had fled the country, he would become a prime suspect. Otherwise, he was reasonably certain he could throw them off the track and that no other fingers would point his way.

"Okay, so tell me this then," he asked Malvolio after a short pause. "How should I go about changing who I am?"

The Sicilian Mafia had once been good at that, Malvolio told him. Malvolio himself had assumed several fake identities while doing his work, because of course he had become notorious as the Cosa Nostra enforcer. Names and identities needed to be created for ownership and loans to set up those fake businesses to launder drug and gambling money. "We used someone called The Mormon. He had a site on what's known as the Deep Web. I'm sure you could pay someone to find him for you."

Like most people, Wheeler had only heard of something called the Deep Web, supposedly a world of Bitcoins and alternate browsers that anonymized behaviour through layers of encryption. Its black markets dealt in stolen electronics, exotic drugs, sex, assault rifles, new identities—just about anything you wanted under the table.

"After you buy a new birth certificate and social insurance number, say, you can do the rest yourself," Malvolio said. "Passport, driver's license, bank account. No credit cards though. You must pay in cash for everything after that. And your appearance and your habits. You need to change them. Wear glasses. Cut your hair differently. Don't run around with the ladies . . . you were always too good at that, my friend. You need to find a wife and lead a much more boring life."

Malvolio took a moment to let that sink in.

"You need to become someone so different that I wouldn't have a hope of finding you, if I tried," he said. "Or at least not as easily as you managed to find me."

Malvolio held up his finger to make an additional point. "I need to read you something, about the other thing, that *memento mori* you wonder about." He struggled out of the comfortable chair and disappeared into the house. A few minutes later he wandered back, holding a book. Wheeler had seen the large bookcase in the bedroom but hadn't bothered to look at the titles. Surprisingly, and Malvolio could always surprise him, this book was Sophocles, *Oedipus the King*. He leafed through the pages and found the passage he was looking for.

Let every man in mankind's frailty
Consider his last day, and let none
Presume on his good fortune until he find
Life, at his death, a memory without pain.

"A good death," Malvolio said. "Preparing for it is what a life is about. This is one of the earliest mentions in literature of *memento mori*." He smiled. "Twenty-five hundred years old, and we haven't managed to figure it out yet, have we, *Cavalletta*."

Wheeler looked out at his old friend's gently swaying olive trees and peaceful property, heard the silence that rolled down the hills.

"I think perhaps you have found it," he said. "Perhaps it's always been right here for you, hasn't it?"

There was more than a little sadness in the answer, and Wheeler thought that maybe Malvolio was tired or feeling the effects of the wine, or perhaps he was thinking back to his old life in Toronto in his thousand-dollar suits, and what he had to do there.

"We spend most of our lives justifying ourselves to others," he answered. "With luck, we can leave enough time to justify ourselves to ourselves." Malvolio looked at him then, traces of a tender smile on his face. "I hope you manage to find a life without pain, too, *Cavalletta*. You seem to have a little more time left than I to do that."

Later, just before dusk made the way back to Castelventrano uncertain, Malvolio hugged Wheeler fondly, and he and Vittoria waved goodbye as his driver pulled out of their rutted laneway onto the paved road. He would make his travel arrangements in the morning—tomorrow, he decided, being his last day as Wheeler and the first day of his life as someone else, someone with no past but with the hope of a future.

Of course, on the way he wondered something else—whether Malvolio's advice for him might have been different if he'd told him the whole truth.

Sicily, he knew, had a long and unhappy history with deception. Wheeler remembered that it was on this island that Ulysses was supposed to have met the cyclops. Greek mythology figured strongly in the tangled history of Sicily, and the hero of the *Odyssey* landed here in Homer's epic. The cyclops were cannibalistic giants with one eye, blacksmiths for the god of fire, who lived in caves near Etna. In the story, Ulysses and his men unknowingly took refuge in one of the caves and were discovered by a fierce, one-eyed cyclops who took them prisoner and planned to eat them. Ulysses knew the monster could not be beaten by force so he resorted to guile. His men gathered grapes and concocted a wine that they presented as the nectar of the gods. The cyclops drank it and fell into intoxicating sleep, allowing Ulysses to drive a stake through his eye, blinding him. Ulysses and his men escaped but were unwise enough to taunt the cyclops from the safety of their ship. In revenge, the cyclops placed a curse and for the rest of his voyage Ulysses incurred the wrath of Poseidon.

Wheeler hoped that was no omen. Where he was going, there would be no margin for error.

CHAPTER TWO

Toronto, Ontario, three years later

Six glossy photographs were pinned across the end wall of the small meeting room, showing well-coiffed men smiling smugly and dressed in expensive suits and tailored ties. They could have been posing for corporate appointment notices in the *Globe and Mail's* Report on Business. But to Hickey, they were imposters, men who'd pledged to do the right thing but did the opposite, criminal suspects who seemed every bit as deceitful and dangerous as soldiers who raise a white flag as they come forward to surrender, then open fire on their opponents.

Very different photos were posted directly underneath, grainy police mug shots of the same men, showing them unshaven and unsmiling, dressed in t-shirts and rumpled dungarees, standing in front of green-painted concrete walls where they'd been rousted late at night. Hickey liked these photographs better—Suspect Balfour, Suspect Terwilliger, Suspect Hodge, Suspect Carson-Whyte, Suspect Burnside, Suspect Jaccobs. All sixty-ish and white, all previously pillars of Toronto's legal establishment. Six men who were finally about to go on trial in this very building, 3-1/2 years after they'd been arrested, each charged with eleven counts of conspiracy to commit murder.

Three other photographs appeared to one side, people who were certainly part of the plot but unable to be charged. Two were dead — a retired judge, Sam Leishman, who recruited the others into what he called the Mandamus Group, and his successor, Morgan Cathcart, one of Toronto's most distinguished tax lawyers until he'd been found shot, an apparent suicide near his wife's grave. A subsequent investigation pointed instead to homicide. His killer was unknown.

The third photo wasn't of a person. It was just a profile of a man's head. At least they assumed it was a man. This was the one who got away, the trigger man the group had supposedly hired to do their dirty work. Someone had playfully scribbled *Jolly Roger's Obsession* in magic marker underneath.

To quote him exactly, Det.-Sgt. Roger Hickey had said something else, looking at the images of the lawyers being put up on that wall, "Someone pulled all those triggers, and it sure as hell wasn't any of these sanctimonious gimps."

Hickey was a veteran detective for the Toronto police cold cases unit, and the man who first noticed similarities in unsolved deaths that had been investigated separately. He would be the prosecution's key witness in the trial, which the tabloid *Toronto Sun* had dubbed *the trial of the century*.

The *war room*, as Chief Prosecutor Sheldon Maddow called it, was one floor above the courtroom at 391 University Avenue where the trial would take place. The room had been set up to prep witnesses and keep the complicated case organized. Listed below each pair of photographs were the names of the witnesses who would testify against them, and below those were brown envelopes into which prosecutors could put notes about the evidence and possible lines of questioning.

On the floor below, a wall had been torn down to amalgamate two courtrooms — the first time that had been done in Toronto. Six glassed-in boxes had been built to accommodate the defendants and extra seats added in the wide gallery to hold the press and the large crowds of spectators that were expected to show up to watch.

"We'll be leading off with you, of course," Maddow, in his shirtsleeves and red suspenders, told Hickey, who'd walked over from his apartment a few blocks away. Since it was Sunday, there were only a couple of clerks and a security guard working besides Maddow. Hickey was short, overweight and fifty-seven, the kind of guy who could walk into a room and not be noticed. He'd been told that was his main investigative weapon—his anonymity. It was easy for felons to forget that his presence was usually contrary to their best interests.

"We want you to take us into the case from the very start, what got you curious and when," Maddow said. They were seated in two chairs facing the photographs.

"The serial numbers on the guns, that's where you want to start?" Hickey asked, and Maddow nodded.

Working cold cases was real detective work, Hickey believed. You never had the crime scene to study, since it was long gone, so you studied the other stuff instead. Sure, all the physical evidence had been gone over carefully by the investigating officers and the hair and fibre people and the medical examiners, but a good cold case officer—and Hickey believed he was one of the best—could sometimes notice patterns that got overlooked the first time. In the Mandamus case, Hickey had examined a gun used by a teenager to commit suicide in his family's garage, a gun whose serial number had been removed, perhaps by acid. Hickey found that suspicious. Why would an anguished teenager contemplating suicide take such a precaution? A couple of months later, he was investigating a drug deal gone bad in which a woman user had been killed—again, a gun had been found at the scene with the serial number burned off. That set Hickey's spidey senses on overdrive, and he went looking for other untraceable weapons found at the scenes of suicides or unsolved homicides. He found nearly a dozen such cases over a two or three-year period. He spent weeks poring through those crime dossiers, looking for any other common denominators—and sure enough, eight or ten of the victims had been involved with either the criminal justice system or some professional regulatory body. They'd either committed a crime or been party to a complaint and had seemingly gotten off lightly.

Maddow was saying that Hickey should maintain a neutral, professional tone in his testimony, avoiding adjectives and speculation, since it was important for the court to trust him as the narrator of the investigation, to understand that the eventual charges against these high-profile lawyers resulted from an airtight and clinical discovery of the facts.

Hickey, though, knew that serendipity had played the bigger role. What he had found were merely interesting similarities, not conclusive evidence that the crimes were linked. His breakthrough moment came when his boss, Jimmy Hurtubise, showed him the letter from that priest, the priest who had apparently heard Judge Sam Leishman's final confession, the priest who was later found dead at a religious retreat called Southdown north of Toronto. It had been listed as a suicide but it was one of the cases Hickey had isolated because the priest had used one of those guns. That's when Hickey knew that he might be dealing with the cover-up of a series of killings, and they had something to do with a retired judge who attended Holy Redeemer Catholic Church.

"When I get to the medallions," Hickey asked, "how much detail do you want me to go into?"

Maddow had said the high-priced defence attorneys the suspects had hired would zero in on any violation of police procedure, and Hickey had cut one corner that might prove troublesome. He'd colluded with a homicide officer pal and had been alerted to some medallions that had been found at the scene of two ongoing investigations. The medallions were etched with a figure of Justicia, the symbol of justice. Cold case officers were supposed to stay away from live investigations.

But the medallions had been a valuable clue, especially when Hickey was shown a mysterious email list the judge's widow discovered in his papers. A logo of that same Justicia figure had appeared at the top of the list, with the motto *Vengeance is Mine.*

Maddow considered Hickey's question for a moment. "I think you're entitled to describe that using, shall we say, a little more emotion." He smiled at his own understatement. "That's when the true nature of the conspiracy sunk in, was it not?"

Hickey nodded.

"Technically, we could be vulnerable on the medallions," Maddow said. "But we want to make a bigger point about them, so don't hold back."

Hickey had worked with Maddow before and liked him. Rangy, ruggedly handsome and six-foot-four, he commanded the courtroom and had been promoted to chief Crown prosecutor at the young age of thirty-six. He was a superstar, rock solid on the law and creative in plotting the strategy and pace of a trial. Hickey knew that Maddow respected him as well. They really didn't need to do an exhaustive walk-through of his testimony.

"Conspiracy," Maddow said, "can be tricky to prove. Lots of moving parts in these cases, for damn sure. But I like our evidence."

Evidence meticulously collected and verified by him. Hickey nodded and accepted the compliment.

"So, tell me, where are you with the other stuff?" Maddow asked, rocking back in his chair and clasping his hands behind his neck, indicating they were about done.

"The Cathcart thing? Now, officially, it's homicide by person or persons unknown," Hickey said, referring to the reopening of an investigation into what had been initially thought to be a suicide in St. James Cemetery. "I suspect that our trigger man killed him, perhaps as a cover-up. Cathcart attended Holy Redeemer, too. He may have been the only one besides the judge who knew the hit man's real identity."

"Yeah, all the others were questioned and said they never knew who," Maddow said. "They kept everything compartmentalized that way."

"So it seems."

"Are you still nowhere on Mr. X?"

Hickey shrugged. "I'll have to take a break from it to testify. Do you think we can get though my part the same day?"

"Count on two at least. There will be cross-examining from all quarters. John Juris will be representing Burnside and you know how thorough he is."

Juris. The man was already a legend in the Toronto bar, famous for winning acquittals in high-profile cases and still sharp as tacks in his early 70s. Hickey never had to face being cross-examined by him in court, but he'd watched him often enough, how his flowing white mane and rumpled silk robes masked a first-rate legal mind that seemed to circle around randomly before stunning a key witness with the kill shot. Juris, senior partner in one of the city's largest law firms, had at his disposal a small army of skilled detectives and legal researchers. Hickey, on the other hand, had only been given one officer very near retirement and an intern to help him look for the assassin, his boss not putting much stock in their chances.

"So what will the defence strategy be, do you reckon?" Hickey asked. He knew the not-guilty pleas all around had initially surprised Maddow, considering how strong the case against the conspirators seemed to be. Hickey had full confidence in Maddow to make the most of the key piece of evidence he had dug up—a clandestine diary of Mandamus meetings, naming names, kept by a seventh conspirator, Carl Barington, whose case had been separated from the others so that he could testify.

Maddow frowned. "They're keeping it under wraps but Juris will take the lead. Think of him as the field general for the defence. If they're smart — and they didn't get their QCs by being dummies — it won't be every man for himself."

"I'm assuming we won't see any of them on the stand, right?"

"Juris will probably put a stop to it if anyone wants to."

"Casting reasonable doubt? Is that what you'd do?"

"The question is what Juris will do. He's always been unpredictable. Either that, or pleading ignorance. Guess we'll find out Tuesday, won't we." Maddow swung his feet so he looked directly at Hickey. "Listen, I know this whole thing is eating away at you. I want the trigger man just as badly, Hick."

Hickey's gout felt more or less benign today so he got to his feet and tapped the picture of Jolly Roger's Obsession. "Remember all those gangland executions back in the nineteen nineties? When the Sicilians were trying to hold onto their turf against the Calabrians?"

Maddow nodded. He'd probably read about it, Hickey thought.

"We're finding similarities."

"What? You mean to our cases?" Maddow asked, raising his eyebrows. "Surely you don't think Cosa Nostra is involved in *this*?"

Hickey shook his head.

"No, not involved, but I'm saying there may be an organic connection. By that I mean the assassin may have once had gangland connections or maybe he's a clever copycat."

"We never had a real line on who the enforcers were back then, did we?"

"No," Hickey said. "But we're scouring old court records, to see if any gun crimes had links to organized crime. Maybe someone got sent away for something, even something minor, and may have appeared before that judge or been represented by one of our bad boys. Sure, I know, it's a long shot, but long shots are what we seem to be down to."

"First time I've ever seen you this way, pal," Maddow said with a grim smile. "Virtually clueless?"

"It's never where I like to be," Hickey agreed. He'd confided in Maddow a couple of months ago when Jimmy Hurtubise mentioned the idea of early retirement to him, said the department was about to offer packages bridging to pension for senior officers over fifty-five. Hurtubise didn't suggest it very strongly, probably had to make the offer to everyone, although Hickey knew Hurtubise had become enough of a bureaucrat to appreciate that cutting the high salaries like his produced the fastest savings. Maddow had agreed with Hickey that they had unfinished business with Mandamus.

"Like, suppose somebody got put on ice for a while and someone in Mandamus thought they could be useful again?" Maddow asked after a moment.

"Yeah, it's possible, it could have happened that way." Hickey made a mental note to get The Squirrel working on that angle, too.

"So, you know we don't need the trigger man to make a case here, right?" Maddow asked.

Hickey wasn't so sure about that. "Look, it haunts me," he said. "You know . . . that the baddest guy of all is still walking free."

Maddow waited a moment to get to his feet. He stretched out his hand to shake Hickey's. "Here's to Tuesday then," he said. "My usual warning, okay? No media, under any circumstances. We've got Ezra Foley for this trial and he's a stickler on contempt."

"Okey dokey, boss," Hickey said, smiling.

"Oh, and about your search for the shooter?" Maddow asked. "I don't think we want to go there at trial. We want to keep the focus on the plotters."

Hickey shrugged. "That's up to you."

"Finding him, however," Maddow said. "I'd say that's up to you."

Hickey knew the news media in Toronto considered him to be an avenging angel, a skilled and dogged detective right out of *Law and Order*, with an obsession for tying up loose ends. He always got good press, even though he did everything he could to stay anonymous and unavailable. It was one of the consequences of working cold cases in a city like Toronto, which still had five daily newspapers, three main local TV news networks and a host of talk-radio stations. More important to Hickey was the esteem of his fellow officers. He still treasured a comment from Cleverley, his old partner in homicide. "Hick," Cleverley had said, "if I was ever lying there shot, and I saw you looking down at me and knew you were on the case, I think I'd die happy."

On his walk home along streets that were still drab and gray in the early March chill, he picked up a copy of the *Sunday Sun*. Their reporter Pete Smythe would be covering the trial, and he'd told Hickey that his editors wanted a profile of Hickey to run in advance. Hickey had refused to be interviewed for it, but Smythe, he found, had done a fair job of piecing together previously published information. He read it in a coffee shop near Dundas and McCall, and he enjoyed the headline. "If you've done a crime and think you won't do the time, avoid being Hickeyed."

The writer only got one thing wrong—the year his wife died. Barbara had passed in 2009, not 2010.

Hickey changed his mind then and headed north to his office. It would be quiet there, and there was nothing waiting for him at home.

Most people in Toronto didn't know that the city had more than 500 unsolved murders, dating back to 1959. The oldest was a twelve-year-old babysitter who'd been found strangled in a snowbank. Hickey's department was close to solving a dozen of them, aided by breakthroughs in DNA technology and social media. Despite the imminent trial of the six lawyers, Hickey considered their eleven victims' cases to be ones that his department still had to solve, mainly because the actual murderer was at large.

He remembered how Stephanie Lord had peppered him with questions about cold case work when he first interviewed her. Initially, he thought it was because she had a stake in the outcome — her ex-husband had been one of the Mandamus victims. Jason Oosherhuis, wife beater and ex-con, gunned down in a hotel bathtub just a couple of blocks from here on Gerrard. Lately though, Stephanie's interest in him seemed to turn more personal, like she was less interested in the case and more interested in him, like there could be a possible relationship attached to it. That made things complicated. He had always kept a wall up between police work and personal relationships, even when he was married to Barbara, and Stephanie Lord was technically connected to an open investigation. So while he wondered what the nice lady might be up to on a quiet Sunday afternoon, and her apartment was just a few blocks away, he didn't think it would be wise to drop over. She'd already made a date with him to have him over for dinner after court on Tuesday.

Sure enough, there was no one else at police headquarters on a Sunday in the sixth floor office Hickey normally shared with six other detectives. He put his feet up and read the rest of the Sun's eight-page special section on the trial.

I've got to get this guy. For sure I've got to get him.

CHAPTER THREE

On the Internet one day, researching his favourite topic, Wheeler stumbled upon a simple drawing made by a notorious American serial killer. It looked like the imprisoned murderer had painstakingly traced the outline of his right hand with a pencil and then drawn in the fingernails and wrinkles on the knuckles to make it more realistic. He'd mailed off this macabre sketch to a fan signed in crude upper and lower printing, *Hi. Jeff Dahmer 177252.*

Dahmer, of course, was the Milwaukee Cannibal, one of the most notorious serial killers in US history. He liked to boil and retain the heads of his victims and have sex with their corpses. He killed 17 men and boys, a real sicko. Wheeler's research taught him that the crimes of serial killers were often monstrous, but the killers themselves were unremarkable. They often had families and homes, were gainfully employed, and seemed like normal members of the community. Dahmer, for instance, was so harmless the Milwaukee police unwittingly returned one of his victims to his care.

Wheeler's interest, naturally, was in how serial killers got caught. In Dahmer's case, it was largely an accident. One of his victims escaped and was seen running down a street screaming with a pair of handcuffs dangling from one wrist. *Duh?* Wheeler thought. The victim naturally led police to Dahmer's apartment where they found body parts and severed heads in his fridge, freezer, filing cabinet, even in a kettle. Dahmer, a thirty-one-year-old former chocolate-factory worker with a history of alcohol abuse and pedophilia, confessed and was sentenced to 15 consecutive life terms in prison.

Before he was beaten to death by a fellow inmate in 1994, Dahmer became famous. He eagerly answered fan mail and entertained book offers. TIME magazine summed up the popular fascination with such crimes. "Viewers are fascinated with these stories less for the gory crime details than for the peek they provide into the extremes of human psychology. We watch to be reassured these people are monsters, not at all like you and me. And to face the fear that in some basic ways they are exactly like you and me."

That was Wheeler's mission — to appear *exactly like you and me.*

The first part was already accomplished. He wasn't Wheeler anymore.

With some technical help, he'd found Malvolio's Mormon within a week of returning to Toronto and simply purchased a fake identity online for $300 worth of Bitcoins. That gave him a new name, date of birth, mother's maiden name, military service record and a Social Security Number, along with an American passport, birth certificate and bank record. It was all fake, of course, which was why it wasn't illegal to sell. But it was believable since the site contained variations of first and last names drawn from US census data, and matched SSN data to actual states and dates of issue, and drew bank records from institutions that had gone out of business.

At the site's suggestion, he'd enrolled in a couple of courses at York University and used its letter of admission to apply for a foreign student study permit at the Canadian consulate in Buffalo. That gave him legal status in Canada under his new identity and, because so many American students were applying to study in Canada, his information was not checked. He used his credentials to obtain an Ontario driver's license and open a student bank account. He had enough left over to pay cash for a late-model used car.

He burned his old ID and deleted his Facebook and social media accounts. He changed his appearance and habits, too, shaving his hair off and sprouting a stubbly beard, choosing lensless wire-rim granny glasses, tossing his preppy wardrobe for second-hand corduroy jackets and jeans, and making a point to avoid the east end bars where he used to troll for available women, and the Danforth where he used to live.

And, since he was determined to follow Malvolio's instructions to the letter, he'd also acquired a wife, or rather someone who had agreed to pose as one.

When he met F—he called her that from the very start, for some reason, and still did—he didn't suspect she was bisexual. She had the kind of body that men drooled over, and she seemed to enjoy that kind of attention. She certainly seemed to enjoy his. After they hooked up through that online site, she'd let him screw her on the second date. And the sex was terrific.

She was thirty-two and black, had a good job in sales that earned her in the upper five figures. That was appealing to him, too, since the best he'd been able to get for himself was a sales job on commission, worth maybe $30,000 a year if he was lucky. Toronto was an expensive city to live in.

So maybe he rushed it a little when he suggested they move in together, after less than two months of dating. You know, sort of like man and wife, they'd get rings and everything, have a ceremony if she wanted. She had a place at Lawrence and Wilson Heights in North York, a townhouse she rented for less than $2,000 a month. Much to his surprise, she said yes, but first she wanted to talk terms. That was when he found out.

She'd dated a lot, she said, and liked variety. You know, real variety. She'd gone out with lots of white men like him and of course her share of black men, and she'd also, like, dated women, too, she wanted him to know. "Of course I've had sex with them . . . isn't that the whole point?" she asked when he asked. "When a man turns me on, I want to fuck him, but it happens sometimes with women, too, okay?" She said their relationship or marriage could be *poly* or *monogamish*, and it took him some time to process that because they were terms he'd never heard before.

"Is that a deal breaker?" she asked him in bed one night.

He said she sounded like she probably wanted that to continue, right?

She said that was right.

"It means that we'd be a couple in a committed partnership but we'd have this understanding that either of us can have sex with other people."

"Either of us?" he'd asked.

"Sure. Why should I have all the fun?"

That didn't sound appealing at the time. But it definitely had grown on him, since his job was boring and he'd always been fascinated by how easy it was to pick up women.

He accepted what he called her *proposal* because she made a compelling case for the benefits. "It definitely removes the pressure of having to be everything to your partner. And it prolongs the honeymoon. You keep having it . . . that tingling feeling of arousal that comes with doing it with someone new."

They'd been living together for 18 months and didn't have many rules. Don't make any babies, don't bring home a disease. That sort of covered it.

"Who knows?" she asked once. "When you learn the kind of people who really get me hot, you could even bring someone home for me. I could do that for you, too. We could surprise each other that way."

"That sure would keep it interesting," he said.

"If you don't ask for what you need," she said, kissing him. "You'll never get it."

His pro-forma wedding to F at Toronto City Hall provided him with one last piece of ID, a marriage certificate—something he'd need when the time came to apply for Canadian Resident Status.

The great thing about F was, she never asked him very much about himself, even though he seemed to have no friends and never spoke about family. Not that he had much to say about that. Both parents had died on the little farm where he'd been raised in Saskatchewan, and he'd been estranged from his brother for years.

His marital *arrangement* meant he was free to check into a hotel room in the middle of the day, like he'd just done now, on a Sunday, choosing the Chelsea because it was just a couple of blocks from his office. He had F's green light to be with other women, and he'd done that a lot, people he picked up in bars or on the Internet. He'd followed all of Malvolio's other instructions to the letter, but couldn't manage to stay away from the ladies. The difference today, he didn't check in with anyone else but instead came with the weekend editions of Toronto's four main daily newspapers. All had extensive coverage of the trial that was about to begin.

The tabloid *Sun* attracted most of his attention because the front page of its Sunday edition was headlined *Mandamus Six go to trial* in big black headlines. Wheeler read the eight pages of coverage carefully. Most of the stories were written by Pete Smythe, the reporter who had broken the story of the arrests three years before. He was particularly interested in Smythe's profile of the chief investigator, Det.-Sgt. Roger Hickey, because it gave him his first look at the man who was probably hot on his trail. Indeed, the profile ended with this—"As accomplished as Hickey's career solving cold cases has been, he's obsessed with the one who got away, the mysterious trigger man who allegedly carried out the grim kill orders from the lawyers now being brought to justice."

The picture accompanying the profile showed a rather unassuming man with a rumpled cop look who looked old enough to be Wheeler's father.

But there was another line in the story that stopped Wheeler cold. It said Hickey kept a rough sketch of a man who could be the killer, pinned to a bulletin board behind his desk. It was described as a composite pieced together from various sources. It didn't go into details, because Hickey was not quoted in the piece, but Wheeler knew that description was false. Only one person could have given him that information—Rachel Leishman, the judge's widow he had been sent to kill but who had bargained for her life in return for the identity of his Mandamus controller, the lawyer he had executed near his wife's grave in St. James Cemetery.

That was the detail he hadn't given Malvolio. That someone was still alive who knew what he looked like.

There was coverage but no additional detail in the *Globe and Mail*, the *Star* and *National Post*, but there was a rather precious editorial in the *Globe* headlined *Betrayal of trust*. It opined that, "Toronto's legal establishment, hiding for years behind a façade of moral and legal superiority, must now face up to the ugly truth. Some of its most noted celebrities stand accused of betraying the law and the public trust. It is time that our lawyers clean up their own house."

Of course, that was Wheeler's main interest in following the trial so closely—what had pushed them over the edge? What had caused some of the city's finest legal minds to betray their calling and take the law into their own hands? Having taken that same step over the line himself—killing people for profit—he was curious about the cause that motivated his benefactors so diabolically. How did they choose their victims? Why had they changed his instructions to start leaving the medallions near the victims—which probably led to their downfall? But Wheeler had other questions that were equally as urgent. How did he know his new identity would protect him from being tracked down? How could he be sure? He thought often about cutting back on the ladies, if *that* might be his Achilles heel, but he needed his pleasures. F was certainly getting hers, in fact she said to him just the other night that was the beauty of sales jobs, "If you found yourself alone with someone you might never meet again, wouldn't you be tempted to do something about it?"

Wheeler remembered how ballsy that Rachel Leishman had been, down on her knees trussed up in duct tape in her living room staring at his gun, and coming up with that deal to convince him to let her live. It had allowed him to get away without a trace but now he worried she might not have lived up to her end of the bargain.

There was nothing in the newspaper coverage that told him what leads the police might have. He hoped not very many. But his plan to attend the trial in person would have to be shelved, he realized. Police would surely be filming everyone who came to watch, and there was the added possibility that Rachel Leishman, if she was there, might accidentally recognize him. After all, she'd been to bed with him. And she had clearly failed to keep her late husband's name out of the Mandamus business. He guessed that didn't give her much incentive to keep quiet about him now.

Perhaps, he thought, his work as Wheeler wasn't yet over.

CHAPTER FOUR

"Hey there, Professor Van Loon!" a voice chirped, and Gwen stopped and reluctantly turned in the hallway.

They must have been waiting in ambush, she thought, two of the third-year undergrads in her Contemporary Canadian Literature course, two of the not-very-good students standing there in their expensive, distressed jeans and light cashmere sweaters, holding coffees and backpacks. Severinson and Gilchrist. She knew what this was probably about.

"Hi, you," she said with a quick smile. "I'm running late for a faculty meeting. Can you see me later? Office hours at two."

They wouldn't be put off. "We've both got Psych then," Gilchrist said. "We just need a sec of your time, miss. We wonder if you'd be, like, good enough to consider, um, a deferral on the synthesis essay?"

"I think you mean an extension," she replied before they could offer any excuse. She relished her habit of correcting students who used sloppy English.

"Yeah, whatever . . ." Severinson shrugged. She seemed to be chewing gum with her coffee.

"A deferral can mean put in abeyance, and I don't think I'm willing to do that," she told them. The assignment, a synthesis of critical responses to Thomas King's *Green Grass Running Water*, was due on Wednesday, worth 25 percent of the final grade. "Besides, you've seen my policy on extensions in the course outline, haven't you? I'm around until five if you want to drop by later."

They signalled by rolling their eyes. *Guess not.*

But she seethed about it as she continued walking briskly down the hall towards the Department of English office. *Why do students today act so entitled? Why do they think that rules, even firm rules like hers, don't apply to them? Why do they always go to great lengths to try to bend them?* Her course outline was clear—*No extensions on major assignments for any reason, even acts of god.* She intended that last part as a joke but she wondered if students took it seriously, thought of her as some middle-aged disciplinarian with an iron rod up her ass. Or was it possible that erecting all these barriers to entitlement had left her prematurely jaded and cynical about the motivation of students? Which reminded her—Wednesday, the due date, happened to be her birthday.

Finally . . . no, way too soon . . . the big Four Oh.

York University's department of English, part of the Faculty of Liberal Arts and Professional Studies, resided in Stong College, a 14-storey tower on the western campus which was named not for a donor but, quaintly, for one of the pioneer farming families of the area. Gwen was one of 35 full-time faculty, although with classes and sabbaticals only about 20 usually attended the monthly meeting. Alicia Bannon, who was nearing the end of her second term as chair of the department, usually kept attendance down anyway, since she belonged to that breed of academic administrators who still believed in collegiality—the fiction that the academy was designed to plod ahead by managed consensus. This meant that the Monday meetings usually got bogged down in administrivia. On the agenda for today, Gwen knew, was membership in the new chair's search committee and debate on an Admin Vice-President's draft proposal for a new pay scale for teaching assistants.

She wondered if her graduate students, all no doubt convinced they were on the fast track to a job in academia that would furnish them with lifetime security and a cushy pension, knew just how boring their day-to-day existence would be.

Gwen slipped into the room quietly and found the seat that her colleague Geruta Goyko had saved beside her. It was across and comfortably down table from where Gwen's dour ex-husband was sitting. Today Gerald Sessions took no notice of her. He had his head buried in what looked like a budget spreadsheet and didn't bother looking up.

Sharing a faculty table with him was still awkward. It had only been eight months since she'd stumbled on the fact that he was being unfaithful, and possibly for quite a long time.

She'd arrived home early one night from class and found dear old Gerald busily humping a naked, red-haired grad student on their living room sofa. She remembered the surprising sprinkle of freckles across the girl's dancing shoulders and how that initially had distracted her from noticing just how familiarly her husband's hands were jamming her narrow hips down into his lap.

That was enough to end their four years of desultory marriage. Her decision to keep her own name when they'd married proved fortuitous. She didn't need to change her business cards or the nameplate on her office door after the divorce came through.

She'd heard that the girl was still living with him, although she wondered how long *that* would last. Gerald, in her experience, was good enough in bed but it was during the long periods in between that he really wore on you. Even horny-as-hell nympho grad students needed their intellectual stimulation, probably. He had unfortunately affixed his academic career to Dostoyevsky and the Russian existentialists, so the thesis he was supervising with her was probably as dark and colourless as the Steppes in winter and not likely to invite much foreplay.

Bannon chose that moment to call on him. "Professor Sessions? Perhaps you can bring us up to date with our proposed budget rationalization." And Gerald popped his head up and happened to catch Gwen's eye for a moment, giving her his familiar dead-fish look. He'd headed a faculty subcommittee on how to cope with one of the periodic and irritating cutbacks that seemed to come down to the academic departments regularly from Kaneff Tower. Gerald, always one to play a moment for more than it was worth, took 10 minutes to explain how they could save the required amount immediately by closing the student writing lab. The faculty present, in a quick show of hands, agreed, possibly because it was well known that students used the lab, and its excellent printer, not for writing but printing, and usually printing nothing that had anything to do with the study of English. Gwen couldn't quite manage to suppress an uncomfortable thought . . . how she and Gerald had at least one thing in common despite their irreconcilable differences—contempt for privileged students. It was a pity about the extramarital sex.

Bannon then handed out her usual monthly array of memos, administrative policies formulated from on high, academic council minutes and one or two academic papers that English faculty had managed to get published. Gwen took a quick look and couldn't imagine anyone reading this one, entitled "Migration, disillusionment and diasporic experiences in Segun Afolabi's *Goodbye Lucille* and *A Life Elsewhere*," a first effort by one of the young Turks. Her own record of academic publishing had more or less ended with the granting of her tenure two years ago, a long, hard struggle that she had no interest in prolonging. She did the occasional book review for Canadian Literature Review, just to keep her annual report current. She wondered what a noteworthy *diasporic experience* might be, and whether it could be anything like the different lives she and Gerald now led as they distanced themselves from the homeland of their marriage. After all, he could get *his* nightly, if he wanted. She, on the other hand, was manless and likely to stay that way, celibate for almost a year and counting.

She fell into step with Geruta as they left the meeting and decided they had time for a quick coffee. That was another myth of academia—the idea that professors, at their leisure, spent long hours flexing their academic muscles in the company of other scholars, usually over sherry in book-lined faculty lounges. Dr. Geruta Goyko's field was eighteenth-century American poetry, focussing on the work of Rebecca Hammond Lard, which meant they had little to talk about besides faculty politics, and there were no book-lined lounges here, just a drab cafeteria.

"The young Turks were quiet today, weren't they?" Geruta asked, when they settled in at a table by the window.

"I expected one of them to speak up in favour of the student writing room, just to be mulish, didn't you?" Gwen asked. It was generally agreed that the *young Turks*, their derisive term for the new hires, a cohort of associate professors still striving for tenure as their busy lives inched closer to thirty, were more student-centred, certainly less jaded. Gwen and Geruta found themselves in the middle of the age demographic in their department, poised between the Turks and the Grandees, who were the over-fifty-fives, the full professors who enjoyed lighter teaching loads and richer remuneration, especially the few past seventy who hung on for the generous annual increments York awarded, not for merit but for seniority.

Drs. Van Loon and Goyko, drawn together by their age and divorced status, had agreed that the most rewarding career path for them might be to survive long enough to join the ranks of the Grandees, whereupon they might be deemed *in the know* enough to be eventual candidates for departmental chair, a job which could give them what they openly pined for — relief from teaching and an extra stipend.

"I'm mentoring a grad student who's asking me a lot of questions about getting a job here," Geruta was saying.

"I hope you're not encouraging her," Gwen said archly.

The average full-time faculty member at a Canadian university worked a 52-hour week, counting teaching classes, conducting research, supervising grad students and serving on departmental and university committees. Most of the teaching, however, was done by part-time faculty members, called sessionals. Their workloads could be even heavier, usually because many loaded up on teaching to earn enough to get by. Many never made it to tenure track, since all that marking and course prep left no time for research, and university hiring committees tend to overweigh research accomplishments. It also meant that sessionals got to bear the brunt of teaching today's brand of privileged and needy undergraduate, although Gwen was unpleasantly surprised this term when Bannon took away one of her graduate seminars and replaced it with a second undergrad course. That meant she had more than 65 of the little buggers to handle.

It was hard to have a life with a workload like that. That was one reason there tended to be a lot of problematic personal relationships in academe—divorces, affairs, burnout, addictions, depression, you name it. If you were a prof cohabiting with another prof, the way she'd been with Gerald the last four years, your worlds sort of metaphorically bumped into each other, all that time you spent together at the office, in libraries and at home. Familiarity often bred contempt, and it certainly had with them. On the other hand, if one were single and trying to date an outsider, the position she found herself in now, there never seemed to be enough time to find anyone and devote to a relationship. And if things didn't happen to work out, students often knew more than they let on.

Gwen was certain there already were catty jokes about her. "Van Loon and Sessions? They used to be Mr. and Mrs., if you can believe it! What happened was, she apparently caught him privately tutoring one of his grad students on the family couch!"

Their relationship hadn't seemed doomed that way when she'd first met Gerald. He was five years older and already had tenure. She was newly hired and working toward hers. She was flattered he was interested, and allowed him to slide his hand up under her skirt the second time he drove her home. They covered up an affair for two years, then secretly moved in together, finally broke down, got married and let everyone know.

"God, second week in March," Geruta said absently, checking her cellphone for messages. "How many more weeks?"

"Three, I think," Gwen said. "Got plans?"

"Plans? This time of year, I'm too tired!"

"Teaching all those little beasties?" Gwen asked, making them both laugh.

"I'm up for sabbatical in September. You'll vote for me, won't you? Say yes."

"We need to stand together," Gwen agreed. "You'll be back by the time I'm up for mine."

Just another three years away, she thought. On her first sabbatical, she'd promised to crack that research she'd begun on the dark novels of Susan Musgrave. Gwen knew she had to spell out her plans in advance so the faculty could decide which sabbaticals seemed worthwhile, and she'd penciled in a month-long trip to Vancouver to scour manuscripts in the UBC library and interview Musgrave. But of course she'd never gone. Gerald required attention in those early days of their relationship. He let her get away for a short vacation with a female friend in Cuba instead.

She asked Geruta what she planned to do with her year off.

"Oh, I don't know . . . try to establish some kind of normal relationship with you-know-who, perhaps?"

She'd started seeing someone named Zuhair, who she said was a grad student in architecture from Yemen. A professor dating a student was okay at York, providing you were in different faculties and didn't have any direct role in supervising a thesis or a class the student was enrolled in. Geruta had certainly brightened up lately, once showing up at a faculty shout-out wearing what she called a *guntiino,* a decorative fabric worn over the shoulder and tied at the waist. From Yemen or Somalia, she said, a gift from Zuhair. Gwen thought her friend, who was thirty-eight, was trying too hard to look twenty-seven, which was how old she said he was.

"That sounds like a good use of time for you," Gwen said.

"I can hardly remember what it's like to have a real life." Geruta smiled.

Gwen had never met Geruta's ex-husband, who worked in pharmaceuticals as an engineer or biologist and who'd been in the habit of keeping long hours, perhaps in the company of someone else. Geruta had divorced him before Gwen joined the faculty.

"How about you? Still the same?" Geruta asked.

Gwen nodded. "I've got a big birthday coming up," she said, deciding not to answer directly.

Geruta's eyes lit up. "No! Not your fortieth! When?"

"Monday. Say, why don't you come for dinner? I could cook something nice for just the two of us, then we could smoke my water pipe into the twilight."

She could tell before the answer came it wasn't going to be a good idea. "Ah," Geruta said. "Zuhair and I were supposed to . . . look, I can cancel that . . . I'm sure he'd understand."

"No, please don't," Gwen said. "I think I'd actually prefer a quiet night by myself, maybe curl up with a movie."

"Make it porno," Geruta said, looking secretly pleased she

was off the hook. "Be good to yourself."

Geruta Goyko, burdened with a Slavic name and disposition, would probably be hard to live with, Gwen thought. Severely intelligent with a spidery kinetic energy, she made friends quickly, not all of them the right kind. They'd need extra batteries to keep up with her. Excitable, determined and exacting, she'd probably have a long list of dos and don'ts for them to follow in bed. She'd have no trouble getting close sexually but emotionally it would be a challenge. The head ruled her, not the heart. No room for fantasy or pushing the boundaries. She was probably emotionally designed to withstand long periods of drought in her sex life. Gwen sometimes wondered if she might be getting that way, too.

The last time she'd directly asked Geruta about her relationship with Zuhair, she'd said it was "Ardent but probably non-permanent, good enough for now." But she'd apparently let him move in.

Gwen looked at her watch. "Oh look, gotta run, have office hours in a bit."

They each picked up their stacks of faculty handouts. "Most of this is just tonnage, destined for the shredder," Geruta said. "But I was told we need to read the revised Turnitin policy. They're tweaking it again."

When she got to her office one floor down, Gwen was relieved that no one had come early. She had some rare time for herself. She shifted a stack of unmarked essays off her desk to the credenza and found the document Geruta had just told her about. *Revised academic policy for Turnitin,* read the stapled-together pamphlet, bearing the imprimatur of Academic Council.

With the emergence of the Internet, many universities found that various kinds of academic dishonesty had become rampant. Students' ability to cut and paste without attribution, and even copy whole essays verbatim, was suddenly un-limited, and universities scrambled to protect academic integrity, which was what everyone was paying for along with the piece of paper they got at the end of it. Luckily, at just the right time, along came an American company, based in Oakland, California, with an internet-based database that could check documents for purloined content.

At York, it worked this way—students were required to submit all English assignments to Turnitin.com, using a course code and password. Their work was then vetted against a database that had grown to include tens of millions of academic journals, essays, citations and documents. The database detected any similarities in previously published work, and produced a report that was sent to both the student and the faculty member. The faculty member received an additional report, called a similarity report, assigning a percentage to the work that was being called into question. Any percentage over 10 was problematic, although much depended on the faculty member carefully analyzing the results to eliminate excusable copying from the percentage—excusable meaning the student had credited the source in a footnote or may have inadvertently copied part of the assignment. If a violation of academic integrity was suspected, the faculty member sent a letter to the student requiring him or her to attend a meeting, and offered some indication of the nature and extent of the problem. No determination of guilt or innocence was supposed to be made until that meeting took place, nor was any penalty determined until the student had a chance to present a case. If the professor decided that the student likely copied material without credit, it was a serious offence against academic integrity. Plagiarism could result in failure in the assignment, failure in the course, or in some cases expulsion.

Gwen had dealt with a few cases where her student, confronted with the evidence, had acknowledged the problem but claimed the lack of attribution was inadvertent. She had merely failed them on the assignment. She suspected she would have caught those problems anyway, since the quality of writing had been one or two suspicious notches above the student's normal work.

Where use of Turnitin got sticky was if a professor was not convincing in his or her presentation of the evidence, and the student appealed, usually to the department chair. With their academic futures on the line, students tended to pull out all the stops, soliciting phone calls from parents and previous teachers, and of course they were entitled to legal and academic representation at that level, usually from an over-zealous student council representative.

Gwen usually tried to impose her penalties at the lower threshold to avoid appeals. But she saw that the university was now limiting her ability to do that. Anything that fit the definition of plagiarism, the new policy stated, would be punished by failure in the course.

She recalled a recent article in the *Globe and Mail* showing an alarming spike in academic dishonesty at Toronto's three universities. Academia usually reacted only if embarrassed, and she thought it possible that this tougher policy was the result.

Out of curiosity, she turned to her credenza and checked the printout of the similarity report for the latest batch of essays from her other undergrad class, one in first year on Twentieth Century Canadian Feminist Literature.

Oh shit. One of her students looked like he was in trouble, all right.

God, 35 percent! She couldn't remember seeing a score *that* high.

CHAPTER FIVE

The Squirrel—Hickey's affectionate nickname for Du-Wayne J. Burley—made his nest in an unused utility room down the hall and around a corner from Hickey's office. Half of it seemed to be filled with DuWayne and his computer equipment, including the 16-gig MacBook Pro that he'd brought from home and on which he could be heard tapping away any time you passed the door in the hallway. A whiteboard filled the far wall, with colour-coded notes in Du-Wayne's cribbed scribble, and to see it properly Hickey had to stand in the hall with the door open, which he was doing at the moment. Hickey had declared the room out of bounds for the cleaning staff, so it usually smelled of perspiration and Three Musketeers, the candy bars DuWayne liked to wolf down as he worked on the decoding of Mandamus Six.

"Found another connection for you, boss," DuWayne said, leaning back.

Hickey remembered the morning DuWayne walked in for his interview, black as spades, maybe two-hundred-fifty pounds with the dreadlocks and the fucking ring in his ear. Hickey figured he had him pegged. This, he said to himself, has gotta be the HR department token. They'd been told they could expect at least one such candidate for every job posting, thanks to the police department's new diversity hiring policy. Christ, Hickey thought before the guy even sat down, should I find out if he's gay or disabled, so we can just check off all the goddam boxes?

But then DuWayne opened his mouth, and everything

changed.

In the six months since Hickey hired him as his research caddy, he'd filled in the facts about what Hickey had only suspected — that the Mandamus Six had selected their victims using personal or professional connections. A good example was the late Morgan Cathcart, who'd taken over the reins of the murderous group after Judge Leishman's death. His wife had been run down in a hit-and-run by the seventeen-year-old teenager who, Hickey believed, was the group's first victim, shot in the head in his family's garage.

DuWayne was a twenty-three-year-old law student looking for summer employment in law enforcement. He said he intended to practice criminal law and wanted to know how cops caught guys and built cases against them that were likely to end in conviction.

"Suppose you're right about that," Hickey had said. "This job is full-time, not part-time."

DuWayne just looked at him. "Okay, that's cool, too. Listen, suppose I told you something you don't know about the case. Would you hire me?"

He didn't even ask what case, said he just assumed the job working for Hickey must be about the Mandamus Six.

Hickey shoved aside his list of prepared questions and leaned back in his chair.

"Why don't you just surprise me then, kid?"

And DuWayne did. Said he was an expert on finding connections. Said he'd created an algorithm which he could use to search legal cases on-line for defendant-lawyer correlations, and another one for law firms, so he could tell if any of the victims had been represented or opposed by anyone from the conspirators' law firms. Said it might be worth him taking a break from his legal studies to work on something that was way more fun.

"So tell me why you want to start there?" Hickey had

asked.

"They're lawyers, man. Where else they gonna find their victims? They couldn't just ask around."

And so Hickey had hired him on the spot. DuWayne was still quite the spectacle at 40 College Street, not only because of his race and his dreads but the way he jangled his way through the lobby at police headquarters every morning, twirling his key chain and dressed like he'd slept on a basement couch. He'd already proven to Hickey that he was the best computer sleuth in the department.

DuWayne had quickly earned the nickname Hurley Burley, but Hickey liked calling him Squirrely Burley better, later shortened to just The Squirrel. He was good at gathering lots of nuts that Hickey could crack. The connecting lines they had drawn between conspirators and victims, he knew, would be an important part of the prosecution.

Now another one had popped up for DuWayne.

"Just tell me it's something on Burnside," Hickey said.

"The big fish, right? Guess what? We may have got a bingo. Turns out he knew the dad of victim number one. Political, not personal connection, but it's a link."

Straight-line links. The Squirrel had a number — three — circled on the top right of his whiteboard, which he now reached up and changed to four. Four of the six defendants now had been linked in some way to their victims. Maddow would be pleased.

Hickey searched his memory. "Sheridan Barrie, the lawyer-lobbyist, right? But he works for the other team. How do the politics of that work exactly?"

"Raises reasonable doubt about whether Burnside was one of the levers the father pulled to get his son off," The Squirrel replied. "Maybe Burnside later had a conscience about it."

"Bit of a reach, son, but suppose we keep it for now." From what he knew about Burnside and the other conspirators, none of them had anything remotely like a conscience.

For the next half-hour, The Squirrel brought Hickey up to date with what he'd found out so far. It was exactly what he'd hired the kid to do but Hickey knew there were still some loose ends in the case. His briefing with Maddow hadn't helped. Conspiracy, the prosecutor had said, was hard to prove because of the intangible nature of the offence. Just talking or acting in general ways about getting up to no good was not an offence. Hickey thought that much of the stuff in Barington's diary, damning though it was, could be written off as all talk and no action, and therefore protected as freedom of speech under the Charter of Rights. To prove conspiracy, you had to prove the Mandamus Six had, beyond a reasonable doubt, specifically agreed to target specific victims for murder, and they had some means to carry it out. Willful blindness or passive acquiescence wouldn't cut it. It was also a valid defence if the accused could convince a jury that he only pretended to go along with the conspiracy.

Second big problem—the charges of conspiracy against Mandamus Six were based largely on emails, documents and other evidence seized as a result of search warrants or production orders. That meant charter protection against unreasonable search and seizure could be used to challenge that evidence in court.

Hickey had asked The Squirrel for a big-picture briefing today because he knew he'd be tied up in court, possibly for the next week. But after meeting Maddow, he had a second reason. With testimony about to begin, and a formidable litigator leading the defence team, this might be a race against time.

"Squirrel," Hickey said, stepping into the tiny room and closing the door behind him. "I said I'd pepper you with questions, so let's start." DuWayne half turned in his swivel and eased his considerable bulk back in the chair to let Hickey have room.

"What's the most notable characteristic of this conspiracy, so far as we know?"

DuWayne popped half a Three Musketeer into his mouth to give him time to think. "I'd say the compartmentalization, different people responsible for different things."

"Right. Like Barington and the money. No one else really knew where he got it."

"Except we now know where that came from."

"Yeah, but no one in the group knew. And shit, with good reason. It may have presented a problem if they did — everyone was Catholic, right, some of them perhaps were even devout. Here was Barington stealing from the church."

DuWayne smiled. They'd spent long enough marveling at the hypocrisy of a bunch of Catholic lawyers betraying their religion and profession by taking the law into their own hands.

Hickey leaned forward over the desk. "Except, what if . . ."

"What if . . . what?"

"Except what if someone knew everything?" Hickey waved his hand at the small pictures pinned to the wall, including the six lawyers facing trial tomorrow, Barington and the two dead co-conspirators, Cathcart and Leishman. "When you think about it, someone almost had to know everything. They had a plan, they found someone to carry it out, they found the means to pay for it, they had something they thought they could achieve, and Judge Leishman passed it on."

Hickey knew he was taking a gamble, putting all his eggs in one basket. But the trial was starting and Hickey knew a clever defence wouldn't miss any opportunity to exploit the gaps in Maddow's case. Hickey's own boss in cold cases was getting impatient and he knew he couldn't count on DuWayne's contract being extended when it ran out next month.

One of the pieces of evidence that Hickey and DuWayne

had looked at most often was Judge Leishman's letter, which Cathcart had read out to the group after his death. It had challenged the others to recommit to their mission but it had said nothing about how it was carried out. To Hickey, that meant Cathcart must have already known. Either Cathcart had found a trigger man, or Cathcart had found him at Leishman's direction, and Cathcart may have been his only contact and paymaster.

But the thing is, Cathcart was a tax lawyer, not a criminal lawyer. Hickey said he thought they ought to concentrate on criminal cases that Judge Samuel Leishman had presided over.

"I need us to find the biggest link of all," Hickey said. He put his hands on the arms of DuWayne's swivel chair and held him straight in his line of sight. "Squirrel, you gotta find me that gun, understand?"

CHAPTER SIX

Gwen Van Loon was celebrating her birthday in her condo alone, certainly not her guest list of choice. Still, there were selfish compensations—a tumbler of Pernaud, followed by a very hot bath, followed by a relaxing toke from her ornate, Moroccan waterpipe, and now, at barely 9 o'clock and feeling what she liked to call *honest*, here she was sitting primly in her naughtiest bra and panties on her velour couch, looking down at herself in the mirror she'd propped against the cushion at just the right angle. It was time to give herself her birthday present.

To set the mood, she'd put on Helen Mirren's reading of Elizabeth Berg's *Range of Motion*. The pot and the Pernaud had ironed out the tension of the day. Gwen's vaguely European face now felt more like Spain than Germany—Moorish and open to passion, accepting of what came to her by her own hand, instead of stoic and resentful that no one else was around to do it. She once thought her impossibly high cheekbones and playful green eyes might make her still attractive to men when she slipped into middle age, but there were no men in her picture at the moment, so it was do-it-yourself.

The voice on the recording said something about being loose and unmoored, as if bumping up against the sides of yourself.

She slipped the straps of her bra slightly off her shoulders, then pulled the elastic front down underneath her breasts, seeing them bulge further as she pressed her arms together. She could stand to lose a few pounds, she thought, but those large, ripe nipples and wide hips tended to give her what the French call *une Bovardaise*. Loosely translated—a ripe, fuckable look.

Helen Mirren's throaty voice said she had the ear to hear now, and the original eye, and there was understanding.

Gwen felt the rhythm of the words start to stimulate her.

She'd purchased the bra and the panties a few weeks ago, shortly before she'd placed the ad. She usually wore quite proper underwear, white and sturdy and buckled in the back, but these were lighter and frillier and there was nothing to undo. They just slipped up, down, to one side, or off. They gave her an illusion of eroticism. That's why she bought them, in hopeful anticipation.

Oh, Mirren's borrowed words were making her anticipate *this*, she thought suddenly, as her pressed-together fingers, carefully painted with red polish for the occasion, nudged aside the crotch of her panty-bottoms. She didn't often do this. Perhaps it was the rather schoolmarmish sense of guilt she'd always feel afterwards. *You're such a prude, Gwen. How did you ever think you were going to find a man in time for your birthday?* But now the sight of her large nipples getting harder in anticipation began to excite her. She still had a nice body. No reason it should go to waste.

Gwen Van Loon, BA, MA, PhD Manitoba—by every measure a successful woman. Tenured faculty position in the English department of a major university, earning $98,000 a year, didn't drive, didn't smoke, had no kids or pets to tie her down. No husband or boyfriend either, now. Plenty of savings to plan solo vacations to places like Costa Rica and Cuba and Fiji and Thailand. Other passions included Canadian feminist literature, Rachmaninoff piano concertos, Pernaud, and subtitled movies. Men? Usually the wrong kind. Women? Little interest, beyond friendship, although for a while in her late twenties she thought she might turn Lesbian. Current state of mind was best described as *clock ticking, horny, frustrated.*

Maybe that explained her ad, which was so unlike her. Why had she written such tripe? *Fine red Burgundy seeks Beaujolais Nouveau. SWF professional seeks virile thirtyish male to wind up her biological clock. Important birthday coming. Please hurry.*

Her voice mailbox at Loving Partners had filled up in a hurry, and she'd patiently listened to each one, erasing the obvious—"Hey, baby, let's mix our juices"—and in the end chickening out and phoning only two back, including one whose office voice mail said he was out of town but was clearing his messages, who didn't call back, and the other, a man named Nick, who, after 10 minutes of small talk, admitted he'd never graduated from high school but had a great cock. Congratulations, she'd told him and hung up. Was she being too choosy? She hadn't had sex in ages. Which is why, as her fingers fluttered across her neglected pussy, Gwen felt gratified that she wasn't—*yet*—the dried-up prune that her fate seemed to suggest. She was already starting to get wet. Perhaps this wasn't going to take long.

Just then her phone rang, and Gwen almost jumped out of her skin.

She'd forgotten to put it on mute. Her first instinct was not to answer. Why should she? She didn't think most women would pick up a ringing telephone when they were just beginning to beat themselves off. But, not being very experienced at this, she found her mood had been shattered by the third ring. *Who could it be? What did they want? Well, it is your birthday, silly.* She withdrew her hand and settled back on the couch, putting Helen Mirren on pause. Call display said *Witherspoon Security*, and she picked up the receiver before her message kicked in, vaguely hoping it wasn't some home alarm salesman giving her a cold call.

"Is this Fine Burgundy?" a man's voice asked.

It took her a few seconds to react. "Yes . . . that's me," she croaked.

"This is Beaujolais Nouveau."

What was she supposed to *say*? It didn't help that she was either a wee bit drunk, or a wee bit stoned. *Could you hang on a minute? I'm busy with something. Actually, I'm in the middle of it. Do you want to help?* Then she thought, how did this man get my number . . . but of course it had to have been the ad.

"I'm not calling too late, am I? I was out of town, just got back and, well, your nice message was waiting there on my machine. I thought I'd call and see if you're still looking. Oh, I know what you're probably wondering. *How*, right? Actually, I have one of those sophisticated answering machines that traces calls. That's how I got directly to you."

Gwen felt herself relax a little. *Of course, he works for a security company.* His voice was actually very nice. Sounded polite, educated, confident . . . she actually thought of another word, one of her favourite words lately . . . cocksure. A lovely, suggestive word. A word that often slipped into her naughty thoughts. She'd decided the ad had been a stupid idea, but now she thought it wasn't as stupid as leaving a message of need on a strange man's answering machine.

James, she remembered. His message said his name was James. His ad had given no age, height, weight, likes, dislikes, marital details, or sexual preferences. She had no idea why they might be a match at all, but she'd phoned just the same and here they finally were. His name was James and he worked for Witherspoon Security. That's all she knew.

She knew she hadn't left her name or phone number on her message. Now, with his voice on her line, she began to feel vaguely excited by the anonymity. This could be the equivalent of Erica Jong's zipperless fuck. He was calling because, three weeks ago, her voice had said she might be available for, well, sex. Sort of.

"It's, um, James, right?" she asked in a low voice, recovering her composure.

"Wow. I'm flattered you remembered."

Now that was nice.

"I'm . . ." For a moment she thought of giving another name, but what was the point? "I'm Gwen."

Saying it, she suddenly didn't like her name, so prissy and old-fashioned. She almost felt the need to assure him she wasn't fifty and on her couch wrapped in an afghan and sipping mint tea.

There was an awkward pause. Then he said, "Pleased to meet you, Gwen. I'm—look, I'm new at this. What are we supposed to do now?"

Do not *say. Why not cut to the chase?*

"Tell me something. Are you married, James?" she asked quickly, and heard the pause. Then the laughter.

"Boy, you get right to the point, don't you?" He replied, "I think I like you already."

It didn't escape her notice that he failed to answer the question. But did it matter? She chastised herself for being judgmental. It's not like you're looking for a *relationship*, girl. You just want a date, perhaps eventually a fuck. Loosen up.

"To answer your question," she said, in a kinder voice, "No, you're not too late. As a matter of fact, you're right on time. Today happens to be my birthday."

She thought then he'd probably ask which one, but he didn't. She liked his tact. *She* would have wanted to know.

He said, "Well, I wish you a very happy one, Gwen. I'm glad I caught you in tonight, to wish you the best." It was so sweet, so straightforward and unexpected that they chatted easily for a few minutes, just small talk, and she got up with the mobile and strolled into her bedroom, where she lay on the bed and wiggled a little more down in her panties. She heard him say he was a security system salesman and liked to travel, lift weights and play tennis. It didn't matter that he said he preferred beaches in the Dominican, which she'd always ruled out because of exploitation and poverty. She said she liked the history in Cuba and liked to spend two weeks there every Christmas, since she was a teacher and could get the time off. Usually, she liked quiet evenings at home. She half-hoped he'd ask what she was doing right now, whether she was home alone, that it was late but perhaps she might be in the mood for a visitor, but instead he said he had a confession to make.

"A confession?" she asked, teasingly. "Already, James? Do you think we know each other well enough for that?"

He laughed. This seemed to be going better—and far faster—than expected.

"I, uh, I hope you don't take this the wrong way," he said. "I may not be exactly what you're looking for."

He had already made her start to think about weightlifters, how lean and strong young weightlifters' bodies looked like whenever she went to the Y. *You seem exactly what I'm looking for, so far.* But instead she said, "I'm not aware I've told you what I'm looking for yet, James. What is it you think I might not like?" She was surprised to find herself flirting with him, so soon. Her nipples were actually starting to tingle.

"I'm twenty-seven," he said. "Your ad sounded like you want someone older. If you do, I thought we should get that out of the way right at the start."

His age sent a little twitch of excitement through her. *Someone who's twenty-seven is actually interested in you, Gwen Van Loonie?* She decided to play it coy. "Or perhaps what you mean is . . . I may be a little too old for you. Is that it?"

"Um no, really . . . no. You see, I'm actually attracted to, well, older women. That's why I answered your ad. I'm guessing you're . . . well, I don't know exactly, but you sound about thirty-five. Is that close?"

She tried to ignore that. "So tell me. Why are you attracted to older women, James?"

"Why are men usually attracted to older women?" he asked noncommittedly. He said it exactly like a fellow English professor might, to encourage further discussion in class about some racy novel, and she picked up his change of direction.

Why not? Why not.

"What if I told you, James, that I'm actually forty?" She let that sink in for a few seconds. "Is that still in your ballpark?"

His voice betrayed his excitement. "That," he said softly, "definitely interests me, Gwen. You mean this, today, is actually your fortieth?" There was a long pause. "Why don't you tell me more?"

"People say I don't look forty . . . but of course I don't expect you to believe *that*. What am I like?" She looked down at herself. Her nipples were poking up like pencils. "Let me put it this way, James. Men find me attractive, but right now . . . I'm feeling something else." She paused, letting him take the cue. "I think it's back over to you now."

"Tell me honestly," he said a little too quickly. "Is this conversation making you, um, a little hot?"

She could have answered yes, but knew it would be more useful to make him guess. The imagination was such a wonderful aphrodisiac.

"Do you mean horny?" she asked, teasingly.

"Jesus. Look, do you mind telling me something . . . what are you doing right now?" he asked. His voice had changed. She could hear the catch of his breathing now.

She decided to be playful. "I don't think I should tell you. Ask something else."

He seemed to choose his next words carefully. "Are you in bed?" She imagined him sitting in his office swivel chair, perhaps thinking about snaking his hand down inside his pants. Phoning her from his office was probably safer for him. Perhaps there was a wife or girlfriend at home.

"Listen, James, I think this is wonderful. Do you understand? It's just that I'm tired and just a little, I think, drunk."

Migod, could we actually do this over the phone? "What would help is, I'm willing to be more explicit, and you will need to be more explicit with me. Do you understand?"

"Or, look, why don't I just come over?" he asked.

"Oh, do you know where I live, too?" she asked, joshing.

"No. But, shit, Gwen, you're starting to drive me crazy."

For some reason, she felt relieved that he didn't know her last name or where she lived. "Then good. Why don't we just talk to each other and see what happens," she said, knowing full well what she *wanted* to happen. And soon.

"Okay," he said. He sounded disappointed, but interested enough to play along for the consolation prize. "What do you want to talk about? Other men you've had? Or other women I've been with? Where the hell do we start with this?"

"Have there been a lot of others, James?" she asked smokily. "Older women, I mean?"

"A few," he said. "How about you?"

She looked across the room, at the slightly chipped mirror over the dresser, at her dress hanging askew on the nearby chair where she'd tossed it after work, like so many other nights she'd spent at home alone. "Me?" she asked, smiling to herself. "No, actually I can't say I've had a lot of older women."

"Ha, ha, ha," he said.

But she wasn't going to let him stray too far from where he seemed to want to head. "Listen, James, you sound very nice, okay? It's just that, at this very particular moment, I'm not feeling like I want to be very . . . you know, *nice*."

"Fuck," he said into the phone.

"Mmm, do you want to say that again?" She laughed, and he laughed back, and she knew that it *was* going to happen.

"You must be, like, you know . . . are you?"

"Like a short burning fuse?" she asked in a whisper, squeezing her toes together. "Something like that, James, yes."

"Jesus. Tell me . . . are you wearing anything right now, Gwen? Are you lying down?"

She felt her throat go dry. For some reason, that always happened just before. She imagined him looking down at her through the ceiling! Her flesh was tingling. There were goosebumps down to her knees.

"What if I told you I just took off my panties," she said in a tight voice.

"All right, all right," he replied. He was at his office, she remembered. Probably with his door locked. "Tell me what you need me to say."

This was better than do-it-yourself—far better. She wondered why she hadn't thought of this before—autoerotic sex by telephone on key birthdays. It was certainly lots easier than what she would have to invent in her mind in order to get off all by herself.

She glanced down, at her nice legs lying loosely open, panties at her knees, at the gentle rounded whiteness of her tummy, at the tuft of light brown hair on her aroused pussy.

"Tell me a story," she said.

"About what?" he asked.

"A woman. Someone you've been with. She may have been married. A housewife, perhaps. Someone older, like me. Tell me exactly what you did with her. Or maybe what you'd want to do to me, if you were here right now, at the end of my bed, looking down at me. I don't know, James . . . maybe touching my bare ankle, maybe starting to unzip your trousers . . ."

"Oh fuck, Gwen. Okay. You want a story? I'll tell you . . . I'll tell you about someone . . . her name is Rachel, okay?" he asked. "I'm thinking of her because she had an old-fashioned name, too."

"Hmm. Go on."

"Anyway, Rachel was married to a client who had to be

away from home a lot. I got to know that so I'd phone, asking to speak to him, and we'd talk. Eventually, one thing led to another and I guess she got interested, or I don't know, maybe she was just lonely. She started saying I could drop in if I liked, if I liked I could drop in, and, well, things happened pretty quickly after that."

"What things? Tell me what you did." Gwen's fingertips trembled as she brushed them lightly across her nipples. She was surprised how big they were now.

"We'd do . . . stuff," he said. "Stuff her husband wouldn't have liked."

"What stuff? Be explicit."

"Boy, you don't give up, do you?" he asked with a nervous laugh.

"All right, I'll tell you. We saw each other for maybe a month, usually in the middle of the afternoon, a few weekdays after work, the occasional noon hour, enough so I wasn't getting much work done. She'd call my cell phone whenever she felt needy and I'd drop what I was doing and rush over. She definitely insisted on being in charge of when. When and what, actually. She was eager to see me, but, when she agreed to do more than just kiss and cuddle, she put strict rules on it. We could never actually have sex, or I guess I should say we could never have intercourse."

It was all Gwen could do to stop from sliding her hand down between her legs, but she knew it would happen too quickly if she did. This was definitely worth waiting for.

"So what kind of sex *did* you have with her, James?"

He took a deep breath. "Well, it started to be several times a week and. uh, you know, I'd go over and we'd . . . there's a word for it but I don't think I should say it."

"You can say it."

"I'd . . . you know, use my mouth."

Her voice was breathless now. "Yes. Use your mouth?"

"Yeah, you know . . ."

She sucked in her breath, and felt an electric shock of excitement run right to her toes. Now she *was* wet. She pressed her knees together and felt her bum move on the damp sheet gathered underneath her.

"That's all?"

"Yeah. That was all she would let me do, but we both looked forward to it. I know I did, and she *definitely* did. She said she'd always been a little Oral Annie. Sometimes, you know, it wasn't always a thing you wanted to do with your husband. That's what she told me. She made it seem so exotic and special. Her forbidden pleasure. I guess, sometimes if you put limits on it, it's even more erotic, eh? Sometimes I would go over there and, you know, just eat her for half the frigging afternoon."

Now Gwen's heart pounded in her chest and she struggled to control her breathing. A couple of times, before she met Gerald, men had tried to go down on her—she tolerated it. Any kind of sex was good, but it never caused her motor to turn over. Once, when they'd gotten very drunk together, the guy before Gerald . . . Ron Sexsmith, a fellow English sessional she was dating for a while, had tried to sodomize her under the table at a sidewalk restaurant in the Beach. They were so drunk she'd let him crawl under the table and work his face way up under her summer dress. Somehow, she'd had enough wits to stop him tugging down her panties. Committing sodomy in a public place, wouldn't that look just dandy on her resume! They'd stumbled back to her apartment instead and he'd fucked her all afternoon. But the idea . . . of having a stranger lick her until she came . . . filled her with new erotic possibilities.

She tried to think of a question, to make him continue the story. "So what happened? Please don't just jump to when her husband walked in on you one afternoon."

"No, but I'll get to that. I want to tell you what I got out of it," he said. "Not much at first. I thought it was so re-pressed . . . that she'd allow a man's face all over her pussy but not his co—" He quickly caught himself. "Sorry, did that offend you?"

"No. You can talk dirty to me, James. I actually prefer it."

"But then . . . well, when she loosened up and, you know, actually came . . . like, she'd tell me what to do to get her off, exactly where to put my tongue, rather explicit instructions actually . . . well, it got me aroused, too. She was an extremely beautiful woman, and I'd go home still tasting her in my mouth."

"So tell me what she was like."

"Jesus . . . bitter blossoms. She said she wanted me to drink her bitter blossoms. She liked to use euphemisms."

She tried to picture a Rachel in her mind, what she might have been like. *Do you like women who are very hairy down there, James? Oh, let's hope so.*

"But did she do anything . . . you know . . . to you?"

"Most of the time, no. Once or twice she would use her hand on me. But she wouldn't . . . she wouldn't give me blow jobs, if that's what you're asking."

Blow jobs. Do you know that's what I'm very good at? But she chickened out saying it.

"Wasn't that frustrating for you?"

"No, not really. I mean, I like it when a woman does that to me, don't get me wrong. But, with Rachel, I would have done it even if she didn't do anything for me. She was thirty-four and had this great body, and she'd let me see everything as long as I didn't touch too much. I would generally go home and take care of myself anyway. I did that a lot, as a matter of fact."

"So," Gwen said quickly. "Are you doing that now?"

Her question surprised him. "Ah, Gwen, shit, I'm sitting in my *office.*" Then he said, half-jokingly, "I'm not sure we know each other well enough for me to answer that."

"Yes we do. Are you?"

"No. Not yet, anyway."

"Are you hard?" Gwen's heart was beating so fast she was afraid she was going to hyperventilate. She was way out of practice speaking with a man this way. There was almost a sense of them hurtling towards something together, recklessly accelerating downhill, with no thought of putting her foot on the brake. She arched her hips, thrusting her pussy up. She could almost feel the trigger there, and how it would go off instantly if she put her finger on it.

"Um, yeah, now that you ask . . .I'm getting huge," he said.

She fluttered her hand lightly across her tummy. "That's good. That's very good, James. Can I ask you something else?"

"Uh-huh. What?"

"What did she do when you got her really turned on? You know, with the licking."

"Okay," he said, and told her about the day she'd opened her back door and she was barefoot and wearing a sexy expensive red silk blouse. Nothing else. "Once she wanted me to just sort of jump her. Usually we had a drink, maybe did a little kissing, a little feeling up, then started taking off things. But this time, she had nothing on but a string of pearls and an undone silk blouse. I guess she was really hornier than usual because hubby was coming home and we wouldn't be able to do it for a while. She jammed her tongue down my throat and sort of dragged me to the couch. We always did it there, on a sheet she'd throw over the good upholstery. Anyway, I'm tearing off my trousers while I've got my face buried in her, and she's moaning and tumbling her breasts inside the silk blouse, and the pearls are rattling and she's all lavender because she'd rubbed cologne down there between her legs."

"Oh, this is a good story," Gwen said, coaxing him to continue.

"And she didn't have to touch me or anything, I could hear her pearls rattling and, shit, you'll never believe what happened."

Gwen, breathless now, her hand poised at the top of her crotch, was barely in control. "Tell me," she croaked.

And he said, "I just had time to straighten up and sort of clutch her against me. I felt myself starting to ejaculate, all over her tummy. I mean, I really creamed her, a few big spurts got way up the front of her blouse. I couldn't stop myself, I just kept coming on her tummy, not letting her twist away, and when I was done she looked down at herself and then back at me, and I could tell she was really pissed, you know, sort of looking astonished and betrayed."

He didn't say anything for a minute. "Christ, you know . . . some women love that. She, however, sure didn't. There was so much on her that I had to get a towel. I thought to myself, *oh fuck, that crossed the line.* She said did I know that was her husband's favourite blouse? How in hell would I have known that, like she'd put on her husband's favourite blouse to get gobbled in, probably the most erotic thing she'd done in her life, and now she was going to have to make up some story to get it dry cleaned. Can you imagine? Like any cleaner wouldn't recognize fucking ejaculation spots on a blouse? She made me leave after that and, when I got back to the office, there was a phone message waiting. She said you can't come over anymore."

"A whisper of silk, a scent of lavender," Gwen murmured, remembering something she'd read in class the other week. She said it almost in a whimper, like he wasn't on the phone listening to her. Her hand slid down to touch the hot inside of her thigh.

"Huh? What's that you said?"

"Oh nothing," she said. But she wondered if he'd ever read *The Crucible*. "It's just a line from a very erotic story."

"I like erotic stories. You'll have to read it to me," he said. There was a pause. "So tell me," he said in a different voice. "Do you?"

His question distracted her from what she was doing. "Um, do I what? Like erotic stories?" she asked, a little puzzled. She certainly didn't feel like a conversation about literature. Not now. Her hand moved down the extra inches, and her finger slid into the slippery fold of her labia.

"No. I meant do you like, you know, *that*?" And he said it for her out loud. "Cunnilingus?"

That was it! Her middle finger pressed down on the hard button of her clit and it was like starting up a car All it took was the faintest pressure, and she tossed back her head and closed her thighs tightly, trapping her fingers there. Her mouth locked open in a silent scream as she waited for it, hung on for dear life, gathered her heels under her and tilted her pelvis up off the bed, sliding her finger eagerly down two or three times into her slippery trench, priming the pump. She closed her eyes and clenched her toes.

"Oh, I'm there *now*, I'm going to—oh, James, yesss! You're making me—"

The phone tumbled off her shoulder and she clutched the bedclothes with one hand as she dug her heels in and with her other hand furiously rubbed between her legs, finishing herself off but not really wanting it to finish, feeling herself break and come and come again, uttering frantic little grunts and moans, imagining he was here with her, on her bed, actually fucking her.

There was a long silence on the other end of the phone as he waited for her to recover and place her cellphone back to her ear. He didn't say a word until her breathing settled down. "Jesus, Gwen, that was unbelievable. Fuck!" It seemed like a voice in an echo chamber, coming from far, far away, a lonely voice in some tin can. She didn't know what to say for a long time.

I can't believe I just did what I did. My God. With someone I haven't even met? On the telephone?

"Yes, okay," she told him when he finally asked and she felt able to answer. She supposed it would be okay for them to meet sometime, maybe even sometime soon.

He said, "You sound like an interesting lady. I think I'd like to get to know you. We don't have to jump into bed together, you know."

Oh sure. Fat chance . . . after this?

They discussed where and when, perhaps Sunday, and she asked if he knew the Starbucks at College and Yonge?

He suggested early afternoon.

"Yes, two o'clock is fine. No, hold on, I've got an errand I have to do earlier in the east end. Listen, there's a Second Cup at Sherbourne and Bloor. Same time is okay." She didn't mention it was half a block from her apartment.

"I'm long blonde, I'll get there early and I'll be reading a book." She didn't want him to know her last name, not yet, she'd see how it went. He said he was six feet, kind of geeky, with shorter hair and glasses. She tried to take it all in, but later found she couldn't remember half of it. She remembered she wrote down his cell phone number, just in case.

"You will be there, Gwen, won't you?" he asked. "I really have to meet you."

"If I decide to change my mind," she said, intending it to be a joke, "I'll try to remember to call."

He didn't find that funny. Made her promise.

As he was starting to say goodbye, she interrupted him. "Oh, and James . . ."

"Yeah?"

"I suppose I ought to thank you."

"For?"

"Well, you know . . . your very thoughtful birthday present."

CHAPTER SEVEN

Hickey arrived early, of course, using his police pass to beat the long line-up of media, victims' relatives and members of the public who would clear security and soon begin to line up eagerly outside Courtroom 4-2. They wouldn't be let in until 9.30, half an hour before trial, first-come first-served except for the relatives, who would be ushered by Victim Services to the first two rows reserved for them on the right in front of him. He chose a seat in the back because he didn't need to pay attention to anything the lawyers said up front. He wanted to study the folks who showed up to watch.

Finally, after three years, the Mandamus Six were answering for their alleged sins.

They'd be brought in the prisoners' entrance soon and take their seats facing the judge in six separate plexiglass boxes. Their fame would not spare them that indignity. There'd be a police officer sitting beside each box, not that anyone expected the distinguished defendants to turn on one other. Rather the opposite, Hickey thought. They probably had excellent reasons to stick together. Some of their legal teams were at the desks nearby, arranging their boxes of Crown disclosure documents, looking friendly with each other, perhaps chatting about golf. Maddow was alone at the Crown table at the far right, fine-tuning his opening arguments, but after a while he turned around, searched for Hickey, and smiled.

Jury selection had taken five days, the defence attorneys

ruling out anyone who was involved with the law or was related to anyone who was. Maddow said he was happy enough with the final panel, since it included five women and three racial minorities. Women, Maddow believed, tended to have more finely developed moral standards than men, and racial minorities, he felt, might be less tolerant of people who take the law into their own hands.

Yesterday, in pre-trial motions, court had ruled on three special requests from representatives of the press. Cameras were ruled out and tape recordings were banned, but Tweeting would be allowed.

Hickey watched as the onlookers began to file in, media with their notebooks and cellphones rushing to claim the front seats to the left. He sympathized with their predicament, having to report accurately on people who were facing away from them in a large room with poor acoustics. *The Sun's* Pete Smyth caught Hickey's eye and waved. Hickey gave him a thumb's up, his way of saying he had no problems with the profile and catchy headline in Sunday's paper.

The gallery was half-filled and he looked to see if Rachel Leishman had shown up, but then remembered that she was on the list of Crown witnesses and Maddow would naturally tell her not to come before testifying. Although she was the widow of the judge who founded Mandamus, she'd given police valuable clues about what the group was up to, even though he had grave doubts about whether she'd told him everything she knew. She was the only person alive who may have seen the face of the assassin, and although she'd co-operated in piecing together a composite sketch of the man, something told Hickey she was holding details back, perhaps in a futile attempt to protect her husband's reputation from further damage, or perhaps, Hickey wondered, out of something more visceral, like fear. Someone — probably her — had identified Cathcart to the assassin, but in return for what? The sketch had not been distributed because Hickey still had doubts about its accuracy.

Victim Services ushered in the first of the relatives of the 11 men and women who had died in the conspiracy, just as the marshals began to usher in the first of the defendants. Hickey marveled at the contrast. The distinguished, rich defendants in expensive suits taking their perches in their plexiglass booths, yet somehow not looking like they belonged there, watched helplessly by the roughly-suited sons and daughters and husbands and wives of the low-life petty criminals they'd chosen to eliminate in a diabolically mad vigilante quest to cleanse the justice system. The public gallery was packed with finely turned-out wives and children and colleagues of the defendants, there to show their support, while the families of the victims hardly filled out a row.

So here we are. Who says class warfare doesn't exist in Canada?

Wheeler was at work but not paying attention to business. He'd called up Pete Smythe's Twitter account and was trying to follow the trial on his computer while keeping a wary eye out for his boss in his glass cubicle at the end of the room in case he got suspicious of Wheeler working so hard.

Long line waiting to get in to Mandamus Six for Crown opening. Case being held amid heavy security at 391 University. #MandamusSix

Victims' families being escorted in by Victims' Services workers. Six defendants in shackles led in by marshals and have shackles removed before jury enters. #MandamusSix

Wheeler wished he could be a fly on the wall in the court room, able to see how the six distinguished lawyers who once

commanded his services were reacting to their public humiliation, whether they acknowledged each other or kept their
eyes straight ahead, whether their families were there to support them, whether it was every man for himself or their attorneys had conspired in common cause. But he knew the
heavy security made his decision not to attend the right one.

*Crown Sheldon Maddow to lay out prosecution theory of the con-
spiracy. Expected to take at least all morning. #MandamusSix*

*Former attorney-general of Ontario Burnside having word with
his lawyer, John Juris, distinguished in his customary rumpled robe.
#MandamusSix*

*All stand as Mr. Justice Ezra Foley enters and calls trial to order.
#MandamusSix*

It was still inconceivable to Wheeler that he'd been taking
kill orders for two years from a who's who of the legal profession in Ontario, including a man who'd held the highest law
office in the province. It surprised him that all six had been
brought to court in shackles, but then he remembered that
they'd all been denied bail. The authorities were really throw-
ing the book at them, arguing that freeing them would dimin-
ish public confidence in the administration of justice.

*Nine Crown and 12 defence lawyers in court today for #Manda-
musSix. Charges being read, each accused has pleaded not guilty.*

*Balfour, Carson-Whyte, and Terwilliger barely look up. Burnside
chatting with his lawyer and smiling encouragement to his wife.
Hodge, Jaccobs stare straight ahead. #MandamusSix*

Six prisoners boxes each surrounded by bullet proof plexiglass, then half-way plexiglass b/t public gallery and lawyers, judge. Finding it hard to hear. #MandamusSix

Wheeler had read that the courtroom renovations cost taxpayers $6 million, not including the cost of the extra security. He guessed there were marshals seated between each of the defendants and more stationed outside to control the spectators lined up to get in. He found it odd they would have skimped on the sound system.

First glitch in #MandamusSix trial — we couldn't hear the judge as he spelled out cautions on reporting and use of electronic devices.

First break in #MandamusSix trial. Recess to test sound system in million-dollar renovated courtroom. 123 test, 123 test.

Wheeler glanced up to find his boss looking directly at him, raising his eyebrows and his shoulders in a silent *What the fuck?* He was supposed to be writing up a new sales pitch and perhaps bossman was wondering what was taking him so long. Wheeler held up a hand to indicate he'd have something in five. He had it already written but stalled for time. It was almost noon and he'd brought something to eat at his desk but his boss always went out. He figured stalling might give him the next hour to himself.

Accused brought back in. Should get underway soon. Burnside is in left prisoners' box, then a gap, Terwilliger, gap, then Hodge, Balfour, Carson-Whyte, Jaccobs. #MandamusSix

#MandamusSix Foley clearly reads out press restrictions. Finally invites Crown Maddow to lectern to lay out prosecution case.

Wheeler remembered his own trial, the intimidating presence of Judge Leishman looking down at him from the bench as the Crown summarized his crime in a matter-of-fact monotone. There was no one looking on from the gallery then, certainly no media, but he guessed the atmosphere at this trial must be quite different. Not a seat empty. Reporters tweeting out every breathless quote. High crimes and misdemeanors. Quite a lot at stake.

Dramatic first words. Maddow quoting the oath all lawyers have to take in Ontario. #MandamusSix

Quotes Section 21(1) of Bylaw 4, Law Society of Ontario, "I accept the honour and privilege, duty and responsibility . . ."#MandamusSix

Maddow turns and looks at each defendant. #MandamusSix

First brutal detail. Victims all shot point blank to head. Guns left at scene. Gruesome photos visible on lawyers' computer screens. #MandamusSix

Wheeler wondered if what they found at his crime scenes had accelerated the police investigation. But what if it had? He was as bound to follow his code of behaviour as the lawyers were supposed to follow theirs, only theirs—as Maddow was reading it out—seemed unspecific, full of high-minded ideals and principles. His, passed down by Malvolio, were detailed and ironclad. *Know your victim. Strike at the moment of least resistance. Always leave the gun at the scene.* He wondered if the vague language of the legal oath had emboldened the six lawyers to step over the line. He glanced up, noticed his boss had already slipped out for lunch, and happily gave tweets his full attention.

Again Maddow reads from the lawyers' oath, "I shall not pervert the law . . ."#MandamusSix

Maddow says lab analysis confirms serial numbers of guns were burned off with acid, suggesting a professional hit. #MandamusSix

Now that one stopped Wheeler in his tracks. Back then, Malvolio had done his work without detection. Mafioso knew of him by reputation but the cops never got a sniff. That's why he was retired and living in Sicily. But if they'd matched Malvolio's methods with what he'd done for Mandamus, Wheeler wondered if they might be closer to him than he thought.

Maddow quotes law oath third time. "I shall champion the rule of law and safeguard the rights and freedoms of all persons . . ." Turns again to stare at defendants. #MandamusSix

#MandamusSix recesses for lunch. Back at 2.

Wheeler marveled at how little time judges actually spent in court during a trial. It hadn't started really until 10.20 because the media and onlookers had to be screened and ushered in, there were the 20 minutes for the sound test and a recess at 12.15, and they'd probably not start up again until a quarter after 2, winding up before 4.

He actually managed to get some work done before his boss got back from lunch and was thinking of checking out to Starbucks with his laptop so he could follow the afternoon testimony without interruption, saying he had to make a house call or something, but his boss had other ideas and he had to catch things as he could. One significant revelation—something Wheeler had wondered from the very beginning—was how Mandamus had chosen its victims. Maddow said the evidence would show that the ten men and one woman were not chosen randomly. Most had a personal con-

nection with one of the plotters, either because he was representing them, or a member of his law firm was, or else they
had some family connection to a victim of their crimes.

That figures. Isn't that how they found me?

Hickey liked the way Stephanie always made sure he was
comfortable first, letting him slip off his right shoe and rest
his foot on her coffee table because she knew it relieved his
gout, asking him if he'd like a drink, even though she knew
alcohol raised his uric acid levels, because she sensed that
he'd had a stressful day. She had the ability to ease his mood
with a joke, like the one she told him just now as she passed
over a glass of his favourite scotch, the ten-year-old Ardberg
single malt. "As long as you're determined to be such a bad
boy, my dear, you might as well splurge on the good stuff."

"Another reason it's good to be here," Hickey said, and
meant it, letting himself relax for perhaps the first time that
day. He inhaled the first sip through his teeth, enjoying the
big-bodied flavour of smokey Islay peat.

She looked as fresh and crisp as he felt rumpled and unkempt, the result of his six hours sitting in court. Nice white
blouse and modest skirt to his undone tie and creased suit.
Times like this, he couldn't help but wonder what a classy
lady like this had ever seen in a misogynistic low-life like
Oosterhuis. He was glad when she told him she had no intention of showing up in court as a relative of a victim. *She* was
the victim, she said.

"I'm dying to know how it went," she said, sitting down
on the sofa facing him with her glass of wine. "You don't seem
too anguished, so I'm guessing well."

"Haven't heard the openings for defence yet," Hickey said,
raising his eyebrows. "Maddow gave quite a performance.
That's why I'm a little early. He didn't wind up until well after

lunch, and the judge turned to Juris and said that's it, you can have tomorrow."

"You admire him, right? Maddow? He did a good job?"

Hickey nodded. "Lawyers say a good opening is the most important part of trial. Grab the jury and engage them there and you probably have them at the end. The job is to make them believe it's all really very simple, that the evidence leads to only one place."

"But you told me this is a very complicated case. How did he manage to make it simple?" She took a sip of her Chardonnay and leaned forward with interest. Barbara used to do that when he was telling her about his day.

Hickey had to think a minute. She was asking good questions, making him draw conclusions that he'd not yet had time to fully form in his mind. "He summarized the evidence they'd get to hear but every two or three minutes he'd quote from the lawyers' oath, what everyone has to swear before they get to be lawyers. The most important principle, implicit but not stated, is *Do no harm*, and Maddow saved that for the very end. He said, and I have to paraphrase a little here, *And so you will find that these men, who swore to uphold the law and do no harm, violated the very principles of their profession.* He paused and looked at each juror in turn, then said very simply. *Your job is to make them pay for it.*"

"Like . . . wow."

"Days like this" — Hickey smiled — "I wish I'd been clever enough to study law."

Stephanie held her glass out to clink his. "Liar." She smiled. "There wouldn't be a case at all without a good cop like you."

Hickey certainly enjoyed being flattered but something made him not want to show it. "Say, suppose a guy was a little hungry. Are you going to suggest another sinful drink or can you tell me what we've got to eat?"

"Only things that are good for you, sir," she said, getting

up. She'd told him she'd researched all about gout on the internet. Something was simmering gently on the stove and there was a big covered pot on the burner beside it. "No shrimp or red meat for you. I've made curried mahi-mahi that we'll have on angel hair pasta." She turned back to look at him half way to the kitchen. "It's always good to stay on the side of the angels, right?"

He'd begun to recognize that Stephanie had the same ability to let him just be himself that Barbara had for all those years. Why was he having such a hard time accepting it? He'd learned one thing during the last seven years of grief — that he was lonely. He had no desire to grow old by himself and the emptiness in his life was starting to wear on him. He knew that was probably why he refused to even contemplate retirement, which sounded like an even emptier life, although he knew that it might soon be thrust upon him anyway.

No, Hickey knew it was more than Barbara's memory that was holding him back from a deeper relationship with Stephanie. It was his duty as a cop. The rules against conflict of interest were ironclad. An old colleague from homicide, Shep Stein, had run headlong into them a few years ago and Hickey had seen him go down. Shep had been working a first-degree murder case and a key witness had died under suspicious circumstances before trial. Defence learned that Det. Stein was having a personal relationship with the witness' wife, and the judge dismissed the charges on grounds that the relationship created a *reasonable apprehension of bias* on the part of the Crown.

The accused, a real estate developer, and his dominatrix mistress, who undoubtedly had conspired to murder his wife, walked free. Shep's career ended prematurely when he was convicted of discreditable conduct.

Hickey didn't want to go out that way.

Stephanie would have to be patient and he guessed, based

on the evidence so far, that she might be.

To relieve his conundrum, he made a special effort during dinner to turn the conversation back to her, asking about her day in as much detail as she had asked him about his, and how her new job was working out. Stephanie, whose beauty salon had supported Oosterhuis' drug habit for years, had gone back to school and learned bookkeeping. She was doing the books for a moving company on Eastern Avenue.

Later, during the taxi ride home, his thoughts were not on the trial, and whether he might be called to testify as early as tomorrow, they were about Stephanie and how he was starting to feel about their cautious friendship, and whether some day he might have to find a gift to give her as precious as the one she was already giving him — faith in himself.

CHAPTER EIGHT

Thomas Wayne Paxton
672 Glen Road
Toronto, ON
M6S 3K5

Dear Mr. Paxton,

I am writing to inform you that a worrisome degree of questionable material, all of it unattributed, was discovered in the essay you submitted to me on March 1, 2019. Numerous passages were identical to those in work submitted previously by others or contained in academic publications. Turnitin identified 35 percent of the content in your essay on its similarity index.

Academic policy established in the Department of English requires me to inform you of this finding and schedule a meeting to hear your version of how this material found its way into your essay, and why it was not attributed. Accordingly, I would like to meet with you during my office hours on Thursday, March 29, at two o'clock in the afternoon. My office is in Room 435, Stong College.

I am obliged to tell you that plagiarism is one of the most serious violations of academic integrity. Penalties can include failure on the assignment, which is worth 25 percent of the final grade, failure in the course, or expulsion from the university. Accordingly, please review Sections 3 and 4 of the York University Student Conduct Code.

You are entitled to be accompanied to this meeting, if you wish, by a representative of the Academic Integrity Office, or the Undergraduate Student Peer Support Group. This is entirely your decision but I ask that you inform me in advance if you are bringing an

observer or adviser.
Yours sincerely,
Prof. Gwendolyn Van Loon, BA, MA, PhD
(416) 736-5865 ext. 435

Though she had sent students such letters before, Gwen always found them awkward to write. She resented the stilted formality they seemed to require. *Who uses a word like* accordingly *anymore in conversation? Why did she feel compelled to inflate her name to* Gwendolyn *and list her degrees?*

Attendance records for AP/EN 1001 3.0 showed that Thomas Paxton had been absent for more than half her classes. She honestly couldn't put a face to the name. She imagined him as one of those disinterested students who usually slumped in the very last row of the small lecture hall and spent class time with their eyes on their cellphones. She couldn't recall him ever contributing to classroom discussions, and he'd turned in undistinguished work. She'd failed him on the initial assignment, which was a critique of a Canadian work of feminist literature, on grounds that he'd chosen *Best Women's Erotica of the Year*, an anthology edited by Rachel Kramer Bussel. She'd criticized his choice as not being feminist, not being Canadian and not being particularly good literature, especially since he chose to focus on one of Kramer Bussel's own stories, a crude titillation called Flying Solo, which was about picking up strangers and having various kinds of taboo sex with them. She had expected him to come see her in office hours to argue for a pass but he hadn't bothered.

His record showed he was enrolled in only her course. Perhaps he had to work to support himself or wasn't yet academically committed. He certainly did not seem to have any interest in feminist thought, beyond possibly getting laid. She remembered his failed essay went on and on about how Kramer Bussel's writing had ignited his curiosity about how best to jump lonely women in bars.

In previous cases of plagiarism she'd handled, the student had usually pleaded forgetfulness and thrown himself on her mercy. She didn't think the new rules Bannon had distributed allowed any mercy, and Bannon had said it might be best to run all such warning letters by her office for the first little while. So instead of popping the letter in the outgoing mail, she put it in an interoffice envelope and directed it to her chair. That, she thought, could waste a week or so, which is why she'd put the meeting date off more than three weeks. Immediately, she felt much better, and let her mind drift back to Monday night and her erotic phone sex with James.

There was a text from Geruta. *Lattes in the faculty lounge. Meet me?*

"I don't know how much I should tell you," Gwen said when her friend noticed her bright smile and asked what was responsible. "Successfully turning forty, I suppose."

But Geruta, who knew her well, tilted her head and wanted to know more. They had chosen their usual table by the window, looking out at the students trooping like ants to class on the busy campus three storeys below.

"I thought you were anxious about it."

"That's true. I was."

Geruta gave her a quizzical look. "I suppose you're waiting for me to ask how your lonely celebration went the other night, right."

Gwen decided to surprise her. "Who said it was lonely?"

Geruta's large hazel eyes widened and she closed her cellphone and dropped it into her purse. "Oh, honey, do tell! I hope it has something to do with a man."

And Gwen told her exactly how it had been—how she'd prepared, what she had on, where she was lying with the small mirror held just so, what she'd only started doing to herself and then the phone call out of the blue, Beaujolais Nouveau, and the delightfully erotic aftermath. She managed to hold several salacious details back, including the exact word he'd said to trigger her stunning orgasm.

When she finished, Geruta bit her bottom lip and began fanning herself in an exaggerated way with a paper napkin, making a few comical faces.

"Ooooh . . . so this took exactly how long?" she asked.

"Listen, I wasn't keeping time," Gwen quipped.

Geruta bent forward in giggles and reached out one hand to squeeze Gwen's arm. "Sounds like you may have set a record!" She said it a little too loudly and clapped a hand over her mouth, but not before a couple of male professors several tables away turned to look. Ribald laughter certainly was not one of the sounds usually heard in the faculty lunch room. "Fine Burgundy and Beaujolais Nouveau?"—she asked in a whisper through her fingers, stifling more laughter—"Oh, I wish I'd thought of that one."

Gwen thought for a moment whether she should have been offended. Was it just Geruta's finely honed sense of irony at work here, or was she being mocked? She was embarrassed enough by what had happened. She didn't need to have it rubbed in her face.

"Speed," she finally asked in a whisper, leaning forward, "is not supposed to rank high on anyone's wish-list, is it?"

That seemed to work. Geruta furrowed her brow a little and, Gwen thought, tried to adopt the tone of a serious academic. "Psychologists might say women of our vintage have been conditioned from our early teens to get our pleasure quickly and silently. After all, most of us grew up in homes where doing such things required speed and stealth."

She let that profound thought sink in for a few seconds. "I've never done it on the phone though. There must be a word for it."

"Cyberbonking?" Gwen asked, a little too loudly. "No, better . . . phoners for boners."

This time the men at the far table didn't turn away.

Over too many glasses of wine in Yorkville the other Sunday, she and Geruta had quizzed each other about their feminism. Gwen had concluded that she might be a 6 on a scale of 10, but Geruta would be a 7-1/2 or 8.

"Do you like men to open doors for you?" Geruta had asked at one point.

Gwen said yes because it shows respect.

Geruta said she expected a lot more from men than opening doors. "Good in bed and a sense of humour for starters. I can open my own fucking doors."

Now Geruta, clearly not satisfied she'd gotten the whole story, asked Gwen if she was feeling any guilt. "Why do women tend to feel guilty if we resort to do-it-yourself? When men do it, everyone takes it as a sign of their virility."

"I don't think I feel guilty about that. Not anymore."

"No. You got your toes curled on your birthday, didn't you? But you feel guilty about something. I'm wondering what it is."

"Well . . ." Gwen could feel herself starting to blush. "I have a feeling he could be married."

"Oh? And so? Him having a wife isn't good if you're looking for commitment, but it can be perfectly jim-dandy if you just want great rollicking sex. Wait. Didn't you say you've already agreed to meet?"

"Yes. Sunday."

"I'll tell you what. This guy, married or not, is batting a thousand in getting what he wants."

"Is that what reeled in young Zuhair?" Gwen blurted out the question. "Just telling him what you wanted?" As soon as she asked it, she knew it came out wrong. Geruta just stared back levelly, a mixture of surprise and dismay. *Perhaps this interrogation is embarrassing me more than I let on.*

"Okay," Geruta said, after a few seconds of silence. "What aren't you telling me?"

Gwen reached over and clutched Geruta's cool hand, mouthing an apology.

"He's . . . well, he's younger."

"Yeah—Beaujolais Nouveau. What you advertised for, right?"

"I mean way younger."

"Look . . ."

"Zuhair's what. Ten years younger? I think this is more like fifteen. I'm not sure I even know how to have a conversation with someone that age."

Geruta choked back a snigger. "Girl, you sure didn't seem to have a problem doing that on the telephone the other night!"

Gwen realized she was shredding the paper napkin in her lap. She let the pieces fall to the floor and sat back in her chair.

"And that's another taboo women suffer that men do not," Geruta said. "When they hook up with younger women, the younger the better, they actually get points for it and people call them sugar daddies and smile knowingly. When we do it, we're scorned for robbing the cradle."

"Okay," Gwen admitted. "Fair point."

"Thing is, it goes on way more than you think. As a matter of fact . . ." Geruta started rummaging in her purse. "You should tag along with me to this on Thursday." She handed over a business card which Gwen saw was for Hemingway's, a chic restaurant in Yorkville. "Next meeting of our little support group."

"Support group?" Gwen asked, looking flummoxed.

"Some of us call it the Cougar's Lunch." Geruta gave her a wicked smile.

Gwen stifled a laugh. "Don't tell me . . ."

"Oh we talk about other things, too, silly."

"But . . ."

"Oh, you should hear some of the stories. Housewives and

divorcees jumping poolboys and friends of their sons. Open season on the young and the hard. If you listen to a few of these women talk, and how easy they say it is, you sort of develop an appetite for culling the young ones out from the herd. It's going on a lot in your neighbourhood, in case you didn't know."

"Really? If I go, I hope I'm not going to meet anyone I know," Gwen said.

"We're not sluts, Gwen," Geruta said seriously. "Most women, especially if they're married, know if they're going to do it, they might as well make it worthwhile."

Gwen nodded. "Tell me about it. Getting that kind of attention from someone so young is certainly . . . well, flattering."

"And he hasn't even *laid* eyes on you yet!"

They collapsed in laughter again, reacting to Geruta's emphasis on the verb.

Just then, Geruta's widened eyes alerted her to someone standing behind her. "I'd like to thank you for the delightful entertainment, ladies," a man's voice said. She turned and saw it was one of those men from the far table. "I'm dying to know what you found so funny." He was leaning forward, and Gwen noticed that he had snowflakes of dandruff on the lapels of his tweed jacket. She had never seen him before, one of the anonymous, middle-aged professors who seemed to frequent the faculty lunch room, perhaps a sessional who had wormed his way in as if he belonged. His companion was not as bold and anxiously looked on from several feet away.

Geruta, as usual, reacted first.

"You're right," she said. "We were talking about you. How did you guess?"

"Stan Gilbertson," the man said, smiling thinly. "I'm history." He didn't offer his hand.

Gwen probably let her irritation show too much. *Just being friendly? Or trying to pick us up?*

Geruta didn't miss a beat. "That's appropriate," she said, flashing Gwen a wicked glance. "I actually couldn't have said that better myself."

The man, tall and slightly stooped with wire glasses and a three-day stubble that he probably thought made him look hipper and younger than he really was, quickly lost his solicitous smile and looked at his companion, who Gwen saw was signaling toward the door.

"Creep," Geruta said when they'd gone. "Wonder if he tries that line a lot on his attractive female students?"

But that quick interchange made Gwen's mind up. Yes, she was apprehensive about meeting James and could still cancel out. But this was probably the alternative — awkward encounters with men she had been thrown together with by reasons of employment or chance, with whom she would have little physical attraction and nothing in common, and whose motives were initially uncertain but probably ranged toward the creepy or predatory. After being out of the dating market so long, she could use a support group. And she really needed to feel that her appetites were not abnormal.

"So," she said, drawing Geruta back to her invitation to Cougar's Lunch. "Tell me what I should expect."

"Great!" Geruta brightened. "You'd probably get along best with Jill. She's newly divorced. Teaches school, but high school, I think. Too busy to date and unsure of the rules. She spends a suspicious amount of time pestering us for referrals — you know, plumbers and electricians and gardeners, always asking us which ones are hot."

"So what else do you talk about, besides home repairmen and how they use their tools?"

"Oh, good one, I'll have to remember that." Geruta smiled. "Actually, I'm sort of a newbie to the group, since I'm relatively new to the game with Zuhair. Been to the lunch only, um, twice. Several of the others are married, they say happily married, although they aren't above a little fooling around. They say it's like the hot pepper you put in the cooking to make an old recipe taste better."

Gwen made a face. "Sure. I remember Gerald tried to use that excuse," she said.

She saw Geruta glancing at her watch. They'd been there more than an hour.

"Oh, hey," Geruta said, fishing something out of her purse. "Are you by any chance following this?" It was the folded-up front page of that morning's *Toronto Star*. Gwen, who'd sworn off the news, glanced without interest at the small headlines about the economy, the latest controversy in the Middle East and local police and crime news. The main story across the top of the page carried a large headline that was just a quote, *Your job is to make them pay,* and featured a photo of someone dressed in his legal robe. A subheading said *The trial of the century gets under way.*

"The Mandamus Six trial," Geruta said. Gwen still looked blank.

"You know, it's those high-profile Bay Street lawyers accused of serial killings, like a vigilante plot. You must have read about it. It's been in the papers for days."

"I might have . . . a while ago. Why? Why are you asking?"

"Well . . ." She unfolded the page and pointed to a picture on page two, a headshot of a pleasant-looking middle-aged woman, captioned with her name and the tagline *Expected to testify.*

"This is one of the ladies who will probably be at lunch next Thursday," Geruta said. "She seems to be a regular, Rachel Leishman. Her husband, late husband, was the judge who supposedly started this Mandamus thing."

"Really?" Gwen asked, raising her eyebrows. "So . . ."

"So you were asking what kinds of things we talk about, besides jumping the hired help," Geruta said, looking a little impatient with her obtuseness.

"Do you think she'll give us a preview of what she's going to say in court?"

"With Rachel, I think it's almost guaranteed," Geruta said, cheerily packing up her things.

CHAPTER NINE

"Is it fair to say, Detective-Sergeant Hickey," John Juris asked in his even, cultured baritone, stepping around the defence table to begin the cross-examination by ruffling his rumpled silk robe behind him like a priest at High Mass. Instead of finishing his sentence, he stopped in his tracks dramatically, 10 feet directly in front of Hickey, looking momentarily lost, like he'd forgotten what he wanted to say next, playing on every one of his seventy-one years to gather the jury's rapt attention.

The crafty barrister was creating his moment, making sure it would be the most dramatic of the trial so far. Then he looked straight at Hickey and said very evenly, "Is it fair and *accurate* to say, detective, that you have absolutely no idea who may have killed those eleven people?"

Hickey had prepared for an aggressive opening shot. "The investigation," he said, as calmly as he could, "is ongoing."

Juris had a reputation for dramatic stunts, and Hickey was on his guard. He'd read a *Maclean's* magazine profile of the defender and learned that he'd once saved his client's bacon in a murder trial by the simple tactic of approving two university professors to sit on the jury. He was quoted as saying afterwards that allowing one academic on a jury was risky — they didn't tend to listen, he claimed — but if you can put *two* on, do it every time. The professors will almost certainly end up arguing with each other and you've got a good chance at a hung jury.

Hickey had spent all morning and into the afternoon taking the jury laboriously through his months-long investigation, ably directed by Maddow. Step by step by step. Now it was 3 o'clock and Juris, who hadn't taken his feet or said a word so far at the trial, was making his debut. Maddow said the defendants would probably let Juris carry the brunt of the cross-examination, and he was famous for tearing holes in supposedly well-prepared cases.

Now Juris dropped his large hands to his side and stared at Hickey, slowly shaking his head back and forth like an aggrieved school master, letting his impressive jowls sway.

"Would you please answer my question for this court, detective?"

Hickey managed to keep his reply in check, even though he seethed at Juris' insinuation that he was being evasive. "The answer is no. No suspects have been identified so far."

"Tell me. Have you ever investigated a serial killing before, detective?"

Hickey shook his head. "No, I have not."

"And have you found any definitive proof that these eleven victims were all shot by the same person?"

There was evidence, Hickey thought, but no proof. He had to say no again.

"No evidence that the victims were in any way related, or even knew each other?"

"Not to the best of my knowledge," Hickey said.

"And you've been investigating murders how long?" Juris asked, raising his eyebrows, holding—Hickey was sure—a copy of his service record.

"Ten years in homicide, another seven in cold cases."

"Seventeen years," Juris said and paused thoughtfully. "And have you ever, Detective Hickey, seen such identical patterns of evidence at so many crime scenes before? I believe the term for it is an MO, am I correct?"

Hickey felt the hairs on the back of his neck stand to attention. He wasn't expecting the question. He really didn't want to go there. It was speculative and he'd only shared his theory with Maddow a few days ago in a very secure room. Then he realized there had been others in the room last Sunday, and he certainly had discussed it with The Squirrel. Or else Juris had sicced his able researchers on the case and come up lucky.

"Detective Hickey?" Juris turned slowly back toward him from the middle of the courtroom, drawing attention to Hickey's hesitation. "Do you want me to repeat the question, sir?"

"No," Hickey said. "I heard it."

"Then we are all waiting for your answer," Juris said, smiling and enjoying the opportunity to ingratiate himself with the jury.

Hickey cleared his throat. He wondered how much he could say. How much Juris really knew?

"Back in the nineteen nineties," Hickey began. "Police found several, perhaps a dozen, guns left at the scene of homicides. Some of the serial numbers had been burned off with acid."

Juris pivoted with surprising agility and approached. "Exactly like the guns you found at the scenes of these murders, you mean?" he asked, raising his thick eyebrows and placing a hand on the railing of the witness stand.

Hickey said yes.

"Would you tell the court what the significance of this fact was, in your opinion?"

Hickey squirmed. "It suggested it might be the work of one perpetrator."

"It suggested?" Juris homed in. "You inferred this?"

"It became our hypothesis, yes. It certainly figured in our investigation in this case, just as it did back then, or so I understand."

"But whodunit, detective?" Juris asked, waving his hands in the air. "And what connection did the killer who burned off serial numbers with acid have with these six defendants?"

"We believe, and shall introduce evidence from Mr. Barington, that they ordered these people killed and hired someone to do it."

"And can you suggest what motive they might have to do that, Detective Hickey?"

Juris punctuated his question by sweeping his hand slowly across the six defendants' stands, each with a recognized member of the establishment staring back defiantly.

"We allege, to take revenge on people who believed they could beat the justice system."

"I see. And would you say that's a hypothesis, Detective Hickey?" He didn't wait for his answer. "Would you say it's a suggestion? Or shall we call it an inference?"

The courtroom fell suddenly silent.

"I believe I called it evidence, counsellor." Hickey stared back at Juris and made sure he didn't blink.

"That," Juris said, walking slowly back to his table, "will be determined by this court, sir." Then he turned on his heel and faced Hickey. "Shall we return to my earlier question then, detective?"

Hickey had to ask which question. Juris, he realized, had spun a web and lost him in it.

"Why, my important question about the significance to you of the untraceable guns found at the scene of all eleven killings, of course. You told me it indicated there was one killer, is that not right?"

"Yes," Hickey said, wondering why the lawyer wanted to let him repeat that point.

"Then I want to ask you what else it indicated, and I draw your attention to what you said about those murders back in the nineteen nineties, I believe—the ones that showed a similar MO."

Hickey knew he now had to say more than he wanted to say. More than Maddow wanted him to. Juris had somehow gotten a leak or been incredibly lucky with his research.

"How else were those cases linked back then?"

"Unlike this case," Hickey began. "The victims then did have common ties."

"Really?" Juris asked, feigning surprise and showing that by turning to face the jury again, preparing them for what he knew was to follow. "And could you tell us what exactly those ties might have been?"

Hickey glanced at Maddow and thought he saw him wince. The careful way he had led Hickey through the evidence that morning and early afternoon, outlining what this case was really about—a group of vigilante lawyers taking the law into their own hands—risked being railroaded by Juris suggesting that they were concealing sensational similar-case information.

Hickey knew he had no choice but to fall into the carefully set trap.

"We learned," he said finally, "the victims were all connected to one branch or other of the Italian Mafia."

Juris swung around to stare incredulously at Hickey, then caught the judge's eye and let his jaw drop open for extra effect. In the public gallery, reporters furiously tapped this bombshell out on Twitter and several spectators turned to each other in astonishment.

"So you're saying they were mob hits?"

"We believe so, yes. Sicilian and Calabrian factions were fighting for turf at the time in Toronto and Buffalo," Hickey said.

"And you are saying to this court that there may be some link from that to this case before us here now?" He said it as more of a bellow than a question and managed to attract every eye in the courtroom. "You're actually suggesting, Detective Hickey, that the Mafia, not a distinguished and respected group of lawyers, could have carried out these crimes? Again I must ask you — is this the product of your hypothesis, your suggestion or your inference?" He stood almost nose to nose with Hickey now, both hands on the railing of the witness stand, letting the silence speak volumes. "I must say, sir," Juris growled. "I am astounded, Detective Hickey. Surprised, astonished and astounded."

Maddow was quick to his feet to object, but the judge ruled against him.

It was a liminal moment, and Hickey was struck with that sinking feeling he'd experienced only a few times in his twenty-five-year career in policing. In homicide, they called it clong. A sudden rush of shit to the heart. When you know you've drawn an ace to a hand but given away one beforehand. Juris had twisted his admission to the defence's advantage by advancing it as an alternative to the prosecution's case. He knew he had to win some credibility back, say something like, "I do not agree with your interpretation, counsellor. I'm saying whoever pulled the trigger in these eleven slayings — our missing assassin — may have been inspired by those Mafia killings thirty years ago, or else could be a clever copycat. I was not talking about the conspirators who caused those crimes to be committed."

But he never got his chance. Juris quickly turned away and said, "I have no further questions of this witness."

Maddow managed to elicit Hickey's rebuttal in a redirect, but they'd given Juris his moment. Hickey left the stand knowing that the headline on the trial coverage the next morning would probably be *Mafia linked to Mandamus Six trial*. Readers might find a few paragraphs of his important earlier testimony deep down in the story.

Wheeler reacted the moment he read Smythe's tweet. *Christ, they may be a lot closer than I thought.*

He'd taken a chance and was following Hickey's testimony from a Tim Horton's on University just north of Dundas, well out of the way of courthouse security but close enough to walk down to mingle in the chaotic press scrum that he knew would happen afterward. He wanted to eyeball this detective who was hot on his trail.

Now he realized that the guns he'd left with his victims' bodies may have had fingerprints on them. Malvolio's fingerprints. The advantage the defence had won by its aggressive cross-examination of the detective mattered little to Wheeler. He didn't care what happened to the lawyers, although he supposed it was better for him if they were acquitted. All he cared about was keeping the hounds of the police off his trail. *And they may be a lot closer than I thought.*

As soon as he read that Judge Foley had adjourned the trial until tomorrow, Wheeler packed up his laptop and walked the two blocks south on University Avenue to Armoury Street, where he saw the sizeable gaggle of satellite vehicles and television cameras and radio reporters with their boom mikes. There may have been a hundred people, including plenty of onlookers, gathered across the street and spilling into an adjacent parking lot, and he figured that would be safe enough cover for him, providing he kept out of the line of sight of the cameras. So he infiltrated his way into the middle of the crowd waiting outside the northern exit of the courthouse.

Wheeler always thought the juxtaposition of buildings here was ironic. The imposing, fortress-like courthouse, where the highest-profile trials before the Superior Court of Justice take place, backs onto Nathan Phillips Square, the civic centre of Toronto. Toronto's iconic City Hall dominates the skyline. But 391 University is also adjacent to Osgoode Hall, where the Ontario Court of Appeal often casts a second set of eyes on Superior Court verdicts and, sometimes, overturns them. All this happens just a few short steps away, one of the few efficiencies offered by the province's sluggish, labyrinthine system of justice.

There was a sudden movement forward by the reporters and camera operators, and Wheeler saw them circling a short, older man who had just emerged from the northern courthouse exit. He recognized him from his newspaper photo—Hickey. His persecutor. His foe. His nemesis. He wasn't close enough to hear him speak but he knew he could find that out later. He'd be questioned about the Mafia connection. He'd be questioned about the aggressive cross-examination. There might even be questions about the hunt for the assassin, and—*Christ. Here I am, standing just a few feet away, you clueless bastard.*

Hickey looked professional, Wheeler thought, as he answered the reporters' questions, and probably they were tough ones after the withering cross-examination he'd endured. After 15 minutes or so, after the TV cameras gave way to the notebooks, the scrum moved forward again, circling a tall, distinguished white-haired lawyer in robes—Wheeler guessed it was either Juris, or Maddow—and Hickey was left momentarily alone. Wheeler thought how easy it would have been for him to just walk up and pop him. He expected Hickey to have a waiting limousine or patrol car to take him wherever he needed to go, but it was nearly 5 and perhaps he didn't need to be anywhere, and Wheeler saw him head off on foot towards Nathan Phillips Square alone. So, without really thinking about it, he decided to follow.

Hickey ambled across the busy square, sped up to cross Bay Street at a convenient green light and headed towards the side door of the Eaton Centre. Wheeler struggled to keep him in sight after he was held up at the light and had to sprint toward the Centre in case he lost him in the after-work crowd. It was Toronto's busiest shopping centre, and if Hickey had turned either left or right, or used the escalator down, Wheeler would have lost him. Instead, luckily, he caught a glimpse of him straight ahead, in the revolving exit door leading out to Yonge Street.

As he fell into step behind Hickey, twenty-five feet or so back, they seemed to be headed east, turning before Dundas and traversing Dundas Square, which was teeming with vendors and Ryerson University students, then continuing east on Dundas. Wheeler was good at surveillance, his techniques honed from tracking the victims Mandamus had chosen for him. He knew the ways to avoid detection and to carefully observe his targets' habits. *Was he or she right or left-handed? Did they move hesitantly or decisively? How did they react to unexpected events, like a car turning in front of them or a person headed the other way in the same path?* As he followed Hickey, he began to think of him as just that, as a target. Actually, a rather guileless target when he was off duty, Wheeler decided. Even though Hickey was a police officer, he never once took the precaution to look around to see if he was being followed.

Old man. Perhaps you're starting to lose your edge.

He wondered how deeply the police had investigated those old Mafia cases. Did they know about Malvolio? They certainly knew his methods. Did they suspect a copycat, or had they looked into old court cases for connections to Mafia guns? The judge who'd sentenced him — might they have started down that path?

Wheeler followed Hickey until he ducked into a coffee shop near Dundas and Sherbourne. He thought twice about going in himself, but noticed through the window that it was a large enough place and crowded. He saw Hickey joining someone at a table, a woman, so Wheeler walked in and chose somewhere he could watch them indirectly, using a mirror on the wall.

He watched them for some time. They seemed to be friends. At least she seemed to be listening sympathetically. Every once in a while she'd reach over to touch him or put her hand on his. Hickey seemed to be doing most of the talking. Perhaps he was recounting his day in court, because he seemed to slump in his seat and avoid eye contact whenever he could. Perhaps he was ashamed of how much he had given away or how clever Juris had been with him.

Perhaps, Wheeler decided, Hickey needed something else to worry about.

After 10 minutes of watching the detective talk intimately with someone who seemed to be much more than a friend, Wheeler decided he may just have found the way.

CHAPTER TEN

Hemingway's on Cumberland was its usual busy noon-time self, packed with expense-account businessmen in thousand-dollar suits and noshing shoppers in dresses fresh from Holt's. "Everyone doing deals or recovering from deals," Geruta cattily remarked over her shoulder as she led Gwen to the stairway and an upstairs room that regulars like the Cougar Lunch girls could reserve.

The others were already there and had drinks. As Geruta managed the introductions, Gwen wondered if any of them had jobs, or was this the way they spent most days, going on shopping sprees and enjoying long lunches of Chardonnay and erotic gossip. Her mind was stubbornly still at York. Her only class for today had ended at 10 but Geruta needed to be back for a 4 PM grad seminar. If it had been any other day, she wouldn't have been able to make it.

The Cougar Lunch mainstays, Geruta had said, were two women best described as being *on the prowl*—Rachel Leishman, widow of the judge, who apparently had a hobby of getting it on with the hired help, and Val Janus, a blowsy redhead with a superannuated model's figure whose lawyer-husband had apparently just left her, and she wasn't waiting for him to come back. They greeted Gwen cheerily and let her know that a newcomer was expected to buy the next round. Also introduced was a Jill-something . . . Holland or Howell, Gwen thought . . . a shy blonde who looked like a *Barbie* doll and, Geruta said, walked in one day and found her husband banging her best friend. The sixth was a thin, stylish woman named Dale Snow, who briskly handed her a card that said she ran a lingerie store in Bloor West Village.

Gwen took stock as a waiter delivered their drink orders. Six well-dressed women, she thought, who were old enough to have children that age, meeting for the purpose of bragging about, or yearning for, sex with twenty-somethings.

If there was a doyenne, it seemed to be Rachel. Even though the conversation was still harmless small-talk, she seemed to direct it. Gwen thought she was much more attractive than she appeared in that newspaper photograph. Geruta thought maybe forty-five or forty-six, but she didn't look it. Dressed tastefully and expensively, she took good care of herself. The jewelry she wore was gorgeously refined.

They ordered their food, Gwen eyeing the pork tenderloin but opting for the salade niçoise, perhaps with her weekend date with the mysterious James in mind.

"Oh, that's Pip's," Val Janus suddenly blurted out, after Jill Something had innocently asked about an after-hours pickup bar that she'd heard about somewhere, perhaps at bridge club. Val swung around quickly to look at Rachel. "Have you ever been back there?"

Rachel shook her head. "No, I haven't. You're forgetting. That's where it happened."

Val looked momentarily puzzled. "Oh right," she said. "I remember he went right for you. I was left with his friend."

"Yes, the Italian stallion," Rachel said, managing a wry smile.

"And how!" her friend said. "When he checked me into that motel, he didn't want to stop. I think I fell asleep as he was going for the hat trick." She did an aside with her hand to the others. "I'd had a lot, and I do mean a lot. At one point I was dribbling tequila from a bottle down my front and letting him suck it off me."

Everyone laughed, and recognized this for what it was, a

warm-up for the main event—the Mandamus trial—and the questions began, because of course everyone had spotted Rachel's picture in the paper and wanted to know more. Geruta told Gwen on the way here that Rachel and Val knew each other from the old days when they may have turned a few tricks as escorts to supplement their salaries as secretaries. Both managed to strike it rich—Rachel marrying a respected judge about 30 years her senior, and Val hooking up with a corporate lawyer. Both were single again and trying to make the most of it.

"That was, what, almost three years ago?" Rachel asked Val. "I didn't know you'd been back since."

"Pip's, yes, a couple of times. Results? Not nearly so good."

Gwen guessed everyone probably wanted to hear every steamy detail about the Italian stallion's first two scores with the rather slutty Val, but their curiosity about Rachel testifying in the trial trumped it.

"Are you talking," Dale Snow asked, chiming in, "about the night you're supposed to be testifying about?"

Now they were really into it, and Gwen was all ears. She'd read the last couple of days' papers and the early testimony astounded her. It certainly was a sensational and unprecedented case. People who had built their careers on upholding the law deciding to turn into murderous vigilantes. In her terms, it was like a university professor intent on good ratings deciding to kill all her students who weren't doing well. She wondered what part Rachel had played, apart from the fact that her husband had been the ringleader. Had she suspected a thing?

Jill Something didn't wait for Rachel to answer Dale Snow's question. "Wait," she said. "You're saying that one of those men on trial picked you up at that place?"

"No," Rachel said. "Not one of *them*."

Right, Gwen thought. The men on trial all seemed to be in

their late fifties or sixties.

"I don't get it then," Geruta, the rational academic, chimed in. "What exactly are you being called to testify about?"

But Rachel was still trying to answer Jill's question. "I think he may have been a messenger they sent," she said.

"Sent? Why?"

"To find out what I knew."

"About . . ."

"Them. Mandamus. You see, I found an email list in Sam's papers and my friend's son thought it would be fun to use it to find out what they were up to." She noticed the shocked looks all around. "I know, I know. That was foolish."

"Wow," Jill Something said, managing to spill a little of her wine. "Did you have any idea they might be killing people?"

She got a withering look back.

Their food was arriving. Everyone admired Jill's sauerbraten, which was a huge serving that she wasted no time in tucking into. Someone ordered two more carafes of Chardonnay.

"So wait," Geruta said, harkening back to Rachel's strange remark about a messenger. "How did you know this guy who picked you up at Pip's was connected?"

"He let me know," Rachel said after swallowing a mouthful of her fettucine Alfredo. "That's what I'll be testifying about. That, and handing over Sam's papers to one of the lawyers involved — he died, he's not on trial — and later, finding that email list."

"That must have been scary," Geruta said.

"What was?"

"When he let you know. How did you manage to throw him off the track?"

"I'm a pretty good actress," Rachel said. "I know how to play it cool with people who may not have my best interests at heart."

"She does," Val assured them. Gwen guessed escort girls had been in their share of tricky situations.

"Still . . ." Geruta wasn't letting this go.

"Look, I was absolutely terrified, believe me."

Gwen knew what she meant. That time when she'd walked into their apartment and found Gerald screwing his grad student, she'd been terrified, too. It wasn't a moment she wanted to second guess. She didn't do hysterics or look away, didn't overreact or underreact. She remembered she'd looked at the girl, who was looking back at her, naked and terrified, from her perch on Gerald's penis, and told her to get out. Then, after the girl gathered up her clothes and left still half naked under her car coat, she'd told Gerald the same thing.

The wine arrived then and everyone refilled.

Someone asked about the trial, how everyone was following it, how it was on every newscast and getting international attention. Wasn't Rachel nervous about that?

"I suppose," she said, turning more serious now. "Especially how much I'm going to have to tell them. I mean, not just going to Pip's wanting to get picked up so soon after Sam's death . . . that's just the embarrassing stuff."

"Yeah, most of our conquests stay on the QT, thank god," Val said.

"Rosedale doesn't like scandals," Rachel added. Gwen guessed she'd lived there for quite some time in the judge's big house.

"So—what else is there?" Gwen blurted out the question, speaking for the first time. Everyone looked at her, as if they didn't know what she meant.

"What do you mean?" Rachel asked, giving her a distant, untrusting look.

"You know, what else are you afraid to testify about? Don't you have to tell them everything?"

"I do," Rachel said. "If they ask."

They didn't know each other. She had no idea if Rachel would be offended if she pressed her, but Gwen had never liked insinuations that were never followed up. She despised them almost as much as she despised hanging gerunds.

"So . . . what might they not know to ask about, I guess I'm asking," she said finally.

Rachel looked unsure about what to say. She wasted some time chewing her fettucine, then said, "You know . . . whether it was the only time, I guess. I hope they don't ask me that."

There was silence around the table. Just the nervous clinking of silverware. Everyone acted as though they wanted to know the answer to Gwen's question but no one wanted to be the one to insist.

Finally, Val turned to her friend, wide-eyed. "What do you mean, Rach. You actually saw him again?"

Rachel took her time patting her mouth with the napkin, then looked around the table. "Listen," she said. "Let's change the subject, shall we?"

"So what did you make of that?" Geruta asked Gwen as they walked out of the restaurant. Geruta had excused herself early, before dessert was served, saying she had to drive back to York to teach, and Gwen decided to leave with her.

She thought Geruta was asking for her impressions of her first Cougar Lunch. "It's not that I don't enjoy sex as much as any normal woman does," Gwen said, remembering the conversation during the rest of lunch, most of it gossip not worthy of any reasonably intelligent consideration.

"I mean, we're both around pimply-faced, fumbly adolescents all day, aren't we?" she asked, snappishly. "Would I ever want to fuck one of them?"

Then she realized her gaffe. She saw Geruta react and reached over and clutched her arm. "Sorry . . . you know I didn't mean Zuhair."

"I didn't mean *that*," Geruta said icily. "I meant what Rachel said."

She knew Geruta was in a rush, and Gwen was headed for the Bay subway and home.

"Following her testimony sure will be interesting. When did she say she was on?"

"No, no . . . I meant the part about her not wanting to say more."

"About maybe there'd been a second time? Yes, that freaked me out."

"Me, too," Geruta said.

"Maybe he didn't get enough? That's what went through my mind."

Geruta checked her watch quickly, then looked straight into her eyes. "Or maybe he wanted something else," she said.

Gwen thought a whole different way about it on the three-stop subway ride home. The widow of the man who started Mandamus had gone to bed with someone associated with the group. Not someone who was now on trial. She may have had another encounter that she didn't want to talk about. Why? Because the sex got more consensual? Or because of something else? Rachel Leishman didn't let on who this person was, but he terrified her. He was sending her a message.

Whatever got into me? Gwen admonished herself as she settled down in her condo with a drink, letting her thoughts stray, to her insensitive remark to Geruta and to her own upcoming date with a mysterious man who hadn't even given her his last name. *I've never used words like* fuck. *I'm practically as straight-laced as a running shoe.* She chalked it up to the ribald tales the other women had exchanged at lunch, and perhaps the Chardonnay.

But then she swung back the other way, remembering Rachel's surprising comment.

A messenger who terrified her. She wondered, of course, who that could be—and if he still might be out there.

CHAPTER ELEVEN

Sunday finally. She got to Starbucks late, dammit, nearly 2.20 PM, her bus down Sherbourne held up by construction. She tried her best not to look flustered but for all she knew he could have gotten there on time, looked around in vain for her, and figured she'd stood him up. *Why did I stupidly forget his cell number back at home?* She looked around the coffee shop for a nerdy single man in glasses but found instead what had to be James, a surprising bit of a hunk, sitting alone reading a book. He seemed to notice her then, too, and waved uncertainly. Gwen shrugged and rolled her eyes comically, nodding, smiling . . . and feeling relieved.

First impression? She picked her way down the aisle to join him. Not what she expected. The book he was reading, she saw when she got near, was Barbara Gowdy's *Range of Motion*, one of her better ones, the story of a woman who starts dating again in her late thirties. She didn't know what she expected a man to be reading who was out to screw an older woman, but the choice of a female author was promising, and the choice of Gowdy, her favourite Canadian author at the moment, almost prescient. *I wonder if he's gotten to the sado masochistic part yet.* He was dressed in a jacket and dark shirt open at the neck, and he had dark eyes and large, capable hands. Definitely not a nerd.

From the quick up and down appraisal he gave her as she approached the table, she figured she'd passed inspection, too. She was glad she hadn't dressed up, just jeans, a white blouse and her red jacket on top, with a new pair of girlish low-heeled pumps. She wasn't tall at five-feet-six, but shorter usually made a better first impression.

"James? I'm Gwen Van Loon," she said simply, holding out her hand. He smiled and got up, without saying a word, and she wondered if he was having trouble imagining her as that screaming banshee having an orgasm for him on the phone a few nights ago.

"James Bannerman," he said, smiling awkwardly. His large hand was soft as he took hers in it. "You didn't phone so I figured you must be on your way."

She chose the chair next to him instead of on the other side of the small table. "I ordered espresso," he said. "It's the strongest thing they have here." He smiled. "I'm afraid I'm a little nervous about this. Aren't you?"

Gwen gave him her languid half-smile. One of her men said it made her look available. James Bannerman, she guessed, considered her attractive. He seemed to be particularly captivated by the sexy little mole on her upper lip and how it tended to give her oval face a kind of lopsided imperfection. Perhaps she'd make him realize she wasn't as wholesome as she appeared.

"That's very honest of you to say that," she said. "I think I'm going to go for a café au lait." She looked at him approvingly. "Don't go away."

All the way back from the counter with her coffee, Gwen tried to show him her curious Nordic coolness, the way she seemed to take in the world around her, as if she could remain unaffected by it if she chose. When she sat back down, he showed her the book cover and asked if she approved.

Gwen arched an eyebrow. She tried her best not to sound like an English professor. "Gowdy's prose is dense, although the themes are interesting. Why are you reading that one?"

He shrugged. "Just picked it up. She writes well, and a friend recommended it."

"It's about a woman who's trying to get laid. She's an older woman . . . are you looking for tips, perhaps?"

He smiled. "I'm glad you said it and not me."

"You have to be careful reading Gowdy," she said. "One shouldn't read that stuff expecting to get any insight into the way all women think."

"Oh? Why not?"

"Because Gowdy always explores the obverse . . . she calls it the perverse mind that lurks within a certain type of woman. All her books are about that. One should read them with a certain sense of licentiousness, I think."

He was looking at her like some of those lovestruck boys in her class occasionally looked at her. "That's an interesting word," he said. "What does it mean, exactly?"

"Licentious," she repeated, wondering if he knew already and only wanted to hear her say it. "It means disregarding accepted rules or conventions."

"Sort of like an exception?"

She shook her head. "Not exactly. More like very moral or immoral. Her books are often about sex." She paused. "Of the perverse sort, usually."

"I haven't got to the perverse parts yet." He smiled. "Will I enjoy them?"

She realized he was flirting with her and that she was blushing slightly. She hadn't done that for ages. She let her shoulders relax and gave him her best smile. "If you're into bondage and that sort of thing. Are you, James?"

"May I say something?" he asked when she'd sipped at her au lait and gotten the foam across her upper lip. Her chin was tilted upward. She tried to look coquettish, but probably failed. Instead, the tip of her tongue darted out from beneath her delicate teeth and coyly licked away the foam. She tried to make it look like she might do that for him when she was doing something else.

"You asked me a question the other night on the phone," he persisted. "The answer is . . . you don't."

"Excuse me?"

"You don't . . . look forty."

She smiled. "Thank you."

She wondered if he felt her hair was right. This length, it always tended to look unkempt. It should be a bob, she'd often thought, allowing her to show off her long, attractive neck.

"I suppose you're right. I'm feeling nervous, too," she said finally. "Do you mind if I ask you something? Did you think I mightn't show up?"

"Gwen," he said, saying her name for the first time. "I'm glad you did."

"But what if I hadn't?"

He shrugged. "Then I suppose I . . . well, I would have called of course. I brought your number."

"And if I refused to answer?"

He looked at her, trying to decide if she was still being playful. "Then I suppose I would have to conclude that you weren't interested."

"Not interested in what?" she asked, teasingly.

He smiled back.

"Shall we say exploring the perverse? Maybe you got cold feet."

She looked back at him steadily. "A little late for that, don't you think? God, I still can't believe we, you know, did that . . ." She leaned toward him, giggling naughtily.

He nodded. Then he pressed forward, his face close enough to smell her faint perfume, the kind that could remind you of yellow spring flowers. "There must be a name for it, mustn't there? Doing it on the telephone like that?"

Gwen laughed, tossing back her head and letting him see her best smile. She knew she didn't look forty at all when she let herself go. Perhaps there was this other woman—a passionate, adventurous, sort of debauched woman—hiding inside her skin, longing to get out. She was starting to hope there was.

"So . . . here we are!" she said brightly.

"Yes, here we are."

The clock on the wall said 2.50. Dear Lord, had they really been talking for three-quarters of an hour? They'd soon have to decide whether to meet again and see what happened, or else leave together and decide what to do the rest of the afternoon. The third possibility — going their separate ways — didn't seem to be in play anymore.

Suddenly she brightened and reached for his hand. "I know what," she said. "Let's make this fun. Instead of reciting chapter and verse about ourselves, let's try to read each other's palms, see what we can find out that way."

The first touch of him actually set off a few sparks.

"Mmmmm," she said, studying his hand for a long moment, then tracing her nail along a diagonal line towards his third finger. "I see you fancy women who are older than you are. Please tell me why."

Say I'm lying back on the burgundy bedspread. My blouse is off and I'm naked to the waist and my eyes have fallen shut. I can hear him moving, discarding clothes, and I can feel his eyes on me. My nipples are hard. One arm is tossed back above my head and the other is curled at my shoulder. I've no jewelry on, I put it all on the dresser. My skirt is bunched at my waist and my knees are bent and I feel his hands parting my legs by my ankles. I arch my back and feel him bend and plant little kisses down from my belly button. Now I feel his busy tongue starting to do its work on me. I'm thinking of ripe berries. I'm whimpering, James.

"I'm not sure," he said, smiling and breaking the spell. "Older women tend to belong to other people. Perhaps I like stealing things."

She decided he had a wicked sense of humour. "I don't

think I actually belong to anyone," she said in a low voice. "So you're not taking me away from anyone. As a matter of fact, you seem to be the attached one here."

She pressed her finger against his wedding band. "Perhaps you should start by telling me about *this*, James."

Okay, yes, he was married, he admitted sheepishly. He hadn't mentioned it before because . . . well, he considered himself *sort of married*. No children. She worked as a real estate agent, but didn't have to. Her father left her some money. She wasn't very good at real estate, she just seemed to like the part about meeting interesting people in bedrooms. She'd developed a bad habit of jumping clients, convincing them her sales pitch might be nicer delivered over a drink without clothes on.

"She's not secret about it," he said. "She tells me everything. She's addicted to sex and doesn't seem to want to stop, so we made an arrangement." He smiled, looking straight into her eyes. "This is the arrangement."

"So . . . it's one of those *open* marriages!" she said, letting go of his hand. She wasn't sure she believed his story, and wanted him to see that.

"What about you?" he asked. "Never ever married, or didn't it work out?"

"My marriage was open, too, I suppose you might say," she said. "I was late finding that out."

He laughed, but sympathetically.

"So now you date. Do you do it a lot?"

"Mostly electronically. Saves time. I have a busy job."

She saw him smile.

"Okay, I ought to confess," she added. "I'm an English professor, up at York. I've *taught* Barbara Gowdy's novels."

He wagged his finger at her, as if to say *you naughty girl you*.

"Okay, guess that earns you another confession," she said,

getting back to his question. "I've added it up. In the time I've been manless, two friends have had babies, one got engaged, and a cousin ran away with her divorce lawyer. I'm falling behind."

"At least you've got a sense of humour about it."

"Oh yeah. Divorce and involuntary celibacy are barrels of laughs, aren't they?"

He was thoughtful for a moment. "You don't find dating works for you, then?"

"Not as a rule. My average seems to be two or three dates, then they go whoosh."

A couple seemed to be arguing mildly at the next table. They acted married and were arguing about whose turn it was to cook dinner. The woman looked tired and cynical. Gwen heard her say, "You can if you want. But I'm getting really fucking tired of spaghetti."

She pinched James' arm and rolled her eyes.

"Gwen," he said, leaning over suddenly so that his face was next to hers, "I'm finding you incredibly . . . um, interesting. Shall we continue this somewhere else? Right now or in the next few minutes?"

She'd already decided what to do. She turned her face and gave him a little kiss on his cheek. "Good idea, sir," she said. "How did you guess?"

"Guess what?" he asked.

"That my place is just a short walk around the corner."

As they rose to leave, he said, "Well, I figured you had an easy choice to make."

"What's that?" she asked, slipping her arm through his.

When they got outside, he said, "As an English professor, you'd probably have to choose how you wanted to spend Sunday afternoon — marking a pile of juvenile essays from students, some of whom probably would like to find ways to get into Barbara Gowdy's pants. Or . . . taking the time to let me convince you to let me into yours."

They both started to walk quicker. "I met her once at a party," was the only other thing he said. "Nice tomato." She realized he must be talking about Barbara Gowdy.

It was only when she was in the elevator with him, heading for the eleventh floor, that she realized how much taller he was. In the low heels of her pumps, she hardly came up to his shoulder. He kept looking over at her with those wild, dark, simian eyes. They seemed either too nervous, or too eager, to attempt conversation and she supposed there was no need to bother with elevator talk. She hoped he thought she had an extremely attractive mouth, with full-red, shiny, fresh lips caught in what looked like an expectant half-smile, with that captivating mole adding mystery and maturity. She'd freshened up in the ladies room before they left the coffee shop.

He almost bent to kiss her, but she chose that moment to raise her purse to fumble for her key. Her blonde hair was tousled a little more than it should have been. She'd quickly run her fingers back through it in the loo. She wondered what she was going to let him do to her, once they got inside.

When she'd started hunting for men again, she'd made an informal rule for herself. No bed on first dates. She enjoyed the dance of discovery, the sweet hunger of seduction, almost as much as the act of sex itself. But this was different. For one thing, there had been her explosive orgasm-by-phone, hardly a prelude to measured conversation or coy flirtation, and she had this recent history of settling for masturbation. When presented with the tall, dark and handsome real thing, she didn't ask herself why. She said why not. So here they were, a lonely professor of English with images of passion imprinted in her mind from countless literary novels, and someone who appeared to be a young, fit, hetero male with wild eyes, a reasonable sense of humour, and the hots for mature women. Okay, he was married, but that didn't seem to be putting any brakes on this and, given her aversion to commitment, perhaps was a benefit. She'd passed inspection, he sure as hell passed inspection, and they were going to her place to fuck. Why not?

She saw him slide something into his mouth, a breath mint perhaps, small like a Tic Tac. The elevator began to shudder and slow, and Gwen slid against his arm with her chin turned slightly upward. Boldness was now called for. "If you want to put something in your mouth to make you feel better," she whispered, rising on tiptoes. "I may have a much better idea." She pressed her warm mouth up against his and parted her lips, letting her tongue slide slowly across his teeth. She let him taste just a hint of her lavender flesh and the wetness of her saliva before the elevator bumped to a stop and the doors slid open.

They practically tumbled into her apartment. All bumping hips and grasping hands. She'd left the stereo on, and the soaring lyrics and melodious voice of Sarah McLaughlin filled the gloomy room. She felt his fingers expertly pinching the bra fastener through her sweater and twisting as she was leaning forward, putting her keys on the table, and suddenly her bra popped apart inside her blouse.

Gwen knew that she really wanted this to happen quickly.

His hands pulled her hips back against him. She thought she felt the hardness inside his trousers, and she turned her head back towards his face, smiling with her lipstick a little cockeyed, some smeared across her cheek.

"That's clever," she whispered. "Let's hurry, okay?"

For some reason, right then, she thought of Barbara Gowdy's *Falling Angels*, which she was making her students read even though she didn't think it was Gowdy's best. But there was a passage in it that was beautiful, describing Lillian having the composure to sit like a lady on the edge of his bed until he stopped pacing.

For some reason, the thought of Barbara Gowdy, a woman, after all, still sexy to men in her sixties, made Gwen even hornier.

He found the spot on her back just below her neck where there was a soft fuzz of girlish down. It had always been one of her erogenous zones. Even that bastard Sexsmith had found it, eventually. She felt his tongue licking her there, sending goosebumps across her flesh to the ends of her nipples, as she hastily undid the front of her blouse.

She twisted around to face him. The only jewelry she wore were those huge round earrings. Too late now to take them off. She started undoing his shirt. She noticed with pleasure that he had a thick whorl of hair from his chest plunging down into the front of his trousers. She enjoyed nuzzling in hair. She had often discovered them in her mouth in the morning, course curlies tasting of her man of the night before.

"I think it's my turn," she said, sliding his shirt apart with both hands. "If we don't take this off, I'm going to get my lipstick all over it. And that may be hard to explain to your wife when you get home."

Like most women, Gwen hoped the horniness showed on her face. Her eyes were faraway and glassy, as if she wanted to go somewhere in a hurry.

She pressed forward against him, letting her bare breasts pancake against his tummy, sliding her soft hands around his waist. "I can see that I'm not going to have time to offer you that drink, am I?"

"Not if you keep that up."

"Hmmm," she smiled, looking down. "You're a fine one to talk about *that*, aren't you, James. Keeping something up?" She reached down and slowly pulled his zipper down over the sizeable lump in the front of his pants.

You need to learn to be a bit of a slut, Gwen. She remembered Geruta saying that to her the other day. *Men want to fuck Madonna, or Pamela Anderson. They want the bad girls. No one wants to fuck Queen Elizabeth.*

For a moment she imagined herself sitting across the room from him, still in her done-up blouse and bra, with her hands folded in her lap and her knees pressed together, wondering if she should let him kiss her, or make him finish the drink and go home. Instead, she slid down to her knees on the floor.

He tasted like Sexsmith. Like oysters. Perhaps all men really tasted the same.

CHAPTER TWELVE

Section 465(1) of the Criminal Code of Canada says that *Every one who conspires with any one to commit murder or to cause another person to be murdered, whether in Canada or not, is guilty of an indictable offence and liable to a maximum term of imprisonment for life.*

When he saw the six defendants enter the courtroom one by one and take up their places again in their plexi cubicles, each of them already looking guilty to him, Hickey recalled those words in his mind and wondered what dark hand had compelled them to risk everything for this—their profession, their families, their reputations, their freedom.

Hubris. But it was only a guess.

Start of the second week of the Mandamus Six trial. Hickey was there, even though he had better things to do. Maddow asked him to attend because they needed to make up for last week's disastrous cross-examination, when Juris had overshadowed Hickey's narrative by grandstanding and offering the red herring of Mafia involvement. Maddow was giving it another shot by calling Detective Ben Cleverley of homicide to the witness stand. His job was to detail for the jury just how police had cracked the Mandamus conspiracy.

The police investigation had been headed by a special task force, co-chaired by Hickey and Cleverley, who happened to be old colleagues in homicide. Hickey was brought in to handle the six cold cases, the early victims of Mandamus who died over a two-year period and had already been investigated by police. Cleverley was in charge of the other five, the most recent deaths that had happened with much more frequency. Maddow explained that, although some of Cleverley's testimony went over the same ground Hickey had trod, hopefully they could handle the cross better this time so those facts would be implanted in jurors' minds with few distractions.

Not for the first time in his career, Hickey hoped Cleverley had his back. He always did.

The explosive testimony of last week had heightened interest in the trial, and a long line of curious onlookers snaked down the third-floor hallway waiting for those admitted to the courtroom earlier to leave. It was nearly noon, and Cleverley had been on the stand for more than an hour. Almost no one had left.

Right now, Maddow was zeroing in on the case of Denyse Scott Hollinger, the druggie shot in the stairwell, which was the first time they'd found something more than a gun at the scene.

"Tell me what you found, hidden under a floor mat just steps from her body?" Maddow asked Cleverley.

"A medallion."

"What kind of medallion?"

"Looked like bronze. Had the figure of justice on it. You know, the lady with the scales and the sword?"

"And what was the significance of that to you, Detective Cleverley?"

"Nothing at the time. But two weeks later, another one turned up, in the office of a doctor who'd been shot and the same kind of gun was found at the scene."

"A gun with the serial number burned off," Maddow said.

"Yes."

"So that linked the murders in evidence?"

"It did, because by that time we'd matched the figure on the medallion with a document that was turned over to us by

Judge Leishman's widow. That contained a logo we took to
be the symbol of the Mandamus group. Lady Justice. It was
identical."

"I see. And you thought the medallion was placed there
why?"

"It seemed to be a calling card," Cleverley said. "It was
meant to be found."

Behind Maddow, Juris rose to object to this as speculation
but the judge overruled him.

"And why do you think Mandamus would do that?"
Maddow continued after the interruption.

Cleverley explained that FBI studies showed that serial
killers often changed their MOs as they went along, either because they grew more confident and couldn't pass up the
chance to taunt police, or because they wanted to send a message. "You know, make a larger point about why."

"Why they might be killing people," Maddow helpfully
added. Finishing his sentence for him, Hickey thought. Juris
let him get away with it.

"Yes," said the detective.

"So at this point, you knew there was a serial killer at work,
or shall we say at least one multiple murderer, but you had
no idea who and you had no idea why that person was tar-
geting victims," Maddow said. "Am I correct?"

"Yes, correct."

"So when did you know?"

In court, the simplest questions always get the most attention, and every juror seemed to be leaning forward for the answer to this one. At first, Hickey thought Maddow was getting a little ahead of himself, and saw Cleverley react. "You
mean, what was the next piece of evidence?"

Maddow nodded and said, "Yes, thank you, that is what I
meant," and Hickey saw that he'd done that deliberately, to
let the jury appreciate how methodical and careful the police

investigators had been.

"We received a letter, a letter written by a priest."

Maddow raised his eyebrows and turned to face the jury. After a short pause, he asked, "Why don't you tell us about that letter then, Detective Cleverley?" He retrieved three pieces of paper from his desk and presented one to the judge and one to the defence table, laying it down firmly in front of Juris. "Crown evidence number twelve, your honour." He delivered the third one to the witness stand.

"Shall I read it?" Cleverley asked, fishing in his pocket for his reading glasses.

"When you're ready, detective." Maddow began a slow, deliberate walk toward the jury, taking time to look each one in the eye, and circled back to his desk, where he turned and leaned back casually on the front edge and crossed his arms, waiting for Cleverley to begin.

The detective took several minutes to read out the letter, which he said was not signed and was addressed to a member of the police commission. The priest, clearly mindful of the seal of confession, wrote without naming the person who had confessed to him, or the name of his church, just that he feared the man may have admitted to terrible crimes, and that those crimes may still be going on.

The press in the front rows stirred into action, tapping staccato rhythms quickly on their cellphones.

Maddow waited for silence. "Did you ever manage to identify that priest, Detective Cleverley?"

"Yes, sir. He was already in our files — as one of the victims."

Now the whole courtroom caught the drama. They were getting their reward for lining up so long. Hickey admired how Maddow was mining the police investigation for shocking facts, so much better than he'd done it the first run through with him.

The courtroom took several minutes to return to rapt silence, and Maddow waited for that to happen. Then he said, "Father Michael Conley, found shot in the head at Southdown Institute near Aurora, where he'd been sent for rehabilitation and reflection by his bishop. A man who defied his church and risked his life to alert you to what turned out to be a serial killer on the loose. He paid for his courage with his life, did he not?"

"Yes, sir. We believe his death was probably part of an attempted cover-up."

"What happened next?"

"I believe I mentioned that we came into possession of the Mandamus email list."

"And that allowed you to do what?"

"We matched the medallions with the Mandamus logo, and we began to take the group's motto, *Vengeance is ours,* much more seriously."

An elderly couple in the public gallery — regulars at the trial — snuffled laughter at the understatement.

"Tell us more," Maddow urged.

"By that time, we'd identified the church, Holy Redeemer, and were in the process of getting records of the congregation when another murder investigation got our attention."

"A twelfth victim?" Maddow asked, stepping back.

"No, no . . . it wasn't connected to this, or so we thought at first."

Cleverley then described how a suspicious husband named Carl Barington, who surprised his wife having sex with their son's best friend, later crashed into their love nest with a crowbar and bludgeoned the boy to death, and tried to do the same to her. Police arrived just in time to rescue her.

"And what happened as you were questioning Mr. Barington about this, detective?"

"We found out he was connected to Mandamus."

"And you subsequently discovered that he'd been keeping a secret diary of their meetings, and from that you identified the others, is that right?"

"Yes, in a roundabout way, that's right."

"Roundabout? Why roundabout?"

"Some citizens stepped forward with helpful information."

Hickey knew that Barington would be called next to testify about the diary, so Maddow didn't need to go there now in any detail. He just looked at the jury and shook his head slightly with a faint ironic smile. "So good police work, detective? Or blind luck?"

"I'd call it luck, definitely. By that time the special investigative team had been formed and was beginning work, but it would have taken weeks to screen the Holy Redeemer congregants, or try to trace the email addresses, which seemed to be well encrypted. But then . . . well, in homicide we have an old saying. When all else fails, wait for luck."

"And perhaps the help of good citizens," Maddow said simply, turning to the jury tellingly before thanking Cleverley and advising him that *my good friend* might have a few more questions. With that, Juris rose with aplomb and stepped forward.

This was the moment the defence strategy probably would be made clear. And as Juris spun it out, Hickey thought it was a clever and audacious one.

"And this diary that you speak about, Detective Cleverley," Juris began, feigning his doddering, older-gentleman demeanor, almost shuffling towards the witness stand and looking down to make sure he understood his notes. "Am I to understand *that* is the only evidence police have to connect these men"—and he waved dramatically across the courtroom behind him—"and to prove they were working together in a conspiracy to commit murder?"

Juris stood back, alert and erect now.

Cleverley seemed momentarily taken aback. "Court will hear from—" he began but Juris cut him off.

"Evidence, detective," Juris thundered. "I asked for evidence, not what court might hear."

Cleverley said the diary was explicit about there being a conspiracy to murder people who felt they had beaten the justice system.

"By these six men?"

"Yes, by these men," Cleverley said.

"And this diary was written by whom?"

"Carl Barington."

"Who I understand we will be hearing from soon."

"Yes."

"Carl Barington, who undoubtedly got some consideration for his agreeing to testify against his former colleagues. A lighter sentence, perhaps? Or a recommendation to the parole board for the earliest possible consideration?"

Cleverley stayed silent until Juris glared at him and gestured that he and the jury were waiting for an answer.

"Was that a question, sir?" Cleverley tried to dig in his heels.

"Yes, Detective Cleverley, it was. He received some incentive to testify, did he not?"

"I wouldn't know about that, sir. If there was, I was not a party to it."

Weak answer, Hickey thought. All the defence had to do was cast reasonable doubt on the evidence, and one way to do that was ascribe ulterior motive to a key Crown witness. Barington might have been a hostile and reluctant witness but he most certainly had an incentive to testify for the Crown at the trial of his colleagues. He was going to face his own trial on these same charges later and had certainly bargained for due consideration.

Conspiracy to commit murder was notoriously difficult to

prove, Hickey knew. Maddow had run him through the many pitfalls, and unfortunately they had already fallen into one of them. All Juris needed to do was convince the jury that Barington was a fabulist, or had a vested interest in concocting evidence of a conspiracy . . . perhaps to cover up his embezzlement of funds from the Catholic Church . . . and everything was suddenly up in the air.

Cleverley's last answer, Hickey thought, made him appear to be an insignificant cog in the justice system that was being exposed for its many flaws. And the next question from Juris drove that point home.

"Tell me, then, detective," Juris said very quietly, his volume rising slowly as the sentence progressed, holding the jury in rapt attention. "Exactly what incentive might these distinguished gentlemen have . . . lawyers, I remind you, who have taken an oath to uphold the law and who have practiced for many years to great acclaim . . . why in God's green earth would they risk everything and turn into vengeful murderous vigilantes?"

It was a question, but a rhetorical one, Hickey thought. Pure Juris. Cleverley unfortunately was not prepared for it, and it was a question he could not answer anyway. No one knew why. No one. And before Cleverley could say a word, Juris turned his back on him and stalked away, saying, "No further questions of this witness then, your honour."

Hickey felt sympathy for his friend.

He looked towards Maddow, slumped forward facing the judge. It took a few moments for him to stand up after Ezra Foley adjourned the trial until tomorrow, and when he did Hickey saw the shadows of concern on his face for the first time.

Wheeler, eagerly scrutinizing every Tweet that Pete Smythe

sent from the courtroom, reacted differently. He was holed up in the townhouse playing sick — F was out at work all day — and he'd spent the afternoon silently cheering Juris on. He hadn't realized until then just how much he had at stake in this trial. If the six lawyers managed to get off, if no conspiracy was proved, perhaps the police would decide to lessen their pursuit of him, or else they'd have fewer resources to do so. Public pressure to bring the killer of 11 rather despicable criminals to justice would ebb. If, however, they were convicted, the chances of one of them trading information about him — if he'd been wrong and someone other than Cathcart knew — would increase exponentially.

From what he'd read about John Juris, they had one of Canada's foremost trial lawyers pleading their case, and so far he seemed to be doing an excellent job.

But Wheeler realized something else, too. According to the testimony, he'd been in the pay of a gaggle of laughable amateurs, men accomplished as lawyers but wickedly inept at conspiracy to commit murder. They'd left so many loose ends that their cover had been blown with remarkable ease. Malvolio would have been as appalled as he was. He, who'd been so careful, who had assiduously followed Malvolio's rules, now risked betrayal by a self-serving loose cannon like this chap Barington, who'd been careless enough to keep a diary spelling everything out. How had they let such a traitor worm his way into their group? He hoped that Juris, who had been like a tiger with Crown witnesses so far, would be positively snake-like in his grilling of their Judas Iscariot.

Hickey, though. He could sense that Hickey must still be hot on his trail, and he had a feeling it was personal with him now, and he wouldn't let up after whatever verdict was delivered at trial.

Perhaps it was time to put in motion his plan to neuter Det.-Sgt. Roger Hickey.

CHAPTER THIRTEEN

Just as Gwen was reaching in her purse for the keys to lock her door shut, her office phone rang and she almost left it be. Students, after all, knew her cell number, but she was early for the meeting and she opened the door and picked up on the fourth ring.

"Stopwatch Gang," he said. "Am I right?"

James. She recognized his quiet, deep, reassuring voice. She was learning that he liked to just blurt out something before he so much as said *hi*, a playful way of putting her on the spot, but this . . . it took her a moment to find her bearings.

"Is this from the other night?" she asked, guessing, still not sure what he was talking about.

"The name of her husband's old gang," he said. "They did it with stopwatches."

She remembered challenging him to tell her something about Susan Musgrave she didn't know. This was something about Musgrave's current husband, Stephen Reid, who was a convicted bank robber. She'd fallen in love with him while reading a draft of *Jackrabbit Parole*, the novel he'd written in prison that she had recommended to her publisher. It was fiction but he'd woven in details from his real life, like the exploits of the colorful gang he used to rob banks with. *Right. The Stopwatch Gang.* James had gone searching on his own, taking up her playful challenge to maybe branch out into Can-Lit further than Barbara Gowdy.

"I'm impressed, sir," she said, relaxing. "You'll have to get an A, and I don't usually give them."

She wasn't used to men who did that—remembered things and followed up. Certainly Gerald had never done it. He never seemed to even listen.

"His gang timed its robberies," James added. "None took more than ninety seconds."

"I told you Musgrave was interesting."

"So, apparently, was her husband."

After they'd had sex at her place the other night, he'd asked about what she was into—you know, besides oral sex—and she'd mentioned Musgrave, how at first it was her poetry and her novels but lately she'd realized it was Musgrave's habit of recklessly heeding her passions, even if it meant suffering the bad luck of getting carried away with ruffians. There was a little of that in her, she confessed, although she thought she lacked Musgrave's courage to grasp it.

He'd asked her if she thought he might be a ruffian.

"Not yet," she'd joked, squeezing his hand and feeling that unfortunate wedding ring. "But you certainly have the potential."

"I'm nearby," he was saying, with more than a hint of need in his voice.

"Yes?"

"I could drive you home, or at least somewhere interesting."

Forty-five minutes later, after her meeting on graduate admissions ended early, Gwen called him back to say she thought she might be in the mood for *somewhere interesting*. He was waiting for her in the parking lot. The memory of what his body had felt like underneath his undone shirt that first night had overcome her inhibitions. She was feeling hungry, but for food or for sex she couldn't really decide. Maybe both? She didn't usually rush into second dates.

Somewhere interesting turned out to be a slightly rundown

motel on Lakeshore that he knew where to find. Just left his car in the parking lot with the engine still running and dashed in to register at the shabby office while she nervously peered out the windows at the rainy twilight. She had no idea what she was looking out for — perhaps it was just an innate fear of being discovered doing something naughty. It looked like the motel had two dozen or so rooms, strung out in a long L, half of them with lights on and cars parked in front. *Busy right after work. Looks like that kind of place.*

"I think you should know, this is certainly a first for me," she told him when he came back with a key on a fob. She leaned over and kissed his ear. "Didn't the clerk want to see who you're checking in with, make sure she's legal age?"

He caught her eye as he reversed and backed in at Number 12. "You're old enough to know—"

"—Better?" she asked teasingly, dropping her hand coyly onto the crotch of his pants.

"I'm helping you work on your Musgrave," he said, changing tack and switching off the engine. "Her story is interesting. Reid wasn't her first ruffian, but I suspect you know that. Apparently she ran away from her first husband, who was a lawyer — actually with one of the criminals he was defending in court."

"Right." She leaned back in the seat and took a deep breath. "Long before *Jackrabbit Parole* there might have been an unpublished draft of . . ." She thought for a moment, playfully. "*Scott Free*? That was first husband's name, Scott. Musgrove's strong suit wasn't commitment. Had a bit of the gypsy in her."

"That's what you like about her, right?" He looked down at how much of her legs the dress was showing. "I think I'd like to be a gypsy with you right now."

Gwen felt a shiver of delightful apprehension but managed to hide it with a smile. "Then you've got the key, mister. Show me to my room."

She waited until he held open the door to Number 12 for her, then scrambled out and held her purse over her hair to protect it from the wet as she stumbled to join him. Once inside, she felt herself pulled roughly against him, felt his hands under her dress trying to tug her panties down, and did her best to find his hungry mouth in the dark.

His friend DM had taught him the drill. Make sure you stake out the right place at the right time from the right vantage point, maybe across the street or some far corner of the parking lot. Wait for a nice car, Lexis or BMW, Saabs, late-model Volvos, something like that. There'd just be some guy or some woman or maybe they'd arrive together, the guy usually driving, the woman either looking like she'd come straight from work or else wearing jeans and no make-up, as if she was a housewife who'd set off to pick up her son from soccer practice and this more exciting thing had come along, and she'd just bundled the kid off to a friend's for a few hours so she could have quick sex in a motel. Sometimes, if you were lucky, it'd be a guy and a guy, that was good, too . . . in fact it could be better.

DM gave him technical instructions, too. Use a good camera, a Nikon D810 or a Canon EOS 5D Mark IV . . . *here, fuck, you can borrow mine* . . . and always, always use the 135-mm lens on sports setting because you want versatility and you want sharpness, because you might only get one chance. Back off the zoom and try to get the motel sign in the first shot, when they're getting out of the car or standing at the door with the key. Zoom in to get the license, otherwise you're shit out of luck, you might as well not do the rest.

Know everything about the layout from there on in, DM had said, DM being a pro at this, boasting that he earned way more this way than from his day job. Know a quick way around back, know how many windows along the alley you need to count to find the room. Bathrooms always face the back and no one is going to shut the goddamn bathroom door because they're so busy doing what they came here for. You can usually shoot right in. Oh yeah, remember not to mix things up. Follow each couple all the way through. You need to keep the pictures of the car together with the bed shot or you can't remember who goes with what. Everyone tends to look the same with their clothes off, DM said.

If the man drives and they've come together, then you only have what DM called a onesie. You go after the guy, you've only got his license to trace. It's better if they come separately because then you can ID the woman's car, too, and some-times . . . *no, fuck, usually* . . . the women are more fun to work with. You can count on the fact they're married, for one thing, otherwise why would they come to a place like this, and sometimes they're married and rich. If they don't happen to be rich, that's okay . . . there are other ways you can go.

DM was David Minh Pham and he'd met him shooting pool and they started talking about what DM called the free-lance economy. DM usually worked the Elmgrove on Fridays, which was the busiest night, but he'd let him take his place tonight because DM's boss at the store was sick. DM said if he wanted to know what Rosedale housewives were doing be-hind their husbands' backs, there were two places to find out—the dress shop at Holt Renfrew, where they usually have their chequebooks out, and the parking lot of the Elmgrove Motel, where they're out for something else.

Tonight was drizzly but the Elmgrove was busy. An hour ago, it felt like a fucking traffic jam. He got a nice shot of one couple stopping for a kiss at the door to Unit 18, almost as if they were posing for it—a button-down lawyer type, had to be sixty, with a blonde young enough to be his daughter. He caught the babe with her hand wedged in the man's crotch, sure not acting like anyone's daughter. Around back, he got a clear shot into the bedroom and, yep, he could see the girl, who looked good naked even from behind, straddling his out-stretched legs, fitting him in and starting to move up and down. The lawyer drove a big Cadillac Escalade, so he was sure to have money and probably a wife. He got back to the parking lot just in time to catch an attractive black lady about thirty-five getting out of a Tiguan SUV and looking around to see that she hadn't been followed before scurrying up to Unit 4. Nice lady dressed in a leotard like she'd maybe just come from Pilates and could fit something quick in before she had to rush home to start dinner. A big guy, looked white, let her in. This time he got nothing around back. Whatever they were doing, they never made it to the bed. He shot them together coming out the front door half an hour later, looking mussed up, like people look after they'd been fucking, and the guy kissed her good night and drove away in a nice-looking In-finiti.

At 6.30, with the light fading, he was thinking about get-ting a beer somewhere, stop for a pop before downloading the pictures, maybe have time to tackle some of that goddamn school work for next week. When a newer-model Honda Civic pulled up and stopped in front of the office, he paid little notice and almost wrote it off. Something, probably the fact that he hadn't put his camera away yet, caused him to fire off a few shots. *Christ, you never know.* The driver, a thirtyish man in glasses who moved like he could be in decent shape, went inside to register, leaving his woman friend in the car. She acted nervous, looking back over her shoulder several times. He zeroed in on the license, made sure he got that. He found himself thinking about how good that beer would be, and watched the man return to the car and back in outside Num-ber 12. He got out first and went up to open the door, then looked back and nodded, the whole thing looking like the guy might be more experienced at this.

He focused in on her as she got out of the car, a reasonably attractive blonde . . . decent legs . . . older than the guy, looks like—wait—

Fuck, Jesus Christ.

He knew her.

CHAPTER FOURTEEN

As soon as Maddow asked it, Hickey's head snapped to attention. He was sitting in his usual back-row seat, scanning the courtroom for new faces, when Maddow suddenly asked Rachel Leishman about the tattoo. He'd asked her about the email list, he'd asked her about collaborating with Sharyn Barington's son to rattle the conspirators' chain with an email message, and he'd asked her about her late husband's concern with flaws in the legal system. He wasn't supposed to ask her about sleeping with the assassin.

Tuesday in the second week of the Mandamus Six trial and Hickey was starting to feel things might be slipping out of control.

Even Rachel Leishman, who Hickey thought of as a great actress, looked taken aback. She asked Maddow could he please repeat the question.

"So this man, this man you met at Pip's who picked you up, you had sex with him after he drove you home?"

She seemed to steel herself for where this was leading. "Yes."

"And at some point you noticed a tattoo?" Maddow, Hickey knew, must have examined the holes that opened up in the Crown's case during the defence questioning of police procedure and decided he had to go there.

"Yes, I did," Rachel said.

The lady was cool under pressure. Hickey had always seen that in her. Probably her past life as an escort girl had required those skills, and they'd been polished by being out in society as the wife of a respected judge. She had the ability to keep a lot hidden when under pressure, which is why he was suspicious of the information she had provided as a seemingly helpful eyewitness.

"Tell the court please," Maddow said, approaching the front of the witness stand. "Did you recognize this tattoo?"

"Yes. It was identical to the logo."

"Which logo?"

"The one I told you about on the Mandamus list."

"Identical? No question?"

"No question."

"And what did that mean to you, him letting you see that?"

"I asked him about it, trying to act playful of course, and he said it was some law school thing but I knew what it was all right, and also what he was telling me by letting me see it."

"And that was ..."

"It was a warning," she said. "Or a test."

"A test? For what?"

"To see if I recognized it. I'm . . . well, good at . . . I mean I think I managed to hide my real reaction from him. I didn't let on it meant anything to me."

"You're cool under pressure?"

"Yes," she said, relieved at the euphemism. "Cool under pressure."

"And he seemed to accept that?"

"Yes, I believe so."

"And he left after a while?"

"I called him a taxi."

"And how did you feel from that encounter?"

"Terrified. Frightened for my life. I took it as warning me off — or else."

"Did you take any action as a result?"

"Yes. The next morning I phoned Bryan Barington and said

I didn't want him involved, that he should shut down our attempt to find out what Mandamus was up to."

"Did he ask you why?"

"Yes, but I didn't go into details. I said something like we may be biting off more than we can chew."

"And from this encounter, at the club and then later at your house, that would have been several hours?"

"I'd say from approximately ten o'clock to, well, after two."

"Four hours then."

"Yes, four hours at least."

"From this encounter you provided police with a description?"

"I did. Yes."

"And this is this the result of that description?" Maddow held up the sketch. Hickey spotted the tiny pinholes at the corners, where he had pinned it up to his office wall.

"That is the man I spent that time with, yes," Rachel said. Hickey gave her his full attention as she said this, and thought he detected a quiver at the corner of her attractive mouth and, most definitely, a momentarily averted glance. *Is she telling the truth, or is this acting?*

"And did this man," Maddow asked, turning dramatically and looking at the jury, "Did he strike you as a law student or a lawyer?"

Juris rose in a flurry to object but the judge overruled him.

"He did not strike me as that type," Rachel Leishman said, having had time to think, concentrating on her words and frowning. "He struck me as something else, a messenger perhaps. There was something sinister about him, like he could be capable of violence."

This prompted the first stir in the courtroom for the day, and Hickey heard the urgent clicks of cellphone tapping as the press Tweeted out the news.

Maddow studied the jury for a long moment, then turned to thank her for her testimony, and Hickey thought he had handled this one brilliantly. Everyone there was probably thinking the same thing he was—could this have been the mysterious trigger man?

Juris, surprising everyone, said he had no questions.

Two kilometres away, following the same testimony on Twitter, Wheeler found himself transported back to that night, remembering how good Rachel Leishman's body had felt, the great sex they'd had, the delicious irony of screwing the widow of the judge who had sentenced him, and then—how she'd fooled him. He'd checked into the Chelsea on the day rate with his laptop shortly after ten. He didn't want to miss anything if he used his office computer so he simply told his boss he had to make a delivery. He'd already popped two beers and had gone through a can of cashews from the minibar. He almost choked on the nuts when the Crown showed Rachel Leishman what he supposed was the sketch of him. She actually admitted she had provided all the information it was based on. *The lying bitch!*

Of course, he also remembered the second night, weeks after they'd had sex, when he'd held a gun to her head. When she'd fooled him again and made that bargain for her life by giving him Cathcart. He'd been sent to kill her, because that was what Mandamus wanted, but she gave him another way out and he took it, naively trusting her to keep her end of the bargain.

Twice a fool. Never trust a perfidious woman.

He had to admire the way she pulled it off though, even that last smoldering look she'd given him, barefoot and pausing halfway up the stairs, letting him know there was more of what he really liked in her bed and he was welcome to stay.

I should have screwed her or shot her that night.

But then he stopped himself cold.

Wait a minute. Why didn't they ask her about the second time?

He guessed she had information about that night that pros-ecutors wanted to know, since they already had the sketch of him but no idea who he was. She could put a gun in his hand and say she was convinced he was sent by Mandamus to kill her, part of the attempted cover-up. On the other hand, if she'd told them about being surprised in her living room and duct-taped up and threatened with a gun, she might have to tell them what she did to save her life.

If she'd told them.

But what if she hadn't?

She gave them my description. Why would she hold back the other stuff? She had no skin in the game anymore because she couldn't protect her late husband's reputation after it all came out, and perhaps she thought I'd gone far away.

The more he thought about it, the more he felt he had to know.

Later that evening, after 9, he dialed the number he'd found for her and heard it ring three times before she picked it up. Her voice still had that throaty urgency that he liked. He wondered if she was alone, perhaps sipping cognac in her waterfront condo, or if she had company and was about to wrap those nice long dancer's legs around someone else. He was glad she wasn't one of those cautious women who lets all calls go to message first.

"Hello?" she asked.

He waited. Then he said in a flat, menacing tone, "Lovely lady. How is it going for you tonight after such a stressful day?" He heard her breath catch. It may have been three years, but she knew perfectly well who this was. Perhaps she'd been dreading this moment all that time.

"Wheeler?"

He spoke slowly. "I'm afraid you've been a bad girl on me, haven't you." He made it not seem like a question.

Perhaps she could see that this was a local call. Perhaps she could sense him nearby. Perhaps she knew now he'd followed her testimony that day and had some important questions.

"How did you find me?" she asked.

"You're in the book."

"What do you want?"

Perhaps she did have company. Perhaps someone was listening to this, wondering why her nice voice just turned to ice.

"Maybe I want to talk about our little deal, and why you broke it."

"That's interesting. What makes you think that I did?"

"I've been following everything," he said. "Maybe I'm wondering about a certain composite sketch."

She didn't say anything for a moment or two. Then, "You haven't seen it, have you?"

He didn't bother to answer.

"You should see it," she said, her voice sounding more confident. "It will probably be in the papers tomorrow. Look for yourself and decide."

He thought about that for a moment and made her wait for his answer.

"You didn't tell them about that second night, did you?"

She didn't answer.

"Nice to talk after so long, Wheeler," she said finally. "I hope you won't need to call me again."

His picture, drawn from her description, filled the front page of the *Sun* the next morning, under the headline *AT LARGE*.

Only it didn't look anything like him.

CHAPTER FIFTEEN

Hickey was reading about Jennifer Aniston in an old *People* magazine when he got the call. Aniston wasn't still pining for Brad, not anymore. She'd moved on from that. Curious, Hickey glanced at the date and saw that it was from late last year—really old news in celebrity gossip terms, and of course he wondered if he'd read this same article before, whether that issue had been here at the time of his last visit. The smell of harsh cleaning solvents added to the antiseptic atmosphere of his doctor's office, and Hickey recoiled at the idea that hordes of sick people had been in this same waiting room, slouching in these same plastic chairs, flipping through these same glossy magazines, leaving their germs for him.

Doc Adamson was a pretty good amateur photographer and his work—mostly rugged landscapes and close-ups of flowers—had been blown up and framed on the far wall. Hickey glanced at the time on the wall clock, calculated he was fifth in line, and he'd probably not get back to the office before noon. He knew there would be a second wait once they were all summoned inside, and assigned to their own little examination room. The peripatetic Adamson, having teed them all up, would duck in for a few moments, chat, deliver his diagnosis, and move to the next room. That was the assembly line he used to collect what Hickey guessed must be seven figures a year from Ontario's taxpayer-supported medical system. But he'd been Barbara's doctor, and therefore he was now Hickey's.

He was here for his gout again, had been lectured by Adamson three weeks ago—no shrimps, no tuna, no red meat and no booze. Adamson joked that those were probably Hickey's four favourite food groups. They were, and he was proud of how much he had been able to cut back. Stephanie's regimen had eased his gout, and the occasional glass of scotch she rationed him helped ease his cranky disposition.

A screen mounted on the wall showed CP24, a twenty-four-hour cable news channel that multi-tasked reports on a split screen about traffic, the weather, the stock market and news bulletins, heavily reliant on police press releases. Not much of an investment in investigative reporting but all you really needed to know. An older couple that had been here when Hickey arrived were growing impatient—the man wearing a natty fedora, the woman with a cast on her left arm—and talked crossly about whose turn it was to drive home.

Hickey, at the moment, was supposed to be at the Monday morning follies, his unit's start-of-the-week update on open investigations. He'd been happy enough to send The Squirrel in his place. Hurtubise couldn't stand The Squirrel but at the same time he couldn't hold him accountable for the lack of progress.

He'd put Aniston back in the magazine rack and was thinking about where they'd have to look next in their hunt for the Mandamus Six assassin, when he felt his cellphone vibrate in his suit pocket.

The screen said *Stephanie Lord.*

She never called him during working hours, and he was pleasantly surprised. He stood up and stepped out into the hallway for privacy. "Stephanie?" he asked cheerily. "To what do I owe this pleasure?"

Her voice sounded thin and high-pitched, like something had frightened her.

"Hickey, can you come?"

He took a moment to react. "You mean right away?"

"Yes. Now!"

He was suddenly all ears. Stephanie wasn't easily spooked. "What is it? Why are you still at home?"

"I'll show you. I have to show you. It's something someone must have slipped under my door last night."

When Hickey got there, 15 minutes later, Stephanie Lord was barely managing to hold herself together and brandishing a drink — vodka and orange juice, from the looks of it, and some spilled when she fell against him and held on. She'd been crying and her cheek was wet pressed against his neck and he felt her shoulders quaking. Her apartment still smelled of breakfast.

It took him a moment to realize it was their first physical embrace. Some of what he was feeling must have found its way to his face, because the first thing Stephanie asked him was if he was all right. Hickey said he was fine.

"Thank you for rushing here," she said. "I just lost it."

And then she showed him why. On the small, antique refectory table in the hall beside her was something familiar — the Mandamus medallion.

"I found it on the floor inside my door as I was going out this morning," she said. "It looks like the one that was in the papers from the trial, doesn't it, the one you found at those crime scenes."

Hickey nodded grimly. "I'm, ah, afraid it is."

"Tell me what this means, Hickey," she cried out, acting more angry than scared now, although he knew she was still undoubtedly scared. Scared and concerned.

He helped her sit on the sofa, took the rest of the drink from her and went to the kitchen to replace it with a glass of water, giving him time to think of what to say.

She didn't deserve this, dammit. She'd gone through so much already with that bastard Oosterhuis, both physical and mental. Now this — an explicit threat from a murder trial that had very little to do with her.

Hickey realized he was angry, too — angry that he hadn't been able to protect her from this.

"I think," he said, sitting down beside her and touching her hand, "this may have been a message directed at me, Stephanie."

He saw her eyes widen in surprise. It probably never occurred to her that having a personal relationship with a policeman carried risks. He'd had his share of threats from criminals he'd put away over the years, and he'd always been mindful to protect Barbara from them. Sometimes, if it seemed serious, he'd get a court to prohibit that person from coming within 300 metres of his house. A few times, he'd warned them directly — if I see you near me, I'll assume you're there to do me harm and react accordingly. And of course, he limited any personal information that was out there on him — where he lived, where he went, who his friends were, what he did outside of work. No smart detective, in his experience, had ever opened a Facebook account.

Now someone was sending him a message by frightening — no, terrifying — Stephanie. *But how?*

Which was what Stephanie wanted to know. "But how did they know how to find *me*, Hickey?"

If it was the guy he was after — and he had to assume it was — then he'd probably been spooked by something said at the trial. Maybe he thought police were closer to him than they really were. Why else might he be trying to send Hickey a message to back off?

"I don't know, Stephanie," he said. "He could have seen us meet and just followed you home."

"You said he. Who the hell is he?"

"The guy I'm looking for? That's just a guess."

"You mean . . . the assassin? Jesus, Hickey. I'm *petrified* now. You've got to do something."

His mind was racing. *The guy is still here. That's good. Something must have spooked him. That's good, too. What's not good is that I've put Stephanie in the line of fire. I've been careless. I care for her and she's not safe here anymore.*

But he imagined the questions Hurtubise would have for him if he asked for round the clock protection for a woman involved in his investigation who had become a *friend*.

"Stephanie," he said. "I honestly don't know what's happening or why but I don't want you staying here. We have to assume you're in some danger because of this." He held up the medallion. "If it's a warning, he could be back."

"To get at you through me?" Tears welled up in her eyes again.

He liked how she was reacting. Some women would have been outraged that he had exposed her to such a threat. And for what? A friendship that may be going nowhere? A relationship with a man she barely knew?

"Look," he said, as tenderly and as firmly as he could. "We're going to pack up some of your things and you're going to stay at my place." When she reacted, he held up his hands. "I have a second bedroom, it has its own bath. You can't stay here, Stephanie. I'm sorry. You can't stay here."

He didn't think he needed to tell her that Barbara had used that bedroom near the end, when she was too sick and in too much pain to sleep with him.

She thought for a moment, then nodded and retreated to her bedroom to pack.

Hickey knew he was taking a huge risk but he didn't know what else to do. He remembered once giving a lecture to recruits at the police college about mixing personal with police work. *Never do it*, he had said. *It impairs your judgment. It holds you back. It makes you do things you're not trained to do.* Now he was doing just that.

"Hickey," she said when she came back, carrying a small carry-on bag. "What do you think set him off, if it's who you think?"

Hickey shrugged. "Something at the trial? Who knows? Perhaps he's been planning it for a while. I would have thought he'd be far, far away right now."

"But what happened at the trial this week that might spook him?"

Hickey thought. "Well, there was the sketch. The one Mrs. Leishman was questioned about. That appeared in the papers." He shrugged. "Frankly, I wasn't completely convinced it was an accurate description, but perhaps it was. That could have been the trigger all right."

"Okay. Anything else?"

"Well, late last week there was the Mafia thing — you know, the similarities of the crime scenes."

Stephanie sat down beside him on the sofa. "Now you're really starting to freak me out. You don't think this was a warning from them, do you?"

"Look, Stephanie, there's no indication the Mafia is involved in this at all," he reassured her. "How would they even know about those medallions, let alone have access to them? No, it's gotta be my man."

"And he's still around, you know that from this, don't you?"

Hickey nodded grimly.

"But why?"

"I really don't know, Stephanie. Perhaps he left some things undone. Perhaps he thinks we're closer than we really are."

"But you're not close at all? Is that what you're saying?"

He didn't answer and she didn't ask him any more during the taxi ride to his apartment. Tuesday was the cleaning woman's day and she'd finished so the place smelled all right. Stephanie inspected the small kitchen and it seemed to pass muster, although he had to admit, her apartment ranked considerably up the scale from this. It wasn't until he showed her to her small room that he discerned a slight sag of disappointment. And only then did he realize he'd never once invited her over. This was the first time she'd even set foot in this place.

He wanted to talk. She said they'd talk later. She had to go to work.

Back at the office Hickey found The Squirrel nesting in his cubicle and got a brief rundown on the morning meeting. The Squirrel wasn't good with administrative details. He just said not to worry, they both still had jobs.

Hickey asked him if there was anything new, and that's when The Squirrel handed him three file folders.

"Suspects, finally, boss, I think," he said with a grin.

CHAPTER SIXTEEN

Gwen was waiting in her office for Thomas Paxton to arrive for his appointment, and he was late. *Not getting off
on the right foot, are we?* She checked the time and called up his
amazingly brazen email that she'd received a week ago. He
must have written it shortly after he received her letter more
or less accusing him of plagiarism.

Dear Professor Van Loon,

*I am writing to ask for your understanding regarding what you
wrote me about, that Turnitin had identified some passages in my
essay that you say were similar to stuff published elsewhere.*

*I know I am not doing as well as others in your class at the mo-
ment, but there are things that I am responsible for that keep getting
in the way. My grandmother is elderly and had a bad fall while I
was researching this assignment and there was not enough time between hospital visits to complete the paper in the way I intended. It
ended up being a last-minute pull-together, just copying my notes
and arranging them in a reasonably intelligent order. I may have
inadvertently missed some citations.*

*I apologize for my haste and carelessness if that proves to be the
case. I am a mature student who is not as aware of academic ethics
and practices as maybe I should be.*

*That said, your harsh judgment of my intentions and perfor-
mance on this particular assignment will probably prevent me from
passing this class. I would be extremely grateful if you would allow
me to complete an extra credit assignment to make up for or replace
the grade you intend to give me. If that isn't possible, I would be
grateful if you would consider dropping this assignment grade.*

I intend to show up at the meeting you have scheduled but I wanted you to be aware of these extended circumstances.
Thank you for your time and consideration,
Tommy Paxton
Student 23099854

She was certainly not impressed. His email showed a complete lack of responsibility for committing what the academy considered a capital sin. His *solutions* demonstrated a failure to understand just how serious his blatant, sloppy plagiarism was. Quite apart from that, his writing was semi-literate. *Extended circumstances*? *He means* extenuating, *for God's sake.*

Now he was keeping her waiting, already 15 minutes late for his appointment.

She was about to put his file back in her credenza when she heard a light knock on her door. "Come in," she said, and in walked a lanky, jeans-clad student with a backpack. She supposed it must be Thomas Paxton. That was just a guess though, because he didn't introduce himself and she honestly didn't recognize him as someone who was from her class.

"Thomas?" she asked.

"Yo," he said, slinging his backpack onto the chair in front of her and slumping down. "I got held up. Are we still cool?"

She tried her best to show him that she didn't appreciate his lateness or his failure to apologize. "I was just about to put your file away."

"So I gotta ask," he said, letting his legs splay out casually close to her desk and slumping back in the chair, crossing his arms. "You got my email?"

Already she didn't like him. His file said he was twenty-six and she'd expected someone more mindful of the need to create a good impression. His long, dank brown hair was tied in a ponytail which he nervously seemed to want to fidget with. He hardly moved his mouth when he talked, and his long, hawk nose gave him the appearance of a buzzard.

"Yes, I did receive it," Gwen said.

"Okay. I just . . . I mean, you never replied."

"Because it didn't deserve one," she said, finally making her frustration clear. "I think you need to appreciate the seriousness of what you're here to talk about. First of all, according to the student conduct code, you have the right to have student council representation. You seem to be waiving that, am I correct?"

"You mean, because I showed up alone?"

"Alone and late."

He gave her a creepy, knowing grin and scratched his head. "Yeah, well, I guess I thought we might be able to, you know, work out something together, Professor Van Loon."

This was not going the way it should. Gwen decided to change tack and remind him about the purpose of this interview. "That's really not why you're here, Thomas—" she began.

"—Hey, you can call me Tommy."

She ignored him. "As my letter said, Turnitin has given us clear evidence that you copied material without attributing it. I am giving you the opportunity to explain how that might have happened. I need to warn you that this is a serious matter that may require me to take drastic action that will affect your academic status."

He looked at her like he thought she must have been kidding.

"Okay, I was careless," he admitted, shrugging his shoulders. "I'm sure you could overlook it if you wanted."

"No, I'm afraid I can't overlook it. I'm still waiting for a credible explanation."

He shifted uneasily in the chair and let his eyes wander lazily around her room before fixing her with a level, challenging stare. She reminded herself of something she'd forgotten—it was always better to tape record these sessions. In fact,

Bannon's new directive strongly recommended it.

"Aww, Miss Van Loon," he said in a particularly smarmy way. "I was hoping you weren't gonna be a tightass this way."

"I beg your pardon?" she asked.

"I did research. I put in the effort. It wasn't like I just made something up. Can't you find a way to at least give me credit?"

"Surely you don't think," she said coldly, "that your grades should be based only on effort."

"Why don't you tell me, then? Like, what else should they be based on?"

"How many of my classes have you actually attended this term, Thomas?"

"Not many. I gotta work."

"Perhaps if you had, you would have read it in the course outline or listened to me explain what I was looking for in class." She gestured with his paper in her hand. "You're re-gurgitating. In university we expect more. We expect you to demonstrate higher levels of learning."

"Which are—"

"Interpretation. Application. You know, make sense of it all. Pass some intelligent judgment on the material."

He shrugged again and scratched his itchy head. "Okay, whatever floats your boat, I guess."

She looked at him angrily. "If you'd delivered a thesis based on even casual research, perhaps you might learn from me failing you on the assignment," she said and noticed his reaction when she mentioned *failure*. "You seem to have fallen short of even that modest threshold. You just borrowed other people's ideas and presented them as your own, with no cita-tions. You lied, in other words. And you stole."

"Wait," he said. "You're saying I'm failed on this assign-ment?" Of course she hadn't handed back his assignment yet.

It was in her hand, filled with critical comments, underlines and question marks in the margin.

"Thomas," she said seriously. "I'm afraid it may be more serious than that."

"What the fuck—"

"Lazy students are easy to fail, Thomas," she said. "Cheats are more likely to be expelled."

He fixed her with a cold stare. All of a sudden, and for the first time in her teaching career, Gwen felt unsafe and vulnerable. He was lots bigger than her, was rough and uncouth and seemed to have a menacing temper. He'd obviously not bothered to read any student code of conduct or even her course outline. And they were in her tiny office, with the door closed.

"Tell me," she said, more to fill the silence than anything else. "Just why are you taking a course in feminist literature? It doesn't seem to be anything that remotely interests you, judging from what you've turned in."

"Can I at least see what you wrote on it?" he asked, nodding toward the assignment she still brandished in her hand. She handed it over and watched him angrily flip the pages, occasionally stopping to read her criticisms. Most of them were just *X*'s and question marks where she noted an unattributed reference that Turnitin had identified. After a minute or so, he picked up on something else.

"Wait a minute," he said. "You're marking me down on *this*?"

She knew what it was. He'd written *mankind* instead of *humankind*—one of the lessons in gender-neutral language that she'd given early in the term. He held that page of his essay out for her to see.

"You see, Thomas, in this department we're supposed to care about how we use the language. It's the English department. We want our students to respect the nuances of meaning that words implicitly have, the assumptions we make, often erroneously, about what these words may mean for the general public, and to be sensitive to our word choices for the sake of writing dispassionately and objectively in our assigned work. If you'd been in class a little more, you would have known that."

He was glaring at her now. She knew he probably saw that as *typical fem-lib semantic bullshit*. The politically correct bastardization of plain English. Part of the conspiracy against macho white males that had filled two-thirds of the seats in humanities departments with naïve young co-eds looking for a future husband.

"I shall have to review my recommendation to the dean based on what you've said here today, Thomas," she said. "But I'm afraid my hands may be tied."

She thought he might react differently, but he just sank back in the chair and sort of smirked—either because he took her reference to being tied up another way, or because he knew they were alone and couldn't be overheard. "I guess," he said, tossing the paper back on her desk. "Whatever moves your mountain, that's it, right?"

Gwen felt herself redden. "You're not helping yourself by acting insolent or aggrieved, I'm afraid," she said. "I shall write you again to tell you what I decide, and what I will recommend to the dean."

He leaned forward and stood up, turning to gather up his backpack. She wondered for a minute why he hadn't pleaded his case more strongly, but then decided she didn't care. He was not going to be back in her class. Probably, his days at York were over. Her only regret was for not reacting more strongly when he accused her of being a tightass.

But he left before she could say a word.

You cunt! Tommy thought, walking out of Stong Hall . . .

You fucking uptight fucking slapper bitch! You've had it in for me since you scrawled that F on my first assignment, haven't you. Sitting there like a prissy tightass and going by the book and refusing to give an inch. Well I've got inches I'd like to stick up your tight cow ass, you motherfucker, and I have reason to know you probably like it that way.

Christ, I really thought she'd cut me a break. A moment there, I thought I saw a flash of something else in those nice green eyes – curiosity? Arousal? Fear? Who the fuck knows? I could see she'd coyly left a couple of buttons undone at the top of her blouse, like it might be a goddamn invitation. Suppose I'd stood up and said, "Listen . . . I'm sure we both know a way to make this go away, professor." – or no, fuck, I'd use her name. "I'm sure we can figure out a way to make this disappear, Gwenny." Maybe pat the front of my crotch to let her know what I was talking about. Who knows, I might have even got a little turned on, imagining those nice long legs spread apart and those knees hooked up over the arms of that swivel chair, lifting her skirt and inviting me to fuck her for grades.

"My hands are tied," she'd said. Yeah, that could be good, too. I can imagine what that would be fucking like.

Getting kicked out of school is gonna fucking ruin everything. No more allowance, no more basement pad, the hounds of the bank chasing me for the goddamn student loans.

Where the fuck did she get off assigning papers in a course that was supposed to be a gut? She'd been a lot harder on me than the other goof-offs, Christ, maybe half the class. And she loved to play those tease-games with them, didn't she? Those short skirts. Crossing those nice legs, making us wait for a fleeting flash of panty.

Christ, she ought to be drummed out of York herself because of all those student comments on Ratemyprofessor.com. Her abrasive manner and by-the-book adherence to school rules. She probably got off on making examples of students like me.

No, no, wait. Hold on there. She thinks she's in control of this? I am. It's just a question of how best to use it. Get me back my academic status but maybe something else, too.

Make her pay. Yeah, make her effing pay.

CHAPTER SEVENTEEN

Hickey had The Squirrel's three suspect dossiers open on his desk, trying to decide how he should deploy his meagre resources and whether time was running out on them. At his command he had just The Squirrel and a sixty-two-year-old ex-fraud detective named Duane Corelli, who Hickey thought someone simply parked in cold cases so he could idle his motor until retirement. DuWayne and Duane. His investigative team. But for how much longer?

"So what's your poison, boss?" The Squirrel asked with more street in him than Hickey thought he wanted to hear. "The mule, the gang-banger or the pervy peeper?"

Hickey looked at him. He had his goddamn Drake t-shirt on today, the black one Hickey hated that said *I just want some head in a comfortable bed*. It had sweat stains under the arms and exuded The Squirrel's fetid body odour.

"You wanna tell me again where you found these insects, Squirrel? Under a rock or something?" he asked.

Squirrel described his algorithm search of Judge Leishman's criminal cases, isolating those five to eight years back, allowing for a jail term of three years or more for a gun crime and covering the time period of the early murders. "If we strike out on these, I'll go back further," he added.

"What about acquittals?"

"That, too, if you want." Squirrel gave his *what-the-shit* shrug, letting Hickey know that he'd already thought about that.

"So tell me why you ruled them out this time?"

"Because this is one bad dude we have here," Squirrel said. "And because gun crimes are usually convictions, especially if we find the gun."

All of these cases had that in common. Corelli, who'd spent more time going through the files than even Hickey, didn't seem to have a word to say about The Squirrel's methodology, nor was he offering any thoughts about who they should start with.

So Hickey asked his law student. "Give me your one, two, three then."

"There's Holmes," Squirrel said right away. "Only one of the three who ever shot at anything."

Antwan Woodruffe Holmes was nineteen and a gang member when Leishman put him away for the crime of shooting a twelve-year-old girl riding in her parents' car. It was a tragic case of wrong place, wrong time. The family was not a target. Holmes and his driver were looking for someone in a rival black gang supposedly driving a similar-looking car. The Crips and Banging Horns were fighting for turf in Lawrence Heights, a low-income neighbourhood better known to cops as The Jungle. The girl recovered from her wounds but Holmes got put away for four years. Released in 2013, he worked some but was put in a gang recovery program as a condition of parole, and he was doing that during the time of the first killings. Home address listed in Scarborough. Gun used was a Hi-Point, a cheap pistol popular with gangs in Toronto but hardly accurate enough to kill anyone in a moving car.

"Corelli?" Hickey asked, and the detective moved his bulk off its perch on the windowsill.

Corelli shrugged *why not*. "Guy should be pretty easy to find."

The Squirrel chimed in. "Only problem is this guy is black. I thought the dude we're looking for is white."

Hickey repeated his doubts about the composite.

"Start with his parole officer," he said.

Corelli nodded and wrote it down. Corelli wrote every-thing down.

"Bank account, cellphone, credit cards, passport, okay?" Hickey asked. "Look and see if Antwan may have met a new friend about three years ago . . . a friend with money." He looked from Corelli back to The Squirrel. "Next?"

"Guess it's Sullenberger. The other guy, the perv, doesn't excite me."

"So what's exciting about Sullenberger?" Hickey asked, flipping the thin file.

"He's that other thing—someone who's gonna be hard to find."

Hickey had already decided The Squirrel should be on this one. Gerald Michael Sullenberger, twenty-three, was sen-tenced to the max by Leishman, three years, after pleading guilty and refusing to divulge who he'd been running a gun into the country for. One of those expensive Glocks, bought in the States, seized from his car at the border. The judge of-fered the guy a deal, but he never talked. Served the full three, out in 2013, no record of any work, no current address.

"So why do you think him?" Hickey asked.

"Guy didn't talk," Squirrel said. "Could have probably got away with one and a half and he took the full three. That's what those mob guys did back in the day, didn't they? That *omerta* shit?"

Hickey nodded slowly. "Bit of a long shot, I'd say Squirrel, but he's yours. I'm more interested in the fact that he seems to have dropped off the face of the earth."

That left Hickey with the perv, Shelby Arthur Swenson, sentenced to three years by Leishman for gun possession and indecent assault, a peeping Tom who took it to the next level and broke into a neighbour's house, holding the pretty wife at gunpoint while he had his fun with her. Got out in 2011, eventually worked for Uber driving cabs, has a current home address in Etobicoke. Gun was a Walther, never once fired. Swenson was a little older than the other two, twenty-seven when sentenced, making him late thirties now. All the evidence said it was a younger man.

"We gotta do this fast," Hickey said. "Let's share what we have on Friday, okay?"

He checked his watch and dashed out. Day eight of the trial was several hours old and he wanted to catch some of Maddow working his last witness. Hickey knew Maddow planned to wrap up the case for the Crown that afternoon.

Carl Barington was sweating, when he got there. Hickey was disappointed that he'd missed Maddow walking him through the clandestine diary he'd kept of Mandamus meetings, the one that his wife had told police where to find once she discovered he was one of the group's members. What he recorded there was key to the Crown case. Barington was the money man. A devout Catholic embezzling money, tens of thousands, from his church and Mandamus had evidently used it to pay for the killings. His diary had identified the other members of Mandamus by their real names.

Part of the sweating, Hickey knew, was due to Maddow's tough questions but the other part was because of the withering, accusatory glares coming from his former conspirators, the men in the prisoners' docks. Hickey knew the expression *No honour among thieves* was not always true. The Mafia relied on honour to keep its secrets. So, too, did Mandamus, Hickey thought, judging from the sense of betrayal playing out here now, the daggers directed Barington's way from the cheap seats.

Hickey wouldn't have missed it. He thought this had to be the best ticket in town.

He looked around the rapt spectator gallery for Barington's wife and son, but they weren't there. His wife, who Barington had tried to kill for betraying him, a crime for which he was serving 20 years for the first-degree murder of her young lover. For that reason, and the fact he'd be tried separately on the conspiracy charges, he'd been declared a hostile witness. Maddow was pulling no punches.

"Was there any doubt in your mind, Mr. Barington," Maddow asked, standing just a few feet from the witness stand, "that your diary was recording the deliberations of men who were determined to commit crimes to achieve their ends?"

Barington shifted uncomfortably in his chair. "No. No doubt," he said quietly.

"And that they had the intention and means to carry those crimes out?"

"Yes."

"Meaning yes, you have no doubt, is that right?"

"Yes."

"That it wasn't just idle talk about what they'd *like* to happen?"

"No."

"And after each *mission*, or shall we say after each execution—"

Jaris bounced to his feet. "Objection!" he thundered.

"Sustained," Judge Foley agreed. But Hickey knew that Maddow had successfully planted the word with each juror.

"After each *action* directed by the group, then, Mr. Barington, what happened?" Maddow asked.

"We were sent an email from either Judge Leishman or Morgan Cathcart saying *mission accomplished.*"

"And what did you take that to mean?"

"That the target had been killed."

There were exhales from the gallery, as if the tension building up all morning had just been punctured. A perfect note to end the Crown's case on, Hickey thought. Maddow turned away from Barington and said to the jury, "Then I have no further questions of this witness," and Hickey thought Maddow managed to work a note of disdain into *this witness.*

Juris rose and, refusing to approach the witness, asked, "This diary you kept, Mr. Barington," and he managed to dangle it from his raised right hand like it might contain some hideous defecation or perhaps a dead rat, held it there for one or two seconds, then let it fall sloppily to his table. "Someone with a suspicious mind might read it differently, might they not?"

Barington looked like he had no idea what the lawyer was getting at. Hickey, however, marveled at the simplicity of the question. Don't answer that, Hickey thought. But Barington did, saying, "I couldn't really say, sir."

"Someone with a suspicious mind," Juris asked, repeating, "might regard it as self-serving, might they not?"

"Self-serving?" Barington asked.

"Yes, designed perhaps to divert attention from the very serious crimes *you* committed, sir."

This time Barington didn't say a word.

"I take it you still consider yourself a good Catholic?"

Barington hesitated, then said, "Yes, I do."

"A good Catholic," Juris repeated. "A devout man who embezzled money from his church. Enough money, if we believe the Crown's case, to pay someone to kill eleven people? And you did so by seducing an innocent young woman, a woman who was on the verge of becoming a nun, for the purpose of blackmailing her not to tell anyone what you were doing. Those were your sins, and your sins alone, were they not Mr. Barington?"

Barington mumbled something about never facing those

charges in court.

"Oh, but you will!" Juris bellowed. Hickey thought he was well on his way to convincing the jury that Barington was a despicable hypocrite, and his next step might be to suggest that he was testifying against his fellow conspirators in order to get a lighter sentence for himself. But Juris instead did one of his famous pivots and approached the witness stand holding Barington's diary, which he had retrieved from his table.

"Can you tell the court, sir," Juris asked, "why we see the word *mission* used again and again in these pages?"

"We, uh, had a hard time agreeing what to call them, so we just said *action* or *mission*."

"Rather than hits? Murders? Executions?"

This time it was Maddow who rose to object, but Foley directed Barington to answer it.

"That's what they meant," Barington said.

"And you had direct evidence that people were killed because of the decisions Mandamus made? Please tell us what that evidence was, Mr. Barington."

Barington thought for a minute. "Mr. Cathcart asked me if I could raise more money, and naturally I asked how much more. He told me that each mission cost fifteen thousand dollars."

"So your source was Mr. Cathcart, was it?"

"Yes, it was."

"Did he ever ask you to sign cheques payable to someone for that amount?"

"No," Barington said. "Mr. Cathcart insisted on doing all that himself."

"You just made sure enough money was embezzled to do the job, is that right?"

"It was deposited into a numbered account. Mr. Cathcart had signing rights. I did not."

"So you never knew who—or precisely what—was done

with that money, did you."

"No personal knowledge—"

"—No personal knowledge, exactly. All your evidence that people were killed with that money came to you from Cathcart, and before Cathcart took charge, I suppose Judge Leishman."

"Yes, because they apparently carried out the group's wishes," Barington said.

Hickey sensed that Juris had more questions he probably wanted to ask, but Barington's use of *apparently* made him cut it short. It was a weak word in the context of sworn testimony because it hinted at hearsay, or Barington's impression, and Juris was content to leave with that gift.

"And *apparently*," Juris said to effect, "both those gentlemen are deceased and unable to verify your account. I think I have run out of questions I need to ask you, sir."

Hickey waited until the judge adjourned the trial to tomorrow and many of the spectators had filed out. He watched as Maddow rose wearily from his chair and took his time packing his briefcase—probably, Hickey thought, because he was in no hurry to face the inquisitive journalists waiting outside. When he turned to go, he caught Hickey's eye and Hickey saw the dark shadow of concern on his face.

Like a man who knew he may be losing the game.

CHAPTER EIGHTEEN

O n Thursday morning, her teaching day, Gwen unlocked her office door and stumbled on a large brown envelope that had apparently been slipped under it. At first she thought it must have been a student's late assignment and set it down on her credenza while she took off her coat. But then she noticed it was addressed to *Prof. Van Loon* and marked *Private*. So she sat down, put her coffee aside and opened it. There was a handwritten note, but instead of an assignment there was a photograph attached to it.

It was an image of herself, stark naked, taken through a doorway, about to go down on James Bannerman. You could only see her face in profile because it was taken from behind but she was recognizable in the buff, slightly thicker in the waist than she'd like, but obviously enthusiastic for what she was doing. She recognized the urine-coloured drapes from the motel room that evening. The note was addressed to *Little Mrs. Cummypants*.

Oh shit!

Gwen felt herself go cold as she read the uneven handwriting.

I know this is a shock to you, but you need to read all of this completely through, and take your time thinking about it. Really take your time, understand? This can turn out okay for you, but only if you follow my instructions exactly. A lot depends on how well you co-operate. If you don't, then you know what happens. Someone else gets to see this one and all the others, so they'll know what a little skank you can be behind closed doors. Be home alone at two o'clock tomorrow afternoon when I call. It was signed, *An admiring onlooker.*

She stopped reading, her mind so completely in shock she could hardly breathe or process the words. Literally, her world—everything, her status in academe, the nice condo she owned in Rosedale, her modest savings, her reputation and social status—seemed to be crashing down around her, all because of an afternoon's indiscretion. *This can't be happening. It can't. Please make this go away.* But she knew that it was very real—at least as real as Bannerman's cock had been pressing against her backside—and that blackmail like this could cost a lot of money. Thousands and thousands, and she wasn't sure she could get her hands on that much. Part of her wanted to break down and cry, but she was just in too much shock. *I need to keep a clear head to think my way through this.*

When she read the note all the way through, it finished with a post script.

I am a person with very particular tastes, Prof. Van Loon. I'm not going to leave it to chance, on whether or not I get what I want. You are going to give it to me. I know that once you've had a chance to think this through, you will understand that doing what I say is the only way to come out of this okay. I will not harm you, and your life can be normal, as long as you obey me. And I do mean OBEY.

Her insides were tumbling, her hands visibly shaking. *Obey* stuck in her mind like a terror, and the ominous phrase *a lot depends on how well you co-operate.* She was not used to being controlled like this, but there was nothing she could do. The note finished with.

If I have even the slightest hint that you've said anything, or if you do not follow these instructions explicitly . . .then your life will definitely change, and not for the better.

Then she thought of something else. The note said be home tomorrow. He knew her schedule. And, she realized, her home telephone number.

Not knowing what else to do, Gwen quickly put everything back into the envelope and hid it in the bottom drawer of her desk, as if she was wishing it away.

The rest of the day — her final teaching day for the winter semester — was a blur. She barely remembered giving a short lecture by rote to her class on the different literary perspectives of Thomas King. She skipped lunch and tried to dole out all the urgent marking to her teaching assistant. And she spent most of the early afternoon trying to think and think and think about what she might have to do. There was the opera fundraiser tonight, she thought with alarm, trying to imagine how she could ever leave her condo at night in an expensive dress while she was being threatened, perhaps stalked, by a blackmailer. He knew where she worked, who she was, what she had done and probably where she lived, and he would make her pay for it.

The tears finally came when she arrived home and took refuge in the shower—great heaving sobs that made her shoulders shake. She began to shiver the moment she turned the water off. This was the first time in her life that she'd felt this kind of paralyzing fear. She let the towel drop to her feet and just pressed her still-soapy breasts forward against the tiles and waited for her sobbing to stop.

No one must ever learn about this.

Of course, she also spent a lot of time wondering who. So far as she knew, she didn't have any enemies, or folks with any reason to wish her harm. The note had been creepy and suggestive — and she thought at first it might be something kinky her new friend, James, might try if he wanted to take her interest in him to an erotic new level. She didn't really know him well enough to be sure about that, but she had given him her home phone number.

Why would he need to blackmail me? Am I not already giving him everything he wants?

The next day, 2 o'clock seemed to take forever to arrive. Gwen spent the morning figuring out just how much money she could get her hands on in a hurry from her bank accounts and credit cards. Counting her personal line of credit, she figured maybe thirty thousand. She had no idea whether that would be enough. She felt a sense of injustice welling up inside her. So many of her friends had done it—cheated on their husbands, at least once, or sometimes shacked up with students, like Geruta had. Why was she the one to get caught?

Then she thought if it wasn't James, might it be his wife? Perhaps he wasn't telling the truth about an open relationship and his wife was having him followed. Jealousy could cause a suspicious woman to do crazy things.

The phone rang on the dot of 2 and she let it ring three times before picking it up. "Hello?" she asked, not able to stop her voice from shaking.

The voice came back at her in a dull, low monotone, disguised somehow—a man's voice and not a woman's. "Good afternoon, Prof. Van Loon. Been a good little girl scout then, have we?" She thought the voice sounded young, but realized there was no way to tell that. He was using some kind of filter that made him sound otherworldly, like a dull, animal growl. But he acted very much in control, like he'd probably done this before.

"I have followed your instructions, if that's what you mean," she said.

"That's very good," he said quickly. "I do want to be proud of you. If this keeps up, we will get along just fine. Do you mind if I call you Gwen?"

She'd never talked to a blackmailer before. "Who are you?"

"Oh, Gwen," he said softly. "You don't get to ask me questions, okay? Are we both going to be clear about that?"

"Yes," she said, trying to compose herself.

"Yes, what?"

"Yes," she repeated. "Yes, I'm clear."

"Say you're sorry then."

"I'm . . .sorry."

"Good," he said, letting his authority sink in for a moment. "Now, I have another question. Tell me what, exactly, you have on right now."

A chill ran down her spine. "I beg your pardon?"

The voice got colder. "What . . .are . . .you . . .wearing?"

She was prepared for blackmail, but not this. She wanted to tell him it was none of his business, just tell me how much you want. But she remembered his ominous note. "Obey," it had said. This was no time to be making him cross.

"Just a skirt and blouse," she said.

"Describe them for me."

"The skirt is gray, my blouse is yellow."

"Tell me, does it show off your nice legs?"

She managed not to say anything to that. *Dear God, does he actually know me?*

"Shoes? Nylons?" the voice asked.

"No."

He paused. "I think I like the idea of you barefoot." She felt another chill go down her body. He was starting to creep her out. She wondered if he imagined her talking to him from the bedroom right now, instead of just standing in the hallway, petrified, wondering what he was going to ask her next.

She tried again. "I think I need to know what you want for the picture you took of me."

"Pictures," he corrected her. "The one I sent you captured the spirit of the occasion, didn't you think?"

"There are others?" Then she remembered his note said

there were.

"I could send you a few more, if you like. They get better." He paused a few seconds. "I hope you don't mind me saying, Gwen, that you're actually quite a beautiful woman with no clothes on."

How long had he stayed shooting pictures through the back window of that motel, she wondered. How long had he spent looking at the pictures? She began to wonder if he might want something more from her than money.

"Tell me what you want," she said.

He didn't answer for a long minute. "In good time," he said. "But first I need to be sure you're really going to obey me. Phones make me nervous. I want your email address please. Not at work. I need your personal email."

She gave it to him.

"I will send you further instructions. Not today or tomorrow, in a couple of days. Follow them to the letter." Then he hung up.

Gwen just stood there for a long time holding the dead phone receiver in her hand.

Most women have rape fantasies. That doesn't mean we want to be raped. It means that it is tantalizing to think about losing control, being forced against our will. I have never been raped, am sickened by the very thought of it, yet some of my most exciting masturbation fantasies involve being taken by force. I know it's a paradox, but women are allowed to think two ways at once. It's okay so long as it's my fantasy, not some sick rapist's.

Was this caller, she asked herself, inviting her to live that fantasy? For a few shocking seconds, she felt her body tingle in anticipation—or was it dread, she wasn't sure—of what was going to happen. But then reason took hold again, and she thought of that phone call from James on her birthday.

Sometimes there can be a wicked little voice that whispers in your ear that you've done it before and nothing happened, so why not do it again? But it's usually a mistake to listen to that voice. No, that's not true. It's always a mistake.

CHAPTER NINETEEN

John Juris proved to be full of surprises. When Monday morning came and the courtroom overflowed with spectators there to hear his long-awaited opening for the defence, he took just 10 minutes to tell the jurors why they needed to acquit the six defendants. Hickey's intuition had been right. Juris was basing his case on two simple points—why would they do it? And there was no proof that they did.

He didn't need very long to say that.

His first witness was an even bigger surprise. Maddow had brainstormed 17 possible people Juris might call to the stand, all of the defendants and a who's who of Ontario's legal profession, including a former premier, Edward Darling, who was now a partner in the city's biggest law firm. Maddow had doubted Juris would dare call any of the accused . . . in fact he gave Hickey five-to-one odds that he wouldn't, Juris, in Maddow's estimation, being far too savvy a barrister to expose an accused to direct attack. Yet when the white-haired lawyer called out the name of his first witness, everyone turned in surprise to watch Desmond Burnside rise from his prisoner's box and walk confidently to the stand to get sworn in. He was impeccably dressed in a pinstriped gray suit that Hickey guessed would be a Gucci or Valentino, and a stylish conservative red tie, which seemed to serve as a talisman for the blue bloods of conservativism who really thought they were preordained to be in control. Burnside's choice of *street clothes* probably cost more than Hickey's salary for a month.

"State your name please," the court clerk asked him.

The province's former attorney-general straightened himself up to his full six-foot-four height and squared his broad shoulders. He raised his hand righteously.

"Desmond Scott Eaton Burnside," he said, then added, "QC," and swore to tell the truth.

Juris greeted him with a short bow and turned to the jury. "Good morning, Mr. Burnside. First of all, would you mind telling the jury what those initials after your name mean?"

It was nicely rehearsed, Hickey thought. Burnside, sitting ramrod straight in the stand, was happy to comply. "Certainly, Mr. Juris. It stands for Queen's Counsel. It is an honour conferred by Her Majesty in recognition of exemplary merit and contribution to the legal profession."

"Indeed. It is considered to be the highest honour a lawyer can receive, is it not?"

"Many of us consider it to be," Burnside said. Hickey remembered that Juris had one, too.

"And how many of your fellow defendants share such a distinction, sir?"

"Four of us." Burnside paused a moment, then said, "Yes, four."

"Four of the six of you, facing trial in this courtroom for the heinous crime of conspiracy to commit murder, happen to be recipients of the highest honour in your profession?"

Burnside did not answer. He tried to look humble for the jury, but Hickey didn't think it was a role he was convincing in.

"Indeed, QC is only one of the many honours you are entitled to list after your name, Mr. Burnside, is that not right?" Juris asked, continuing.

"I don't usually list them all," Burnside quipped.

"Nevertheless, I would ask you to list off what they are and what they mean for the jury."

So Burnside turned to speak directly to the 12 citizens who

held his fate in their hands. "Well, LLB, of course. That's the degree that entitles you to apply for the bar. I earned mine at Queen's University in nineteen seventy-eight. What follows are titles for education and bestowed honours but none, curiously enough, for a former member of the Legislative Assembly of Ontario, nor for the two years I served in cabinet as attorney-general . . ."

Juris interrupted. "You were head of the legal system for Ontario, in other words. And being a former cabinet minister means that you are entitled to be introduced as *The Honorable*, is that not so?"

"When I was in office, yes, but apparently not in perpetuity," Burnside said, glancing over at the jury again with a faint smile, as if the very idea of being introduced in such a formal, archaic way was embarrassing. "Not sure how I'd feel about being introduced that way today."

Hickey recalled some of the background he'd gathered about Burnside and the others. Most had attended expensive private schools like Upper Canada College or Trinity College School or Appleby, and their classmates had been likeminded sons and daughters of the entitled rich, used to joking about their privilege in a clubby manner like this. Hickey thought this might backfire with the jury, although a couple of them rewarded Juris by smiling like people tend to smile when they've been let in on the secret.

"And OOnt and OC?" Juris asked, reading from what may have been Burnside's CV.

"Order of Ontario, Order of Canada."

"How do you get those honours?"

"The Order of Ontario," Burnside said, "is conferred on someone for high achievement in any field. It's the province's highest honour. The Order of Canada is the same thing for the whole country, given for service to the nation."

"On the recommendation of whom, sir?"

"Actually, the Ontario one is conferred by the lieutenant-governor on the recommendation of an advisory council, which includes the chief justice of Ontario and up to six previous recipients."

"So, in other words, your peers."

"I suppose so, yes."

"So tell us," Juris said, approaching the witness gravely. "How did a person of your august stature get involved with this Mandamus group?"

"Judge Leishman was an old friend. He asked me."

"You attended the same church, am I correct? Holy Redeemer Catholic?"

"Yes, that's right. The judge organized a Saturday discussion group that several of us were drawn to. One of the topics was shortcomings in our justice system, and at some point Judge Leishman suggested a separate group made up of just lawyers."

"So what made you, someone sworn to uphold the law and indeed someone who administered this province's legal system at the highest level, what led you to join a group that was conspiring to subvert it?"

Juris let the question hang in the air for a second or two for effect, wanting the jury to wonder if he might be about to cross-examine his own client.

"Mandamus wasn't anything like that," Burnside said. "Do you think I . . . that any of us . . . would have anything to do with something like that? Yes, we were concerned about shortcomings in the justice system, but our discussions focused on how to reform it, not how to circumvent it."

"So you were not vigilantes, as the Crown is suggesting?"

"Good God, sir. No. Never. My whole career . . ." And Desmond Burnside, once known to his political opponents as *Old Ironpants*, bit his bottom lip and appeared to falter, as if overwhelmed by the outrage of having to face such ridiculous and contrived challenges to his sterling reputation.

Juris made sure he waited a few moments for Burnside to compose himself.

"Yes? You were saying about your career?"

"Sir," Burnside said, looking suddenly remarkably in control, "my distinguished career in law and politics speaks to the impossibility of me knowingly participating in a scheme of this sort. Yes, we often discussed cases of failed justice. We were lawyers, after all, and part of our pledge to uphold the law is to seek ways to improve the legal system."

"You did not," Juris asked, going on, "recommend certain criminals for elimination?"

"No!" Burnside thundered, bringing his hand down hard on the railing in front of him, sending a shot through the courtroom.

"And you did not direct either Judge Leishman or Morgan Cathcart to hire someone to carry out your kill orders?"

"There *were* no kill orders—"

" —But the jury heard from Mr. Barington, sir," Juris interrupted. "Did he not keep a diary saying you did all those things?"

"The man is a scoundrel, lying through his teeth."

"You mean you never discussed those things?"

"Some of it, some of those criminal incidents, may have been mentioned, but only as examples of the things we were trying to fix."

"Fix?" Juris lowered his voice, facing Burnside from less than two feet away. "And precisely how did you intend to fix them?"

"By lawful means. Only by lawful means. Advocating for new legislation. Minimum sentences for certain offences. The sort of thing I managed to press Ottawa to do when I was attorney-general."

Juris held eye contact for a long moment, then turned and

marched over to his desk, returning to the witness stand holding two thick volumes. One was the Bible. The other, he pointed out for the jury's benefit, was the Criminal Code of Canada.

"You've sworn on your honour, Mr. Burnside — once on the Bible to tell the truth, and once on your bar admission to uphold the law." He held both volumes up in the air. "Swear to us now, you remain true to those pledges. Swear to us now you have committed no crimes. Swear to us, sir, that you are telling the truth."

And the Hon. Desmond Burnside, QC, LLB, OOnt, OC, held up his hand again and so swore.

The very personification of entitlement, Hickey thought as Burnside glanced over to the jury to gauge their reactions. He'd read about psychological experiments that demonstrated that people of wealth and privilege were more likely to regard themselves as more worthy than others, more likely to feel righteous about their decisions and more willing to exploit others. But this had been something on another scale entirely — extreme arrogance that entitled this man to lie about his actions and even to place himself above the law.

Now it was Maddow's turn.

They'd prepared for this possibility, of course—if one of the defendants actually decided to take the stand. Now one of them had. Hickey knew the entire trial probably now rested on whether the jury believed Desmond Burnside, a man whose picture they'd seen not too long ago on the front pages of newspapers. Maddow's job was simple—he needed to destroy him.

Whereas Juris had been armed with props — Burnside's resume and the Bible and the Criminal Code — Maddow approached the stand casually, with his hands in his pockets. His first question seemed almost an innocent one.

"Good morning, Mr. Burnside," he said with a smile.

"Please tell us, including your two years as attorney-general, how long did you serve as a member of the Legislative Assembly of this province?"

Burnside seemed surprised. He thought for a moment, as if trying to figure out what kind of trap it might be, then said, "Eight years."

"And during that time, you naturally would have done your share of constituency work—that is to say, dealt with problems that the voters of your riding brought directly to your attention?"

"That was certainly part of the job, yes." Burnside allowed himself a puzzled frown.

"You gave advice, and occasionally intervened with bureaucracy to speed action?"

"Yes."

Hickey imagined those kinds of favours would have be sought frequently at the Albany Club, a Burnside hangout, where he often broke bread several times a week with his fellow establishment Conservatives.

"And in performing those duties," Maddow asked him, "did you ever encounter, or offer advice to, a person named Sheridan Barrie?"

Hickey saw Burnside's demeanour change, a stiffening of his arms and a narrowing of eyes, like he now understood where this was leading.

"Yes, I did," Burnside said. He was aware, as Hickey was, that Sheridan Barrie was in the courtroom, as he'd been most days, sitting with the other relatives of victims in the front row.

"Can you tell the jury about those particular meetings, please? What advice did you offer? What help did you give?"

Burnside cleared his voice and Hickey noticed that he was making a conscious effort not to look at Barrie.

"Sheridan Barrie is a lawyer and a lobbyist. He happens to

be of a different political persuasion but as a constituent of mine, when he came for help, I was happy to hear him out." Burnside squirmed in his seat before continuing. "It was a particularly tragic case—his son, a fine young man on the cusp of attending university, was involved in an automobile accident and was facing charges. Serious charges. Had I still been attorney-general, you understand, I could not have intervened. But as an MPP, well, offering advice, even legal advice, came with the territory."

"You mentioned it was a tragic case," Maddow said. "Can you tell us why?"

"A woman unfortunately died. A pedestrian."

"And the fine young man who killed her . . . he was drunk and fled the scene, did he not?"

"Yes," Burnside admitted.

"And as a result of your advice, what happened?"

"Oh, I can't vouch that I had that much to do with it," Burnside said. "But the charges against him were dismissed."

"Why?"

"The search of the boy's home was apparently done without a proper warrant."

"And your advice to Mr. Barrie was to challenge that evidence?"

"Sir, as a lawyer . . . you understand, surely . . . solicitor-client privilege. I cannot answer your question."

"I understand," Maddow said, glancing at the jury. "So the boy got off. Got off on a technicality at the age of seventeen." He stopped and looked back at Burnside. "Can you tell the jury what became of that very fortunate young man?"

Burnside now was nervously crossing and uncrossing his arms, starting to look flustered. He, and Hickey, knew perfectly well what was coming next.

"Unfortunately, a few months later, he was found dead in the family's garage. Initially, it was thought to be a suicide.

But that later changed."

"It changed how?"

"I believe police linked the gun found at the scene to those other ones, the ones without serial numbers."

"And his death is listed among the Mandamus killings, is it not? It fit the pattern."

"So the police say," Burnside said.

Maddow approached the stand. "Do you, a former attorney-general, question their finding, sir?"

"No," Burnside said after a pause. "I, of course, have every confidence in the thoroughness of police investigations, as a general rule."

Maddow turned and walked over to the Crown table and picked up what had become familiar to everyone, Barington's well-cited diary.

"It's interesting," Maddow said, walking back towards the witness stand leafing through its pages. "Do you not find it so? That the case of Peter Wilton Barrie, the seventeen-year-old son, is recorded in Barington's diary. You discussed him at one of your meetings, did you not?"

"Yes, I believe it was mentioned," Burnside said quickly, seeming to dismiss it.

"In what context?" Maddow asked.

"I'm afraid I don't remember."

"Did you perhaps bring it up? Is it possible that you, Mr. Burnside, cited his case as an example of shortcomings in the justice system?"

"I don't remember. I don't believe it was me, no."

Maddow placed his hands on the railing at the front of the witness stand and looked Burnside in the eye. "Because you would have been conflicted if you had, wouldn't you."

Burnside actually blinked and averted his glance. "I don't know what you mean by asking me that."

"I mean," Maddow continued, "you gave his father advice,

the charges were dropped, the boy walked free. It would have been awkward for you to claim it was a travesty of justice. *Because you made it happen.*"

"As I said," Burnside said, trying to recover. "I do not believe I participated in that discussion, if indeed there even was a discussion."

"But a few minutes ago," Maddow said, "you admitted there was."

"I meant—"

"The transcript will make clear what you said, sir."

Hickey wished he could have seen the look on Sheridan Barrie's face. He was leaning forward in his seat several rows directly in front, no doubt staring at Burnside with a grieving father's outrage. Burnside's shoulders, Hickey noticed, had slumped forward. His bespoke suit seemed to hang from his shoulders.

"The important point, Mr. Burnside, is that you were connected to at least one of the victims of the Mandamus conspiracy. The Crown has already alleged that those eleven victims were not chosen randomly, but were plucked out of the files of people that you or your law firms represented and that Mandamus decided were worthy of elimination. Your victims were all known to you, weren't they?"

"That is not true," Burnside spluttered.

"*Vengeance is Mine,* Mr. Burnside. Was that not your group's motto?"

"That is . . . taken from the Bible, sir."

"And so it is. As the word of God," Maddow countered. "You were using it differently though — as justification to seek vengeance yourselves."

"That's ridiculous . . . I had absolutely no reason to seek vengeance on young Peter Barrie!"

Maddow, halfway between the witness stand and the jury benches, stopped in his tracks and held one hand high in the air for a second before sweeping it down by his side. "Exactly, Mr. Burnside. Exactly. But I am going to suggest one obvious consequence to you, sir, from that answer. And it is this—that there must have been another reason for your group to target that seventeen-year-old boy for elimination, another reason for Mandamus to take out its righteous vengeance on him."

Burnside chose to say nothing.

"It was to honour the victim, was it not?" Maddow asked as he turned slowly to Burnside again. "The innocent woman who died as a result of young Mr. Barrie's tragic misjudgments, for which he escaped punishment with your help. Perhaps you can tell the jury who he ran down at Sherbourne and the Danforth that October night."

"I'm afraid—"

"Marlene Elizabeth Cathcart. Do you recognize that name, sir? Marlene Elizabeth Cathcart?"

Burnside glared back at him.

"Answer me. Do you recognize that name?"

Burnside said, "Yes, I do."

"She was the wife of Morgan Cathcart, who was a fellow member of Mandamus—in fact, Judge Leishman's putative successor and the man you, sir, nominated to take over leadership of this murderous group. A man who certainly had good reason for vengeance, would you not agree?"

Burnside looked shell-shocked.

"Again, answer my question for the court!"

Burnside, looking much older than his sixty-two years, croaked out his answer.

"And on July twentieth, twenty fourteen, the day after Peter Wilton Barrie's body was found in the family's garage, you and the others received a message directly from Mr. Cathcart. Perhaps you can tell the court what that message was."

"I . . . don't—"

"Mission accomplished!" Maddow bellowed. "Mission accomplished! Is that not right, sir?"

Burnside's answer was barely audible and Maddow made him repeat it, so the jury could hear.

"Yes, we received that message."

Hickey heard gasps in the courtroom and noticed one of the jurors with her mouth agape.

Sheridan Barrie's righteous eyes, Hickey imagined, must have at that very moment been boring deeply into Burnside's treacherous soul.

CHAPTER TWENTY

Four ninety-nine Kennedy Avenue turned out of be one of those faux-Tudor bungalows on a thin lot that a thirty-something couple expecting a child might buy as a starter home. Close enough to Bloor West that you could walk to a Starbucks for your morning latte before catching the subway at Runnymede to get to work downtown. But too close to escape the constant hum of traffic that would disturb your sleep and make you too tired to enjoy it. Gwen hadn't really read the listing so didn't know what was inside, whether it had one or two bathrooms or two or three bedrooms. She didn't give a shit about the house. She was there because today it was advertised for an open house.

Listed by Frieda Bannerman.

She had methodically gone through the real estate sections of the Saturday papers, not really expecting to find anything, and was surprised when her listing turned up in the *Globe and Mail*, in a house ad for Royal LePage. James' wife had fortunately chosen to take his last name. Her picture showed a wide, handsome face, with sloe eyes, Gwen thought very sexy. Probably got a lot of customers that way, just from the picture.

There was another thing, a thing that frankly surprised her because James hadn't mentioned it. His wife was black.

Of course, he hadn't mentioned lots of things, like where he was living, or where his family was from, or that he was married to a very attractive woman. Finding her picture made

Gwen put Frieda Bannerman at the head of the line of suspects that was forming in her mind.

A person who might have a motive to blackmail me.

She hadn't told a soul about her predicament, of course, not
even Geruta, because at first she thought it might be James
and she was embarrassed to suspect him with no evidence.
Then, when she'd thought about it, that didn't make sense,
because he'd actually appeared in the blackmail picture and
no blackmailer would do that, let himself be photographed in
rapture as the person he wanted to blackmail was about to
give him a blow job.

But his wife? His attractive wife? Perhaps what he called
his *open marriage* was just a convenient lie. As soon as she saw
Frieda's picture, Gwen thought she could just as easily be an
extremely suspicious, jealous and long-suffering spouse, who
may have twigged to her husband's odd hours and lengthy
absences and decided to do something about it, find out what
he was up to besides work. Perhaps she'd hired someone to
follow him. Perhaps they'd been followed to that motel. Perhaps it wasn't money from Gwen this woman wanted but
something else—the goods, perhaps, or retribution, or
grounds for divorce.

So Gwen developed the plan she was now carrying out,
dropping in at the open house to see if Frieda Bannerman,
who by now would have seen them, recognized her from the
pictures. She supposed it wouldn't be too hard to tell. Either
her eyes would widen in surprise at the first sight of Gwen,
or she'd treat her as just another curious stranger, and if it was
the latter, Gwen figured the most she'd lose was half an hour
of her Sunday wandering around a house she didn't want.
She hadn't worked out any plan if it went the other way.

In Toronto, the real estate market was more or less divided
by Yonge Street. You were either an east ender or you were a
west ender, and rare were the people who crossed over. You
wouldn't buy Kennedy Avenue unless you were a west ender

and Gwen, who'd lived in her Rosedale condo for a decade, was a committed east ender. If she needed an excuse, she'd simply have to say she was looking for something bigger.

Gwen took her time strolling the neighbourhood block near Kennedy, watching people arrive and depart, biding her time until the last half-hour when she figured there'd be fewer people competing for Frieda Bannerman's attention. At a quarter to four, when she walked in, the agent was talking to a couple who appeared to be the only viewers left in the house. Gwen slipped off her shoes at the door and smiled down the short hallway. Frieda gave her a quick look and continued where she'd left off. " . . . and if there happens to be an offer this weekend, can I call you at this number?" She was talking to an older couple, a man in glasses who was putting a measuring tape back in his holster and a graying woman who looked like she still needed convincing. They looked at each other and the man finally nodded yes.

Gwen came close to touching shoulders with her lover's wife as she showed the couple to the door. She stepped into the living room to let them pass. Frieda Bannerman flashed her one of those level, friendly looks that professionals use to tell you they're working hard at their jobs. No hint of recognition at all. But a stunner, Gwen decided, even prettier than her picture, five-two or five-three with the kind of body you were used to seeing on track athletes — narrow waist, an upholstered, jutting backside and a sleeveless sea-foam green jumpsuit that showed off long, toned, ebony arms. She wore enough jewelry that, when she walked, she jangled like a wind chime.

"I'm Frieda Bannerman," she said, slipping past and offering her hand fleetingly. "Welcome to Kennedy Avenue."

"Pleased to meet you," Gwen said. "I was walking by—"

"Just finishing up, be half a sec," Frieda said quickly, wanting to turn her attention back to the couple at the front door.

"There's my brochure for the listing in the kitchen. Please sign the register, then make yourself at home. Catch up with you in a jiff."

No sign whatsoever that she'd ever laid eyes on Gwen before this. No hint that she knew this was the woman her husband was fucking.

Gwen didn't give the living room much of a glance, thinking that she'd probably slit her wrists if she had to live in such a place. There were faux-Tudor beams criss-crossing the walls, making the room seem even smaller than it was. The stuffed, patterned sofa and chair didn't help, and there was a small cheap gas insert in the fireplace. A door led to the kitchen from the small dining room and she grabbed a brochure and didn't sign the register. A glance at the full-colour listing said this house had been built in 1952, which she guessed was when Swansea really developed as a village that was worth being gobbled up by the surrounding municipality of Toronto. It mentioned that Lucy Maud Montgomery had once lived in the neighbourhood, but Gwen guessed the author did not live anywhere near this busy, nondescript street. Once heavily Polish and Ukrainian, Swansea had lately become younger and more multicultural. A toney Montessori, no doubt swarming with BMWs and Volvos at pick-up time, occupied part of the west side of Kennedy just below Bloor.

Gwen was frowning at the sadly neglected backyard outside the master bedroom window when she sensed she wasn't alone. A rustle behind her, a slight closing of space, a hint of jasmin perfume. She half-turned to find James' wife in the doorway, seemingly very interested in her neat white legs and crimson toenails. Her sudden presence made Gwen jump.

"I have a habit of surprising people in bedrooms," Frieda said, looking coy when she said it, but using a tone of voice that made you wonder if it just slipped out that way or it was a deliberate double entendre.

Gwen was being inspected, and it made her uncomfortable. *What is this woman up to anyway? I'm reasonably sure she isn't my mysterious blackmailer but what else is going on? If I wasn't so out of practice, I'd swear she's trying to hit on me.*

But when Frieda spoke again, her gaze had shifted beyond her to the window. "I think with a little imagination and, oh, a hundred thousand dollars or so, you could push this wall out into that dreadful backyard and make a sitting room, don't you?"

Gwen allowed herself to relax a notch — a little too soon, as it turned out.

"That's if you think bedrooms are for sitting in," the woman said, crossing her feet casually and playfully jangling one of her hoop earrings.

Gwen recalled something James had said, that his wife was a gypsy-type. He never knew what she might be up to. She decided he was right about that. Now in the same room with her, Gwen felt awkward and foolish. Frieda, on the other hand, looked like a cat ready to pounce.

Normally, Gwen enjoyed the dance of seduction, if that's really what this was. She was just out of practice. She recalled that more than her share of men, and even a few women, had resorted to the same methods, and their playful double meanings and insinuations could speed up the music. This particular adventure, she thought, could either end up at the front door with a cool goodbye . . . or flat on her back on that bed over there with a frisky black real estate agent all over her. Sale or no sale.

But the moment passed. Either, Gwen thought, because she hadn't passed inspection or she hadn't given the lady a green or amber light — something, in other words, to make her risk, if her radar happened to be wrong, a potential complaint of unprofessional conduct to RECO.

"So," Frieda Bannerman said, "I can see that this isn't turning your crank." For some reason Gwen took her to mean the house and not the flirtatious possibilities, although she'd recently read a story about real estate agents who liked to proposition clients in empty houses.

"I'm looking for something bigger, I'm afraid."

"Oh," the agent said, stepping forward and placing a small, warm hand on Gwen's arm. "There's no need to be afraid, love."

Gwen could feel her arm tingling after Frieda squeezed gently and let go. She hoped she wasn't letting on that she felt an embarrassing arousal—embarrassing because, while Gwen didn't think she was up for a roll in the hay with another woman, contemplating doing it with the wife of a man she was letting screw her opened up erotic possibilities.

"Take my card. I'd be pleased to show you other places. I'm sure we can get you into something you'll like."

When they shook hands at the front door, Gwen felt another telltale parting squeeze. *Get me into something I like. I'm sure you could.* She walked down the short walkway and turned back to the house when she reached the street and caught that elfin, brown, attractive face darting back behind the drapes.

Well, James, you've certainly been honestly right about one thing. Being married to Frieda Bannerman must be a very open, gypsy experience, mustn't it?

Open to just about anything.

She took the subway across town to meet Geruta for a pre-arranged early dinner and drink at Café Bruxelles, their favourite bistro at Broadview and Danforth where they liked to enjoy Belgian mussels and frites and the fine Chardonnay house wine. Geruta lived nearby and they made it their practice to get out one Sunday a month away from school to talk about whatever was going on in their lives. Gwen arrived still a little shaken by her encounter with Frieda Bannerman and still in the dark about who might be trying to blackmail her. She wondered how much she should confide but if Geruta suspected she was on edge, she didn't let on. She had other things on her mind.

"So tell me, are you following that trial?" she asked when Gwen had settled in. Geruta, punctual to a fault, always arrived first.

Her distracted mind took a moment to connect. "Oh, that," she said. "No, actually, I'm not."

"You should," Geruta chirped, sitting forward confidentially. "There's a lot coming out, but not always what you'd expect."

"Tell me what you mean?"

"Well, Rachel Leishman testified the other day, and to say I was surprised is an understatement!"

"Was it juicy?" Gwen remembered only bits and pieces of the woman's story from the Cougar Lunch. "I think you've just kindled my interest. Please tell." She'd been impressed most of all by the attractive woman's hidebound loyalty to a much older husband who may have been a scoundrel. She couldn't remember doing anything similar for Gerald when they were together.

"The surprise," Geruta said, "was not what she said but what she didn't say."

They were regulars at Café Bruxelles, so Philippe the waiter was on them immediately for their drink orders. They chose a carafe of the house Koonunga Hill and took up his suggestion to glance at the blackboard on the back wall to check for specials.

"We should place our orders," Geruta said, looking around. "The drink crowd is starting to arrive."

"I thought we were the drink crowd," Gwen quipped.

"Ha. Good one," Geruta said. "Listen, I forgot to ask. How's the love life going these days?"

"Well, we've been to our first motel." Gwen could feel herself blushing slightly. "Tell me if that's good or bad."

"I wondered if he was still in the picture." Geruta gave her a symbolic thumbs up. "And it's very, very bad, actually. Congratulations."

"Do you and Zuhair still do those things?"

"We're starting to go out for long dinners instead." Geruta made a regretful face. "We don't seem to have the energy for very much else. He's doing his oral next month. It's cut out the shagging a bit."

Geruta caught her bemused look. "Yes, regretfully the oral part is being directed elsewhere."

"Oh, sorry."

Geruta flipped the menu open impatiently, pretending to study the regular entrees they both knew so well. Gwen got the message and pretended to do the same.

"I'm hungry, and right now," Geruta said, motioning for Philippe. She ordered mussels marinieres with langoustines, and of course another carafe of wine so they wouldn't have to wait for it when they finished the first one. Gwen, still flustered, ordered the same dish.

"So back to the trial, then," Gwen said. "I'm curious, mainly because of what happened at that lunch, but I honestly haven't had time to follow what's happened since."

"So," Geruta said, draining the last of the first carafe into her glass. "On Thursday, when she was on the stand, I actually followed it live in my office on Twitter but her story didn't come together for me until I read the fuller account in the *Globe* the next morning. Everyone's covering it, of course, but I like the *Globe* because lawyers are sort of in their demographic target group, right?"

"Even crooked lawyers?"

Geruta ignored that, possibly because of the way the conversation had gotten sidetracked a couple of minutes earlier.

Gwen thought it was exactly how Gerald used to behave with her in his serious, condescending way, refusing to get caught on the shoals of her playful asides.

"So Rachel, turns out she had to testify for most of the afternoon — mostly answering questions put by the Crown — about turning over her husband's papers to that lawyer . . . Cathcart I think his name was, right? The one who was found shot at his wife's grave that they thought was a suicide? Turning over the papers and then later finding the mysterious email list and using it. She told us all this at lunch."

"I remember," Gwen said. "But she later got a warning because they thought she must be the leak, right?"

"Yeah, by the guy who picked her up at that bar, the guy with the Mandamus tattoo. That was the warning. She said in court she was terrified but . . . I think she's probably been in similar situations before and knows how to handle herself."

"Wait, so she testified about that? I thought you were saying she held stuff back."

"Okay, remember there was another encounter?"

"What did she say happened exactly?"

"That he came back. The same guy came back. He tied her up in her house one night a few weeks later and it scared the shit out of her."

"Now I remember. She didn't go into any details, just said they came to an understanding, whatever that means."

"Do you remember her face when she said that? Like she was just, I don't know, whistling past the graveyard."

"You think her life was actually in danger?"

"Not something you'd let slip your mind, you think?" Geruta said, leaning closer. Gwen saw Philippe coming with steaming bowls of mussels in each hand. They let him serve them, reminding him again about the wine. Gwen was starved but she asked Geruta what she was getting at.

"That's what surprised me most," Geruta said. "She didn't

mention a word about him coming back in court."

Gwen left her fork poised over her mussels. "She told us but not them?" she asked finally.

"Exactly. Strange, isn't it?"

"I'll say," Gwen said, starting to eat slowly and trying to remember more from that lunch. Rachel Leishman had said the younger man hadn't looked like a lawyer, that he could have been a messenger. She remembered Geruta wondering afterwards whether he could have been the one the police were still looking for.

"The defence questioned her, too, but not about that. They were more interested in challenging the description she'd given police. I think they were probably trying to knock holes in her story, make the jury think she was unreliable. In any event, no one heard about that second encounter. As far as this case is concerned, it never happened."

"You're right," Gwen said. "That sure doesn't square with what she told us."

Geruta had deposited the larger pile of shells in the common shell bowl in the middle of the small table, and summoned Philippe to clear it away.

"If you're right," Gwen said, "and this guy's still at large, she may be scared he'll come again."

"Whatever deal she made—Christ, the guy was supposed to have always left a gun at the scene, didn't he? He could have been sent to kill her."

"Because, like, she was the leak, wasn't she. And she wanted to keep the judge's name out of it, I remember her saying that."

"Okay but it didn't work out that way, did it," Geruta said. "The police found out."

"Right."

"But maybe she—I don't know, the police seem to be treating Cathcart's death as a homicide. Rachel—just think about it—she could have been the link. She could have given him Cathcart in return for her life."

Gwen was listening so closely that her remaining mussels were turning cold and unappetizing. She patted her lips with the napkin and sat back.

"Wow. Wheels within wheels. You are really into the conspiracies of this thing, aren't you?"

Geruta shrugged. "She's got to be afraid of what could happen if he thinks she broke her deal with him. He could come after her again."

"Really? You don't think he's still around, do you?"

"Who knows?"

"But Rachel gave police a description of him. She did cooperate."

"Unless—"

"Oh, I get it. You're saying she might have given them a misleading description?"

"What would you do? Let's say her life was really on the line and she gave him something in return—something that would help him get away?"

"A deal with the devil?"

Geruta smiled. "A devil with a tattoo, it appears."

Now Gwen remembered Rachel talking about that at lunch, and the Cougar Lunch had been a few days before she went to the motel with James. Remembering how she and James spent some time discovering each other's bodies after the sex, him kissing the mole beside her navel and asking about the faint scar from her childhood appendectomy, her tracing the birthmark on his chest with her finger and finding traces of what looked like a tattoo. And what he had said about it when she asked—that it was something connected to an old girlfriend and he'd had to get it erased before getting married.

"Lots of men have tattoos these days, I guess," Geruta said

finally.

Gwen watched her finish off the second carafe, then said, "I suppose. Lots of them are devils, too."

But her thoughts were drifting miles away, to the Elmgrove again, trying to remember every detail about their night together, wondering if the blackmailer had gotten shots of what happened later, when James flipped her over and came at her from behind.

Strange. Until now she'd forgotten all about the traces of a tattoo on his shoulder.

Chapter Twenty-One

She read his email first thing Tuesday morning with a sense of dread.

It gave no clue to her stalker's identity. Hotmail accounts were easy to contrive, she knew, and his just read *cocksure*. His message rudely alluded to the photo he'd sent her. *You seem to have a preference for blow jobs. I like that. I like that a lot. But what I really want will have to wait. I'm not sure I can trust you, so we'll have to go through something first. You're going to go on a shopping trip.*

She wondered how he knew she was free today, that Tuesday was her day marking at home. He listed the items he wanted her to buy and warned, *I may be watching*. Ginseng tea and Johnson's Baby Oil at No Frills on Broadview south of Danforth. Three linen scarves at Frida on Wellington. Lavender soap at The Body Shop, The Atrium mall on King. A package to be picked up at Booty's, 506 Queen St. W. with instructions to try it on.

There was already ginseng in the house. She'd grown accustomed to drinking it strong with lemon juice and honey, to induce a restful sleep. It was also supposed to be a good aphrodisiac, which she guessed was more his line of thinking. She would have to go out for the other things. But then there was a second email ten minutes later, telling her what she had to wear, and a warning. *You must carry out these instructions to the letter, today.*

She took the subway one stop to Broadview and bought the baby oil. Since she was due for a food shop, she tossed some broccoli, tomatoes, lettuce and chicken breasts into the trolley, too. She realized at cash-out that she'd forgotten something on her list, and had to go back for it. Following his instructions, she was wearing no panties under her skirt. She'd never gone out in public before with nothing on underneath, and it felt wicked and oddly stimulating in the late-spring coolness. She thought about him constantly, but not in a good way, wondering if he was somewhere nearby watching, and how he might tell, you know, whether she was following all his instructions. But then she found out. Her cellphone rang when she was looking for riper avocados and it was that garbled voice again, asking her to lean over just a little more. He needed to check for himself, he said. She looked around the store when she straightened up, but no one was watching her and she felt embarrassed and foolish. To her consternation, she also could feel her labia involuntarily starting to swell.

All he said to her was, "Good girl."

After dropping off the oil and groceries at her condo, she subwayed downtown to pick up the lavender soap, then walked over to Frida for the linen scarves. She wondered why he'd instructed her to buy three. She kept looking around to see if someone might be following her. She'd changed on his instructions into a slightly shorter skirt, and as she walked west on Wellington the noontime sun warmed the backs of her legs, and she pressed her shopping close to the front of her to guard against a gust of wind accidentally revealing her scandalous secret.

He phoned her again and asked if she liked to shave down there and she said no. "That's fine," he replied. "I won't ask you to. I like women with lots of hair on their pussies."

He was getting bolder and more explicit.

When she finally got to Booty's, just after 2, and asked if a package had been left for her, the clerk handed over a Rene Rofe box and asked if she'd like to try it on. She took it into a small fitting room and opened it apprehensively. Her *gift* was a garter body stocking with black net strings and an open crotch, and only a tiny red G-string panty to cover the rest. When she managed to wiggle into it, the strings cut uncomfortably into her fleshy breasts, her nipples and navel peeked through the mesh, and her dark brown pubic hair bristled out the top of the skimpy G-string. She'd never even thought about wearing such a thing in her life, and it made her look more or less like a prostitute. But another surprise awaited her at the cash. This was no gift. She was expected to pay for it—$258.99 plus tax.

When she arrived home, another email directed her to shower with the lavender soap, brew herself some ginseng tea and drink two cups, put on the girdle-thing and take the scarves and the baby oil to her bedroom at precisely 5 PM. He said he'd phone on her land line but asked her not to forget her cellphone. She had to remember to take her cellphone to bed, too.

The last of the day's warm sunlight illuminated the floral curtains, warming the room. Obediently, Gwen lay down on her bed. The bath and the tea had relaxed her body but her mind was racing ahead, wondering what the three scarves were for, what was supposed to happen with the oil, what he would ask her to do when he called. She assumed he'd call. She prayed he wouldn't suddenly knock on her door.

Gwen lay as still as she could manage and stole glances down at herself. Her nipples were actually roused and standing at attention, poking through the body stocking. *Dear god, are you mad? I don't want this happening to me!* But at the same time, despite what she knew she should be thinking, Gwen found that she was getting sexually aroused.

His call came on the dot of 5.

He made her wait several seconds without saying anything after she answered. "You've been a very good girl so far,

Gwen," he said in that garbled voice. "I hope that's going to continue."

She knew there were men who got off on doing things like this, creepy sorts intent on humiliating women and making them obedient, even women they'd never met. It gave them a misplaced sense of power. They were misogynists, of course, but would never screw up their courage to go the conventional route and ask you out. Most of them were not dangerous, as long as you managed to avoid them. Something told her this was different, and she'd better be on her guard.

"I wanted to show you that I can obey," she said.

"Gwenny, Gwenny," he said. "You do understand the predicament you're in here, don't you? I think you must be a very smart woman, and you've figured it out by now."

"Yes," she said. "I believe I have."

His voice took on a menacing tone. "Please understand . . . I have a darkness inside that I need to unleash. Tell me you get that."

"I understand," she whispered back. "Just tell me what you need me to do."

"You can ask me questions, that's all. You can't disobey."

"Questions?" His strange comment left her momentarily confused.

"*How* questions. *What* questions. *Where* questions. No *who* ones though, not until I'm ready to tell you."

"You will . . . you'll tell me that?"

"You have no idea, do you?"

"No. No idea whatsoever."

"It's good to keep it that way for now, I think."

She couldn't help but think back to that other phone call, the one from James on her birthday, and what he'd made her do for him.

"Have you had your nice tea, Gwenny?" he asked. "And do you smell all lavender?"

"Yes."

"And are you lying on your bed like I said to do?"

"Yes."

"Good," he said. "Now start taking off your clothes. Take your time. It's better if you do it slowly."

"I . . . I'm wearing that thing you made me buy," she said, reminding him. "There's not much to take off."

"Oh, my dark soul wishes I was perched in your ceiling, looking down at you spilling out of that mesh, Gwenny," the disembodied voice said. "You can start with the panty-thing."

Gwen reluctantly raised her hips off the bed and hooked her thumbs under the thin silk G-string, then slowly drew them down. The sensation of silk sliding down her thighs actually gave her a smattering of goosebumps, up her legs and across her tummy. She tried to think about that time she talked to James on the phone like this, tried to imagine it was his voice directing her to do this, but then remembered she was angry at him for not calling her after that night in the motel.

"Snap them for me, so I know they're off," the voice said. His tone was commanding, and it shouldn't have shocked her, but it did. So as soon as she raised her feet and slipped them off she did as she was told. She obeyed.

"I can imagine what you look like now, I really can. How does it make you feel to be naked for me, Gwenny? Are you still frightened, or could you be getting just a little turned on?"

She thought about the best thing to say. *Play along,* a little voice inside said. "Perhaps . . . you want me to be honest? A little of both."

It helped that he seemed to know what he was doing. He'd done this before, probably. He was commanding her, not asking. Making sure she knew he was in control. *I certainly am not!* She realized she was starting to give him more than he asked for, and wondered what had happened to make her want to flirt with him like this.

"Do you usually wear panties when you go out, Gwenny?" he asked.

"Yes," she said. "Always."

"I'll bet you do," he said. "What was it like not to? I imagine you've thought about doing that once or twice, right? Riding the subway or even showing up for work wearing nothing underneath?"

She thought of saying, *It was a little drafty, to tell you the truth*, but thought better of it. "No, I've never thought about doing that."

"So how did you feel finally doing it?"

"Vulnerable," she said after a pause. *Why not tell him the truth?* "Like I was keeping a secret and someone might find out about it."

"I can almost imagine what that must have been like." He seemed to be purring now. "Did you get a lot of looks?"

She didn't answer. Predictably, he took her silence for permission. "Gotta tell you, Gwen. I think I'd find you hot. Really. Really. Hot. See, I got this raging hard-on thing . . .and I don't want you to take this the wrong way, it's a compliment . . .I just happen to have the hots for . . .well, older women who look like you. And do you know what else I like?"

You probably want to fuck me, don't you? Or make me give you a blow job. Maybe you're into that. She remembered all the things she'd let James do to her in that motel room, how they'd even got around to some role play, pretending they were strangers. She'd wrapped the sheet around her and called herself Desiree. He gave her $100 and said he wanted a blow job.

She was good at that. Sexsmith had instructed her meticulously in the do's and don'ts. *Don't be an Eight Second Annie,* he'd told her. *It's a sex act. Pay attention to foreplay!* Sexsmith claimed that the longer you held a man at full-throttle *erectus*, the greater the volume of his ejaculation—and he certainly demonstrated it conclusively with her several times. It was Sexsmith who taught her to use lots of saliva, particularly under the glans, where it is attached to the shaft of the penis with a sensitive little muscle. It was Sexsmith who showed her how to use her tongue to stimulate erection, how to rub the thick underside vein lightly with her finger to hurry things along, how to gently tumble the testes, stimulating them tenderly with her long nails, when and how to talk and slow things up, and how to surprise him in different ways when he came. When she did it to James that night, he said, "Perhaps you need to be Desiree with me more often."

The heavier breathing on the phone pulled her attention back.

"What . . .else," she said weakly. Her bottom lip trembled a little in anticipation of his answer.

"What are you like?" he asked. "Describe yourself for me right now. Look down at yourself."

"Nipples," she said breathlessly. "Hard."

"Good. Don't touch them. I know you probably want to. I'll tell you when to do that. When to do everything, okay? Now I want you to use the baby oil, okay? Put some of it on your pussy, Gwen, and smear it around, and some on your chin, so it shines."

Gwen realized what that was for. When she'd done it, she told him.

"Now the scarves . . .you have them . . . take your time . . . tie both ankles together. A nice tight knot, like someone would tie if they wanted to keep you hostage."

He was starting to give himself away, too, she thought. She sat up, feeling the netting tighten around her, and bound up her ankles like he said.

"I'm not," she began to say.

"Not what, Gwenny? Not a hostage? Or not *like that*?"

"I'm . . .not anything like what you think I am," she said firmly.

His voice hissed back at her. "But maybe, just maybe, you want to be, don't you, Gwen? Maybe you're just aching to be that kind."

She was still on the phone. That must tell him everything.

"Do you know what I'm going to ask you to do now?" he asked quickly.

She waited.

"Put one hand behind your head." His words were suddenly condescending, and she obeyed with the sensation of being a child all of a sudden. "Is there something to tie your wrist to?"

"The bedpost," she said. She was very aware of how helpless she was now, and very aware of how this position caused her to arch her back and offer her breasts upward. Her face was burning as she tied the scarf, and she realized how wanton this would make her look if anyone saw her like this.

"I need to know you're actually doing it," the voice said. "I want you to take a selfie for me, Gwenny. Use your cellphone."

She froze. "Why?" she asked, turning cold with fear. "You already have pictures of me."

"Oh, but not looking anything like I imagine you're looking right now."

She picked up her cell and tested the angle. He'd want to see her pussy. He'd make her take another one if she didn't show that. "What kind of expression do you want to see on my face?" she asked.

She thought he'd be pleased she was being obedient but she heard him laugh. "Oh, Gwenny, I'm not interested in that part of you."

Has your body ever reacted to a sudden situation or event like an electric shock flowing through your genitals? Okay, I'll admit that

I'm more than a little turned on by this situation. How could I not be? A stranger has the goods on me and is having his fun. Things are getting hotter by the minute. He hasn't said a word about money. He seems to want a hostage for his sexual gratification. And I have no way of knowing how this is going to end.

If this turns out to be James, I will kill him.

Gwen raised the cellphone up with her free hand and obediently did what he asked, making sure she gave him a sexy pout, like she wanted this, she really wanted it.

"Okay, I did it. What now?"

He gave her instructions where to text it. So she did.

"Is . . .*that* . . .what you want?"

"Just a sec. You've sent it?" Then, after a few seconds, she heard him again, in a gentler voice. "Oh, Gwenny, Gwenny, you're so fucking *naughty*, aren't you?"

Something about this definitely matched up with the role play at the motel. So she said, without really thinking that she might be mistaken, "Please, tell me now . . . is this really you, James?"

There was silence for a few seconds. "That was his name, wasn't it? James?"

"Oh," she said, almost to herself. "Oh shit."

She heard a different voice on the phone then. The voice was normal, or as normal as it could be if you didn't move your mouth much. He must have dropped the filter. "You never swear in class, Gwenny," it said.

Tommy Paxton's voice.

And she knew what he wanted.

"Exhibit A," he said. "Is a compromising picture of you on a student's cellphone. What do you think the faculty code of conduct says about that, Gwennykins?"

CHAPTER TWENTY-TWO

The Squirrel got right to the point, as usual. They were meeting just before 6 in Hickey's cluttered sixth floor office and no one else seemed to be at work yet. Squirrel already had coffee brewing when Hickey arrived and they were careful to save enough for Corelli, who ambled in late as usual, yawning and bleary eyed.

"My vote," Squirrel said without being asked. "Sullenberger. I think he's our man." He slapped the thinnest of the three files down in front of Hickey and stood back against the wall with his arms crossed. He was wearing a black rapper t-shirt that had a lighthouse on it and the slogan *I am a beacon of intolerance.*

"Okay," Hickey barked. "Dish. Tell me why."

Hickey's due diligence on his guy, Shelby Swenson, the perv, hit a dead end when Swenson's live-in companion, a girl who looked maybe eighteen and had facial piercings, including a fascinating round silver stud in her tongue, vouched that she'd been with him during Murders No. 4 and 5. Hickey didn't bother to ask what they'd been doing.

"Reason number one," Squirrel said. "I already checked with Corelli and it ain't Antwan. While someone was killing Vic number ten, the cat was at some kind of gang recovery retreat in, shit, where was it? Guelph?"

Corelli verified that with a nod. It was too early to expect him to talk.

"Number two—and this is the interesting part—Sullenberger left the country two days after Cathcart's body was

203

found in the cemetery. That matches with your theory, boss — that killing Cathcart might have been the assassin's getaway card. Like he was banking no one else in Mandamus knew his identity."

"That seems to be right," Hickey said. "Tell me where he went?"

"Far, far away," Squirrel said, explaining the passport records had come in late yesterday. Hickey liked the fact that DuWayne had everything in his head, just like a good police detective does. He'd already decided The Squirrel would make a better cop than a fucking lawyer. "He visited Thailand, then Australia, then Turkey, and get this — then Italy."

"Italy?" Hickey's head jerked up. "Was he doing the usual tourist thingy?"

"Rome, yeah. But he also took an internal flight. You'll never guess where."

Hickey just raised his eyebrows.

"Sicily, boss. Sicily."

"No shit."

"I'm checking hotels, that kind of stuff. I'll get back to you on that."

"Okay, good."

"Number three, number four seal the deal," Squirrel said with emphasis, sliding two photos across the desk. One was a mug shot, Hickey presumed of Sullenberger, because he'd served those three years and it showed him in a prison brush cut. The other was of a man standing in front of a house. He had one of those old-fashioned mullet haircuts, shaved at the sides and long at back. Hickey thought the men looked remarkably alike.

"What's this — before and after?"

Squirrel pointed to the mug shot. "Sullenberger," he said. Then he pointed to the mullet. "And Mr. Sullenberger's next of kin." Squirrel waited for Hickey to look up. "Guy happens to have an identical twin brother, boss."

Hickey said no shit again.

His first thought was that neither picture looked anything like the composite sketch the police artist had worked up from that Leishman woman's description. So he'd been right to question her reliability, and he'd have some hard questions for her when he brought her in. If *this* was what the Mandamus killer really looked like, if The Squirrel was right—and Hickey thought he very well could be—they finally knew who they were looking for.

"So, Squirrel," Hickey said after trying to reconcile his conflicting thoughts. "What exactly does this tell us?"

"I spoke to the brother by phone last night. Name's Gord, lives on the family farm in Biggar, Saskatchewan. Says he had a falling out with his bro six years ago, about the time he went to prison for the gun. Had no contact with him while he was in, has no idea what he did or where he went when he got out."

"Shit. Did he tell you anything we can use?"

"Well, they were identical, right? I asked how the family told them apart. He said the only way—and I know you're gonna like *this*—Gerald had this birthmark. Right here." And The Squirrel drew a short line across the right side of his chest just below the nipple. "Bright red birthmark—that's the only way the mother could tell which one was Gerald."

So they had a photograph and a physical characteristic. Not a whole lot to work with but a start.

"What about credit cards, bank accounts, credit rating, the financial stuff?" Hickey asked.

Squirrel shrugged. "Everything was closed down shortly after Sullenberger arrived back from Italy." He grabbed the file back and checked the date. "December of twenty twelve. That's when everything disappeared. Sullenberger in effect ceased to exist."

"So now he's someone fucking else, is that what you're telling me?"

Squirrel put out his hands facing up. Raised his eyebrows. "He could be dead."

"What did his bank account show before he closed it?" Hickey asked.

"Just getting them sent over, maybe later today," Squirrel said.

"Corelli," Hickey said. "You'll have that job now, *capiche*?" Corelli took a moment to write it down in his notebook.

"Squirrel, let's get this photo out there with a description. Just say wanted for questioning without saying what case. Mention the birthmark."

"All media, boss? Special advisory?"

Hickey thought for a moment. "Better let them stumble on it all by themselves. It's all circumstantial right now."

"Cellphone records might give us some info to follow up on but it looks like we won't find anything in the last three years."

"Yeah, shit," Hickey said, slumping back on his chair and feeling his hopes sag. "I was hoping it wouldn't be like this."

"If our guy has a new identity, we may have to start from scratch, boss."

And all Hickey could think about was how best to break this bad news to Maddow.

That night, finally, he managed to have his even more important talk with Stephanie. Things had been cool between them for days, Stephanie showing signs of cabin fever or perhaps claustrophobia, probably feeling trapped in this strange new situation, living in the same apartment as him before either of them was ready for it.

"It's . . . well . . . complicated, Hickey," she said when they sat down across from each other in the living room to finish their wine from dinner. Stephanie had made her delicious chicken marbella, definitely one of Hickey's favourites. At least he'd been eating better since she moved in.

"Is that why we've waited so long to clear the air?" he asked her. "You find this hard to talk about?"

"Something like that, yes."

He tried to lighten things up. "You know, I've always thought women get us wrong. The average man is a lot simpler than the average woman, I think. For instance, you're always asking me what I'm thinking about. Chances are I'm not thinking of anything. There's a little box in our brains that's called the Nothing Box, and men spend a lot of time there."

"It's hard for me to imagine you keeping your mind in idle."

"Women tend to complicate men," he quipped. "I don't think we're that complicated."

She reached across and squeezed his hand. "But this is."

Three weeks ago he figured his apartment was big enough that they could each have their own space, she might get used to that. There was a swivel chair in her bedroom that she could sit in to read. He had a TV on the wall in his room where he could lie in bed and watch the Leafs. Mornings he usually left early, before she was up and about. She had a book club or yoga classes that kept her out late a couple of nights a week. But she wasn't, he knew, getting used to any of it. They'd had words about his messes. He'd complained about her leaving the door unlocked once.

She suddenly had trouble meeting his eyes. "I've decided I'm moving back home, Hickey."

He thought about it and nodded. What could he honestly say back to her? She was right, and he'd never liked people who beat around the bush.

Chapter Twenty-three

Anxiety. Disappointment. Confusion. Anger. Loneliness. Abandonment. A few aching horny spells. The blues.

Borderline depression, actually.

A week without hearing from James had made Gwen feel all these things. But the moment her cellphone rang and she heard his voice, she put them in the back of her mind.

"It's been seven days," she said, trying not to let on how desperate she was for his attention. "I was afraid you might turn out to be another of those disappearing men and I'd scared you off."

They'd talked, or rather joked about it — how men, when they grew tired of a relationship, tended to just walk away. No calls. No notes. Just poof, they're invisible. It had happened to her enough times. She considered herself an expert.

Women, in her experience, did not do that. If you were seeing someone, and the sex was great but you just weren't into *him*, you'd talk to him about it, maybe suggest you should just be friends. Not that you really wanted to be friends, but just to avoid hurting his feelings. Offer him a consolation prize. But with men, there seemed to be no consolation prizes. They were either there for you, or they weren't. If not, they just seemed to drop off the face of the Earth.

"Something came up," he said, not giving her the apology she hoped for. "I need to see you." There was something strange about his voice, she thought, an edge to it instead of the teasing and humour she was used to.

"You told me something once — that men are often attracted to the way women make them feel. Is that it?"

"Is that — what?"

"Did I say something or do something to make you feel bad?"

He sounded exasperated. "Look, I want to see you *now*, so I'm not sure what we're arguing about."

"Are we arguing, James?" Her pride made her determined not to let him off the hook this easily.

"You sound pissed off."

"And you sound insensitive."

"Wait," he said. "Just because I didn't call for a few days, you think I'm blowing hot and cold with you?"

"That's one possible interpretation."

"What's another?"

She hesitated. "Okay, I'll say it. Are you seeing someone else, James?"

That seemed to clear the tension out of the shadow dance they were engaged in. He laughed and his voice changed. Back to the old James, she thought. "No, lovely lady. I'd say my life is already complicated enough!"

At least he still knew how to make her laugh. He had an exasperating clueless way about him that made him easy to forgive, and she tried again to not let that show. "The last time we met, you took me to a cheap motel. Why don't you tell me first what you have in mind?"

It was 2 PM. She'd just had lunch with Geruta in the faculty room. She had marking and office hours were from 3 to 4.

"How about a nice quiet diner," he said, more sweetly.

"I'm tied up until four."

"Is that a yes?"

"Say pretty please."

"Pretty please," he said. "Please, Gwen. Okay?"

When she met him in the parking lot outside Stong shortly

after 4, he gave her a rather perfunctory kiss and acted preoccupied. His familiar, musky masculine scent was the same.
She'd tasted it on his skin when she nuzzled up after all that
sex at the motel. But his attitude wasn't the same at all.

She wanted to say she missed him but instead said, "So
what's been happening with you, stranger? You seem to have
lost my scent."

"Work," he said, rather dismissively, turning the car for the
exit. "How are things with you?"

"It's almost end of term," she said. "I'm happy I can finally
see the finish line."

"So, any plans?"

It was almost like they were strangers again. She could tell
he wasn't that interested, perhaps wasn't asking in order to
find out if her plans included him. She couldn't say yet
whether they did or didn't. She was still feeling strange about
the day before, the shopping trip and what followed, getting
all worked up suspecting it was James disguising his voice,
then discovering it was that creep Tommy Paxton, and stupidly—so stupidly—giving him the ammunition to force her
to submit to him, give him whatever he wanted.

She also felt ashamed of the way she'd allowed herself to
get mildly turned on by the things he'd asked her to do. She
tried to convince herself she only did that because she thought
it was James. She hoped that Tommy Paxton, who she certainly had no interest in fucking, might only want his grades
manipulated. She had no idea what she'd do if he wanted
more.

"No, no plans," she said finally. "Why? Do you have some
suggestions?"

He was headed down Dufferin Street and she didn't know
where they were going, especially when he took a left at Shep-
pard.

"Listen," he said. "I've got to stop by home for a quick

shower and change. What do you feel like eating?"

Gwen looked at him like he must be kidding. The very thought that she might willingly go anywhere near Frieda Bannerman's home stomping ground, after having shown her face at that open house? She couldn't imagine what she could say to explain what she was doing in the Bannerman home in close company with her husband.

"Ummm, this could be very awkward for me, James," she said. "Are you sure that's a good idea?"

It was 4.30. He turned south and made a few more turns. Gwen lost track of the streets.

"She's got showings. Said she wouldn't be home until eight. We're cool."

Gwen wasn't convinced. "It wouldn't be good if her plans happened to change, would it? Arriving home early to, you know, find your husband's doxy there . . . woo, I don't think I'm ready for fireworks!"

"Don't worry. She always phones if that happens. It's one of our rules."

Right, she thought. They had that kind of arrangement.

He pulled into a driveway and turned off the engine. Despite his assurances, something felt very wrong about this.

The townhouse was one of those two-storey yellow brick duplexes that look like giant windowed-up double garages, parking around back. There were hundreds of them in the spider-web of streets that criss-cross North York, a thick band of density stretching across the top of Toronto just north of Highway 401. She'd had a small house there with Gerald when she was doing her post-doc, and hated it. He held the door open and let her walk up the stairs ahead of him, and Gwen took each step with a sense of dread, imagining what would happen if his wife, running late, happened to meet her half way down. "Oh, hi again," she might say. "Gwen, isn't it?" Then turning to her husband and saying something cheeky like, "James, you'd better finish her off quickly before I come back—otherwise we may have to share."

And of course she thought of what she'd say to *him*—or rather what she should have already told him. *I checked out your wife, James, because I thought she might be the one who's blackmailing me. Wait, you'd probably say, you're being black-mailed? And I'd have to tell you that, too. About getting the picture of us having sex in that motel, and the phone call and emails, and how I guessed that it was you and it was a joke but I was so, so wrong.*

His flat, or rather the one he shared with Frieda, was done in elegant Ikea. She guessed it was her choice, rather than his, because there were a couple of those Georgia O'Keeffe vulva flower prints on the walls. He drew close and gave her a longer, reassuring kiss once the door was closed, and she could feel the perspiration on his shirt back and a little of the hunger for her in his mouth. He took her coat and invited her to sit down while he fixed a drink. She stared at the vulva over the mantle and tried to relax, happy the coast was clear. Perhaps they needed to just talk tonight.

"So how long have you been married?" she asked him.

"Ah, two and a half years, I think." He said he had gin. What did she want it with?

"You're not sure?"

"I'm guessing, but I'm going to say tonic, okay?"

"I meant your marriage, silly."

"I'm reasonably certain it's been that long," he said lightly, showing her he was having fun with her question.

"I feel like Italian, I think," she said.

"Fine with me. Why don't you find someplace reasonably near and make a reservation. Give me five minutes." He set down her gin and tonic on the coffee table in front of her and headed for the shower.

She heard the water running in the other room and thought for a minute about joining him, just slipping out of her dress and underthings and surprising him like that, pressing up against his soapy chest. Fear of Frieda walking in put that thought on hold. Instead, she took a couple of gulps of gin and tonic and decided to try to forget about the tribulations of her predicament.

After a few minutes, she started to feel drowsy.

Then everything started to happen in rapid succession. She was searching for Italian food on her cellphone and, try as she might to concentrate, the listings kept fading in and out of focus. Her fingers seemed to be operating independently, and she tapped a few wrong commands. She felt like that time she'd been about to pass out drunk. She checked her glass and found she still had two-thirds of the drink so that couldn't be it. She began to get increasingly confused and anxious, not understanding what was happening to her. After a few moments she gave up and slumped back on the sofa to try to rest her head, which was starting to spin in lazy circles. She felt like she was falling off a cliff into a dream. Then she could no longer hold the phone to see what she was doing. She tried to speak but no sound came out. The last thing she remembered was trying to call out his name.

She had no idea what happened while she was passed out, or whether it was for 10 minutes or an hour. Coming to felt like coming out of anesthetic, that time she'd had her laparoscopy surgery and was in the hospital recovery room. She felt groggy and confused, waking a little, then drifting off again, then waking up a little more, trying to remember — what had happened, where was she, who was she with. Her memory seemed to be playing tricks. All she was aware of was that something seemed to be touching her, lightly touching her flesh in the vicinity of her tummy and upper legs, something soft and whispy, either coaxing her back to consciousness or doing something else. She felt a sudden panic because she couldn't see what it was. The room was dark. No, that wasn't it. Something was covering her eyes. She felt the tightness of something, a bandana perhaps, tied around her head, and when she tried to move her arms to take it off she couldn't because they were secured to something above her head.

Then she remembered where she was.

"James?" she asked in a croak, scarcely recognizing her voice. She got no answer. She could sense his presence in the room though. Not nearby but he was there. His scent was there. *Why isn't he helping me? I think I need help.*

She heard a woman's voice instead. A voice that seemed familiar, even though she couldn't make out any words. Maybe there were no words, just sounds she heard, and heavy breathing.

She felt feathery hands sliding slowly up the sides of her legs like a caress. And something like hair, long fine hair, whisping across her thighs and tummy like someone was straddling her, sweeping her off. Then realized with alarm—someone had taken all her clothes off. Someone had tied her to a bed. Someone was doing things to her against her will.

"James?" she asked again, more insistently, since her tongue had started working again. "What the hell is going on?"

This time he answered, but he was not speaking to her. "I think you can take the mask off now." And she felt small capable hands reaching up and sliding the bandana off her head. She caught the faint scent of jasmin.

The brightness blinded her for a few seconds, and when she could focus she found herself staring directly at Frieda Bannerman.

Who was also buck naked, legs parted across hers, her chin already slippery. She didn't want to know what with.

"I don't often get to do this with any woman I've met show-ing a house," she purred. "What were you trying to find out, sweetie?"

James, still holding a towel around his waist from the shower, was watching from the foot of the bed like a voyeur, seeming to enjoy the sight of his wife poised over the pin-ioned legs of his white mistress.

Gwen felt the moistness in her groin and wetness down the insides of her upper legs and realized what Frieda must have been doing. The woman's dark Nubian nipples were aroused and her eyes seemed dilated, as if lost in Lesbian predation. She slowly and deliberately wiped her chin off with the back of one hand and eased back on her haunches, catching her breath, and Gwen understood what the wetness between her legs was from.

It must have been one of those date rape drugs, Gwen thought, slipped into her gin. Xanax or perhaps Ketamine, which some of her more sexually active women students called Bump. Her head still felt like it was filled with cotton batten. But she was starting to think more clearly.

"You need to untie me and let me go, James," she said, looking at him. "Right fucking now."

But instead of answering, he walked slowly around to the side of the bed and looked down at her like she was scarcely worthy of attention. "Why don't you answer my wife's ques-tion instead, Gwen." Then he added, "Or I might just let her finish her work."

She felt Frieda's soft hand press possessively down on her abdomen. "It's the first time he's ever done this," she said, smiling. "Brought someone back for me."

Gwen felt nauseous now, like she might want to throw up. She'd never been to bed with a woman before, and was grate-ful that she couldn't remember anything that had happened. That would certainly change if she didn't co-operate. Frieda, she guessed, judging from her carnal appetites, would be an enthusiastic and voracious lover.

"I thought it might be your wife who was blackmailing me," she said, looking at James.

"Oh, have you ever got it wrong, honey," Frieda said, rather mockingly.

But James just stared at her. "You mean, you got pictures sent to you, too?" he asked.

"I was going to tell you, really, I—" But then she realized what he was saying. They'd taken his car to the motel. Tommy probably traced his license plate. He might have even received his picture before she did.

What is he so afraid of? The wife doesn't seem to give a shit that he plays around, I doubt his employer cares, what secret could he have that would make him turn on me and subject me to THIS? I have lots more at stake than he does.

Frieda said something then that made Gwen realize he had kept her in the dark. "Wait. Pictures? What pictures? Can I see them?"

James sat down on the side of the bed and casually circled each of Gwen's nipples with his index finger, playing her like a toy. He seemed to be thinking hard about something, not really paying attention to what he was doing. She usually craved his touch but now she felt sour disgust. Finally, he looked like he'd made up his mind about what he was thinking about, and leaned back and gave his wife a long, lingering kiss that seemed to involve most of her tongue. Then he turned to look at Gwen.

"I think I like tasting the scent of you on her lips," he said.

"Bastard," she said.

He quickly clutched her face, his hard grasp paralyzing her jaw as he squeezed tighter than she'd ever been squeezed before. "Why don't we talk about who wants something from you? Or shall I have my wife resume your pelvic examination?"

She could feel Frieda eagerly rocking back and forth on the mattress in anticipation. "Oh, I really think she's hotter than shit for me right now, babe. Sorry," his wife said, looking down hungrily at Gwen's body. "I think I could turn into a fucking feral animal with her right now."

He just smiled.

Gwen thought of her options. She really had no choice but to tell him everything. About the phone call and the emails and the shopping trip and finding out it was her student and what he wanted. She had no idea what he might want from James. Perhaps money.

"This is getting kinkier by the minute," Frieda said after hearing about the erotic telephone call and the part about Gwen stripping off the G-string.

"It's one of my students," she said. "A student in academic trouble, and I guess I'm going to have to let him off the hook."

James looked at her coldly. "So how does that help me, lady?"

"I've been avoiding meeting him," she said honestly. "He's a creep and I'm frightened that he might want a little more than a good grade. I need your . . . help."

"You want me to protect you?" James asked, smiling and looking at his wife looking hungrily down at her again. "I've not done a very good job of that so far, have I?"

Frieda certainly looked primed for another go.

James, however, said he had a better idea.

"I think I've thought of a way to get rid of all our problems. Shall we try that instead?"

Chapter Twenty-Four

W hen the cab arrived for her — and she almost couldn't believe they were just letting her go — it was idling in the plaza where he'd driven her and James was holding the door open. When she clambered in, he leaned in quickly and kissed her, sloppily and possessively. Gwen did not move her lips or reciprocate, and the cab driver must have picked up on her hesitation because he'd scarcely driven a block when he turned and said, "That man, he not good for you I think, lady."

He looked Middle Eastern or perhaps North African and he spoke with a thick accent. His cab license on the visor said his name was Hussein. Muslim, probably. Lots of Muslims seemed to be driving Beck taxis in Toronto these days. She looked closer and noticed a small, telltale Muslim insignia hanging on a thin chain from his steering wheel — the green star in a crescent moon — and Gwen wondered why she'd noticed, why it mattered. Then she thought, of course, it's another miserable relic from her marriage. Gerald adamantly refused to ride in Muslim cabs.

"Why would you say that?" she managed to ask him. She still felt in shock because of what had happened back there. She knew her disheveled look must have said a lot.

"Man no gentleman," the cab driver said.

The wisdom of cab drivers. At least James had allowed her to shower. She'd used extra soap to try to scrub Frieda Bannerman off her skin, but she still felt the teasing press of those tiny fingertips on her thighs and hips, as if they were still violating her underneath her dress. She knew she looked mussed up. There hadn't been much time to dress properly and she was so afraid James would change his mind.

The cab driver kept stealing glances at her through his rearview mirror, and Gwen sensed his concern.

"You may be scared of him, lady?"

Yes, you're damned right I'm scared of him.

She knew what James planned to do, and he'd made clear what he was expecting her to do to make it happen. He'd told her this after shooing Frieda out of the bedroom, so she knew his wife wasn't meant to be in on it. Frieda's attention seemed to be focused on something else anyway, and that was whatever James had allowed her to enjoy when Gwen had been unconscious. James had other goals, and he'd made clear to her, when Frieda wasn't there to distract her, that he expected Gwen to deliver her student to him, and that he was going to make sure they wouldn't hear from him again.

"But why is he a threat to you?" Gwen asked again. "It's me he wants things from."

And James had looked at her with his frigid eyes and said, "That's none of your concern, Gwen."

But she knew it must have been something important. He'd given her just three days to set it up.

"Or?" she'd asked as he started to untie her.

"What do you mean — or?"

"Or what?" she asked with her heart in her mouth. "What if I decide I can't do what you want?"

He stopped what he was doing and leaned menacingly close. "Gwen, you do not want to be in that position. Trust me, you don't."

He'd insisted on driving her to the Retail Plaza on Wilson just west of Dufferin rather than having the cab come to the house. She thought about his threat all the way home.

Her shock didn't really wear off until she closed the front door of her condo and secured it with both locks. She just peeled everything off, dress, then bra and panties, and left her clothes strewn in the hallway behind her as she stumbled for the bathroom. She'd never been raped but she knew rape victims did this—they showered and showered, soaped and scrubbed, again and again. And as she felt the water cascade over her shoulders, it all came back to her in a crash of cognition—being drugged, falling unconscious, waking to find herself tied up in a bed being sodomized by her lover's wife, James' betrayal and her own still-felt shame and humiliation. But the one compelling image, the one she would hold in her mind forever as her nightmare, was the predatory face of Frieda Bannerman, chin wet with saliva and perhaps pussy juices, rising satiated from her groin, catching her breath before she planned her next plunge into muffled ecstasy.

The water was still running when Gwen felt her insides start to quake. She stumbled out of the shower and fell to her knees on the slippery tiles in front of her toilet and threw up.

Two hours later, after a steadying drink, she phoned Geruta and asked for Rachel Leishman's phone number.

"You okay?" Geruta asked, noticing her shaky voice.

"Yep," Gwen lied. "I just remembered her talking about something at that lunch that I want to know more about."

Geruta naturally wanted to know what.

"Pilates," Gwen replied quickly. "I think she mentioned doing it at the Y. I read somewhere that Pilates is better than yoga for losing an inch or two around the hips."

"Sex is supposed to be good for that, too," Geruta said.

Well, there'd be no more of that for me, Gwen thought bitterly. Certainly not with James Bannerman.

She had to leave two messages before Rachel phoned her back.

"I was out all afternoon," the older woman explained when they connected shortly after 5. "It was nice to come home to your message. Actually I'm glad you reached out. I was meaning to call and arrange something myself. You asked me a very good question at that lunch, and I'm not sure I fully answered it."

Gwen had to ask which question was that.

"You know, the one about things I might be afraid to testify about."

"Oh."

"You seem to be someone who likes to cut right to the point, if you don't mind me saying," Rachel said. "Geruta said I'd like that about you, and I think I do." Might they get together for lunch sometime soon?

She sounded a little surprised when Gwen asked how about tomorrow.

They met downtown at Arcadian Court, the meticulously restored Art Deco restaurant and event space often called one of Toronto's hidden gems. It occupied several hundred square feet on the eighth floor of The Bay department store at Yonge and Queen. It was Rachel's choice. "A reminder of when Toronto stood for the best," she said when Gwen arrived. Gwen hadn't been there before and found herself overwhelmed by the size of the place, large enough for big corporate events and weddings but open Tuesdays and Thursdays for lunch as just a restaurant. For a time after it opened in 1929, it was called the Men's Grille and women weren't allowed, but Gwen could plainly see from her fellow diners that women had splendidly taken over.

The Arcadian Court was where the debutantes of Toronto's rich traditionally were introduced to society, and Gwen remembered it was used as a setting in Margaret Atwood's dystopian novel *The Blind Assassin*. She supposed it was a fitting venue for a chat about vulnerable women and dangerous men.

"I should apologize to you," Rachel said when they'd ordered—just a light salad for her but Gwen opted for something more substantial. After all, she wasn't going to have to suck her tummy in for anyone for a while. "You asked for the lunch and I went ahead and suggested the topic of conversation."

"Oh, don't worry. I probably would like to hear about that, too."

"You first, okay?" She thought Rachel had a warm smile and probably did not want for male attention.

Gwen took a moment to collect her thoughts. "I'm interested in that message you said you got—from that young man who picked you up at the bar."

"You mean, how did I know he was part of Mandamus?"

"Well, yeah . . . that—"

"May I ask you a question first?"

"Of course."

"Why in the world would you want to know that?"

Gwen felt momentarily flummoxed. She wasn't sure how much to tell. Probably not a lot. Rachel looked like she had problems of her own, probably related to her testimony at that trial the other day. "Let's just say I may have had a similar experience—not with the same man, of course, but with someone I suspect could be dangerous."

Rachel looked at her with interest, switching her gaze from one eye to the other, taking her measure. "Bad date?" she asked.

"I'd call it a rather short-lived affair," Gwen replied. "He was married."

"Aren't they all?" Rachel raised her eyebrows and shrugged. "It all depends on the sex being good enough to let you forget it. Mine was . . . or it was until I spotted that tattoo."

"Right. I wanted to ask you about that."

"Have you ever gone for triples on a first date?"

"You mean—"

"Yeah, vaginal, oral and anal, not necessarily in that order. He wanted it like that, treated me like I was some Olympic event. It was very intense. Rough even, especially the anal, which I found . . . well, I'm just not into that very much."

Gwen remembered that long evening at the motel, and what James had tried to do.

"Tell me more."

"He spent a lot of time admiring my body—lots of men never get past my tits, but his interests were definitely lower. He asked me to describe him at one point. You know, say we were separated in a mall and you had to tell people *I'm looking for . . . what would you say?* So I told him—tall, handsome, athletic, stylishly long hair. And then I asked him the same question. How would he describe *me*? You know what he said? *I'd say a woman with big tits and delicate features, in a flawed, accessible way.*"

"That's pretty crude," Gwen said.

"Honest, though. A lot of men might describe someone that way if they'd just talked them into anal sex." They both laughed, Gwen a little ruefully. She was not into anal at all, and she'd stopped James with her hand that night.

"You said when he let you see his tattoo, it scared you."

"It did. It scared me even more when he came back for me."

"That's the part you didn't tell police, right?"

"Actually . . . I had to spend most of yesterday afternoon telling them all about it."

"Huh?"

"Detective-Sergeant Hickey called me in. He accused me of lying and giving false testimony."

"Wow. That's serious. Lying about what?"

"The description I gave them," Rachel said. "He found out it wasn't accurate."

"You lied about that? Why would you do that?"

"Because I had to make a deal to stop him—he said his name was Wheeler—from, like, killing me. He tied me up in my living room and held an actual gun to my head."

"Oh my God."

"I think Mandamus ordered him to kill me. They'd had a leak and it was reasonable to trace it back to me. I had to think quickly. I didn't have time to consider all the complications. The biggest complication is that, if he thinks that I'm helping police find him, my life isn't worth a dime. He even phoned me after I testified. I'm sure he knows where I live. He could come and kill me at any time."

"Wait," Gwen said. "How did Hickey know you lied to him?"

Rachel looked at her. "He has a picture of the assassin! He showed it to me. I mean, it was *him*. And it sure didn't look anything like my description."

"A picture? They know who they're looking for then?"

Rachel nodded.

"But the trial is just about to wrap up, isn't it? Why was Hickey raking you over the coals?"

"He needed confirmation—you know, that the photograph really was the guy with the Mandamus tattoo."

"And you confirmed that for him."

"I did. I had to."

"God, Rachel, I don't know what to say. That's terrifying."

"As long as I was forced to co-operate, I figured I better tell him about the second visit, when I could see that this Wheeler had probably killed people before. My radar should have told me he was dangerous that first night. Men who have sex like that tend to be bad boys."

"My . . ." Gwen honestly didn't know what to call James

anymore. "My date, my cheating husband, my whatever . . . he was like that, too. He didn't want to stop when I said he was hurting me."

"You're not still seeing him, are you?"

"No, not anymore. At least I don't think so." Then Gwen remembered another thing she wanted to ask. "He had a tattoo, too, but an old one, one he'd tried to erase." She reached around and pointed to the back of her right shoulder. "Right here."

She saw Rachel's eyes slowly widen in surprise.

"That's where it was on him, exactly," she said. "Lady Justice with the scales."

Oh fuck, please God, no.

Chapter Twenty-five

I f Hickey had been in court, listening to the last day of testimony, he would have missed her because she just dropped in. But he was in his office, unable and unwilling to waste his morning listening to a who's who of the law in Ontario vouching for the good character of Burnside and his friends. Juris, wrapping up the case for the defence, had scheduled the highest-profile character witnesses he could find, including Edward Darling, the former Conservative premier. Burnside had served as attorney-general in his cabinet. The hard-right men's club that had nearly torn away the province's social security net during its time in power was still thick as thieves.

It was 9.30 when he got the call from downstairs. There was someone who needed to see him, said it had something to do with the Mandamus case. He asked who and they said some professor who thinks she may have dated your man. Hickey was preparing the press release for a news conference he was about to call for early afternoon. He was going to release Gerald Sullenberger's picture and announce that police had reason to believe that he was the Mandamus trigger man.

He put that aside and asked them to send her up.

Police had a word for them. Walk-ins. Just like a homeowner who opens his or her door to a knock in the middle of the day, you never knew what you were going to get. It could be the frigging Jehovah's Witnesses. Some of Hickey's cold cases had received valuable information this way, but most often the evidence that people thought they had was irrelevant or not very helpful. But with the trial about to wind up, and the outcome so uncertain, Hickey decided not to take a chance of missing anything.

His first impression when she walked out of the elevator was—classy lady. Stylish dresser. Not someone you'd expect to want to share a bed with a serial killer.

She introduced herself with a firm handshake, said she was Dr. Gwen Van Loon and a friend of Rachel Leishman. That got his interest. He invited her to sit down.

"I'm told," Hickey said, "that you might have reason to believe you know a gentleman who's of great interest to us."

She looked at him coldly. "I don't believe I used the word *gentleman*, detective."

Hickey shrugged and allowed himself a faint smile.

"Rachel told me you showed her a picture. Of the man you think killed all those people. She said you seem to know who he is, and I want to check to see if it's the same person I've been seeing."

"And why do you think it might be?" Hickey asked, opening his drawer to get Sullenberger's file.

"He sort of matches the description she gave. He has an old tattoo in the same place, for example." She pointed behind her shoulder.

"What kind of tattoo?"

"It's hard to make out. He said he tried to get rid of it but it wasn't completely successful. Also, he's done things that make me think he could be dangerous."

Hickey didn't ask her what. Perhaps it was embarrassing.

"Ma'am, does the name Gerald Sullenberger mean anything to you?" he asked instead.

He could tell from her face that it drew a blank. Perhaps this was going to be a waste of time.

"No, I don't know anyone with that name," she said, and he tried to decide if her frown was one of relief.

He reached in the file and extracted Sullenberger's photograph. Might as well make sure. He slid it across the desk and the moment she saw it her expression changed. "My God, I think that could be him!" She looked startled but gave it another look. "He's changed his appearance but . . . oh my God!"

Hickey was so surprised he momentarily forgot what he needed to ask her.

"He goes by the name of James Bannerman," she blurted out.

"Wait," Hickey said. "Are you telling me you know him? That you know where he lives?"

Gwen waved her hands in front of her in confusion. "I can't remember the address. Somewhere in North York. I was only there once and he drugged me."

He looked at her. "You said he's changed his appearance. I need to know how."

She examined the photograph more closely. "He's shaved his head, no brush cut, wears wire rim glasses, has one of those short, three-day beards. It's the eyes I recognized. Those cold, unforgiving eyes."

"You mentioned he had a tattoo, ma'am," Hickey said. "Any other marks or scars that you noticed?"

"Yes, I remember a birthmark or something, right here," she said, drawing a line under her breast.

Hickey just sat back in his chair and left Sullenberger's picture facing her on the desk. "Then, ma'am, I sure am all ears. Tell me anything you can about your Mr. Bannerman, please."

She tried to add more but began to tremble and tear up, so Hickey reluctantly excused himself to fetch her a glass of water from the cooler down the hall. *Dear sweet Lord. Just when you give up hope, good shit happens.* On the way back with it, he stopped to rap at the door of The Squirrel's cubbyhole. The

Squirrel popped his head out. "You got that press release ready yet, boss?" he asked Hickey. "I oughta get it copied for the press conference. Are you sticking with two o'clock still?"

Hickey pointed to his office. "Something just came up that may pre-empt that, son. Stay tuned for now, okay?" Squirrel saw a blonde woman sitting in front of Hickey's desk. "Oh, and, Squirrel," Hickey said. "Get that artist, what's his name? Branscombe? Tell him to come quickly and bring his laptop."

In the next half-hour, Hickey drew the story out of Gwen Van Loon, how she'd hooked up with James Bannerman despite her misgivings about dating someone who was married, how they'd been photographed in the motel in a compromising position, how she'd been contacted by a blackmailer who turned out to be her student, but apparently Bannerman had been contacted, too, and he'd freaked. She was afraid he was capable of killing someone and he wanted her to set up her student. By then the police artist had come and they updated Sullenberger's picture and added his new identity.

"He wants to hear from me this afternoon, detective," Gwen said when Hickey was all done. "What should I do?"

Hickey was already thinking two steps ahead. He held up his index finger for a moment and brought it down on a red button on his phone. It was his direct line to Hurtubise. "Boss?" he asked when Hurtubise picked up. "How many officers can you give me to brief in the next hour?"

Hurtubise said, "Don't fucking shit with me, Hickey. Tell me what's up?"

And Hickey told him, "Maybe you're about to give me my retirement present."

"Professor Van Loon," Hickey said when he finally put the phone down. "If you're willing, this is exactly what we'd like you to do."

Chapter Twenty-six

The first call from her told Wheeler nothing very much. She said she had to leave a message for her student to call her back, but there was no answer. She'd called three times. That had been just after 1.30. "You're home?" he'd asked, and she said yes, and he wondered if university professors ever went to their offices once classes were over. He, on the other hand, was pissing away his Saturday day off because, for him, this was life and death. He couldn't risk being discovered, not now, and certainly not by some amateur blackmailer with the hots for his teacher.

The second call came an hour later. He was almost going to call her because he'd said call me within the hour and she'd pushed it to the limit like women always seem to do. Still nothing, she said, and she didn't know what to do. He could hear fear in her voice, which was good. Apparently the kid lived with his rich parents somewhere in Forest Hill. He didn't have anything to tell her except she'd better fucking set this up, and quick.

By the third call, Wheeler was convinced that she was trying her best. She'd been in touch with her student and he was willing to meet. She'd suggested her condo, which is what Wheeler told her to say, thinking he could hide on the balcony or in a closet. The guy was probably going to be too horny or antsy to check the place for an intruder. She said the student's name was Tommy. She said Tommy was going to get back to her.

He congratulated himself for the idea that had made her so

compliant—zonking her out and letting F have her fun. Gwen, he was sure, was hetero but F had a way of making someone forget her sexual preferences. All he needed to do to keep Gwen in line was to have F primed and ready, and she was eager enough to do that.

While he was waiting, Wheeler wondered again why he hadn't gotten a call from Tommy himself. The envelope with the blackmail photo had been stuffed through his mailbox four days ago, with a note saying, *Someone would be in touch.* So Tommy knew where he lived. But nobody had gotten in touch. Nobody had phoned or left another note. Wheeler thought it should be easy enough to trace his cellphone number but then he remembered he was still cycling through burner phones and Tommy might not have caught up. Besides, the kid was preoccupied with Gwen, and who could blame him. Gwen was probably quite a nice little wet dream for a struggling university student. Shit, sending her on that erotic shopping trip, spending all that time on the phone with her suggesting all that shit. Why wouldn't he like the real thing?

Wheeler said to make it sound like you might fuck him if he handed everything over. Guy like that, he should be easy to deal with.

Wheeler knew he couldn't risk procuring a gun so he'd made a rope garotte wrapped with tape at the ends, and he figured he'd wait until Tommy, who sounded like he didn't need much encouragement, was in bed with Gwen and strangle him from behind. What he'd do with the professor, however, was another matter. She would have to be taken care of, too, although it might be a stretch to set up a scene in her condo to make the cops believe she was having an S and M affair with her student and things got out of control. Maybe Gwen would have to take a leap into the Don Valley ravine from her eleventh-floor balcony. Something like that.

His fourth call from her came just after 4, and there was a problem.

"He doesn't want to come to my place. He said no fucking way."

Wheeler didn't like it. Not one bit. Once his plans were made, he never changed them. He didn't like people who did. "So tell me where he said instead."

"You're not going to believe this," she said. "He says to meet him at the motel."

"Fuck, the Elmgrove?"

"Yes. Same room. I couldn't remember which one but he knew. He wants me to meet him there tomorrow at four. Room twelve."

"I don't see how that's going to work," Wheeler said.

"I told him I didn't want to do that but he's insisting. What are we going to do?"

"What did you tell him?"

"Like you said. I said exactly what you told me to. The deal was always he'd give me the pictures if I agreed to drop the plagiarism. Now, who knows? I'm afraid he's going to expect something more."

Wheeler kept his voice menacingly calm, but with a hint of a sneer. "I certainly understand him wanting *that.*"

"Why don't we talk about how you are going to help me?"

"What if I said give him what he wants?"

"You bastard. You don't actually expect me to be alone with him, do you?"

"Why not—you have this thing for younger men, don't you?"

"Look, I'm not going to do this—I'm not—unless you can tell me where you'll be, and it had better be very close."

But he had no intention of telling her that. "Relax," he said. "If you play your part right, you'll be off the hook, too. You won't have to compromise your precious academic reputation."

"And how do you think you can accomplish that?"

"Just leave it to me, okay? Less you know, less you'll worry."

After he hung up, Wheeler decided to walk to Lawrence and buy a *Saturday Star*, maybe grab a bite at Sawyers Deli. F was going to be out at showings until at least 7, she said, and then they'd talk. F was chafing to know when she might get her next shot at Gwen Van Loon.

Once you get a taste, it's like fucking catnip.

On his way, he wondered about the risk of taking care of the kid at such a public place. The Elmgrove had been like a parking garage the night he'd taken Gwen there, but tomorrow was Sunday and bound to be quieter. He guessed even lonely Rosedale housewives needed their day off. Gwen would be a problem, though, especially if Tommy wanted a roll with her and he was late coming to the rescue. Then he wondered if maybe he could use F in a creative way to keep her occupied.

At Sawyers he ordered pastrami on rye and managed to claim a couple of sections of the fat Saturday paper. *The Star* couldn't hold a candle to the *Sun* for its coverage of the trial but it had a columnist, Rosie DiManno, who seemed to think the conspirators had a chance of getting off. She based that on Juris' devastating cross of the cops—Cleverley and, shit, even Hickey. Wheeler thought she was so intent on being provocative that she downplayed the Crown's later undressing of Desmond Burnside. He'd have to wait until the morning to read Pete Smythe's more measured weekly sum-up of the week's testimony in the *Sunday Sun*.

Pity about Prof. Van Loon, he thought, tucking into the thick pastrami that sort of reminded him of the sharp taste left in his mouth after going down on her that night at the motel.

Fuck, the lady was a bit of a prissy dresser but not too shy about what she let herself get up to in bed, and he'd broken his rule and gone back for seconds.

Such a pity the nice lady had to check out before he fully broke her in.

Chapter Twenty-seven

If Tommy Paxton believed he was good at nothing much, at least he knew that he was excellent at one thing — watching. Hadn't he proved that by getting those photographs? Hadn't he proved it by successfully stalking Gwen Van Loon that day he sent her shopping, lagging back for the most part but once venturing so close he could actually smell her hair. She had a scent like sandalwood. He liked that. Now he was watching again, knowing she was waiting for him in there.

He knew she was alone because forty-five minutes ago he'd seen her arrive by cab and check in, dressed disappointingly, he thought . . . light coat, black tights, tall boots, nothing revealing at all.

No one had joined her. Tommy, scrunched down in the front seat of his car across the street from the Elmgrove, was particularly looking out for a late-model Civic with a license that ended in 9113—James Bannerman's car, because that would tell him this was a trap. Bannerman, that one time he'd seen him, looked like he might be able to take care of himself. Of the half-dozen cars in the parking lot this early hour, none was familiar. Tommy knew she could have also gone to the police, but didn't think she was that stupid, and there was no sign of surveillance.

People don't look around anymore. That was his experience. They look at their cellphones and they look at their TVs and they look at their own reflections in windows. They're so self-absorbed they don't notice people who tend to blend in, like he did, and might be following them, or stalking, intent on doing harm. The body's natural defence mechanisms have been disabled by atrophy.

She had told him 4. It was now half-past and he wanted to be sure. He was still trying to figure out why she'd suggested meeting here, surprising him by telling him on the phone yesterday afternoon. "Why don't we talk about what you really want?"

He thought he'd just finished telling her that. He'd put all the pictures in a zipped drive and he'd hand that over, once she gave him back his plagiarized paper marked with an A. He suggested dropping by her office Monday morning.

"What do you mean?" he'd asked.

"Why don't you just say it?"

"Look, you sound like you're trying to make a point and I'm not getting it."

"Oh, I think you get it," she said. "The point is, maybe it's something we both want."

"Yeah?" he asked, not really taking her seriously. "Shall we make it your place then?"

There was a long pause. "How about your favourite motel?"

That stopped him. He didn't know what to say. He remembered asking her about her shopping trip, whether she'd been scared or else a bit turned on, and she'd said *maybe a little of both*. He hadn't taken her seriously, figured it was her way of playing obedient and getting him off the phone. *Now? Fuck.*

"Same room if we can manage it," she said in her cool voice. "Otherwise I won't be able to compare, will I."

"Are you shitting me, lady?"

"Your pictures showed you what I like," she said. "Aren't you curious to give it a try?"

Now, playing it back in his head, Tommy knew something wasn't right. *Fuck, students called her The Ice Maiden behind her back.*

Just then a man came outside from the motel office with a

broom and half-heartedly pretended to sweep the entrance, but he seemed to spend most of his time looking around. His buddy, DM, had told him the front desk clerk had worked there for years, guy in his late fifties named Stover who used a cane and was bent over like Quasimodo. This guy looked way different.

Tommy thought Prof. Van Loon might have to wait a little longer for him.

Gwen looked at her watch again. It seemed she'd been doing that every ten minutes, every five since it passed 4 o'clock. *Where is he? It's half past.* She was lying on her back on the bed waiting and her high boots hurt but she dared not slip them off. She dared not slip anything off. Better to just wait on the bed — the same bed — for her blackmailer to come calling.

The bedsprings made noise as she shifted her hips. They had that night as well, the night James had been all over her and she all over him. "A boneshaker of a bed," he'd called it. "Good thing there's no one listening downstairs." *That should have been what I said, not him. I'm the one who should have cared about that, someone finding out what I was up to.* But then she corrected herself. Back then, she didn't know. She didn't know that James was not really James, that he was someone else. A killer. That he was using her to lure Tommy Paxton here and kill him.

She studied the ceiling for the exact spot she'd focused on when he had his hungry face buried between her warm thighs, and she was trying her best not to come too soon for him. He'd been good at doing that to her, very, very good. The room had one of those dappled, old-fashioned stucco ceilings with spots and swirls that looked like things, and in a few minutes she found it, just to the right of the urine-coloured light, a shape that reminded her of a vagina. Perhaps what he'd been doing made her imagine that. They'd left the light on in their haste for sex and she remembered it wasn't very romantic. Somehow the spot looked different now, and she glanced instead at her watch again. *Four thirty-six. Jesus.*

She hadn't heard from James, and that worried her. She assumed he must have been nearby, waiting for his quarry to arrive. She wondered if she should risk phoning Hickey again—this wasn't going according to plan—but she knew where he was, in that room facing hers on the other leg of the L, and he'd know what to do without her coaching or freaking out.

And you are freaked out, she said to herself. Her stomach felt like it was tumbling in loops, that unwelcome queasy feeling when there were too many unknowns competing for your attention. To distract herself she looked up and studied the tacky motel picture framed above the bed. She hadn't noticed it that night when she'd been occupied by James. It looked like a bad impressionist print of some gay street scene in Paris or Brussels, and it seemed out of place in this seedy room that smelled of disinfectant. She looked over and saw the chair by the bathroom door where he'd draped her dress and cardigan after the first time, picking them from the floor and leaving them there until 6 in the morning when he'd offered her the shower first, that drippy, moldy, cramped shower, and he'd slipped in and joined her there. She still couldn't remember how many times they'd had sex. She hadn't bothered to count all the condom wrappers he'd left on the floor beside the bed.

She knew that Tommy, when he arrived, would probably expect sex with her, too. Perhaps she'd been too explicit about that, made him think she was up for it, or was there something about this drab room that made men assume they were entitled to it? No, she knew it was all because of what James had coached her to say, to ensure her student showed up. She still wasn't sure what he might be showing up for. *But he wasn't showing up, was he. Perhaps he was watching, like he had watched that night, only now he suspected this might be a trap.*

She studied the ceiling again, trying to find a pattern that didn't suggest part of her anatomy. Her mother had told her you can do that — choose your own reality. Widen your perspective, dissipate your fears. Focus on something else. She hadn't thought about her mother for a long time. How strange to think of her now. Mother certainly wouldn't have approved of her waiting for a man in a motel — not that night with James, not now. "Good girls don't check themselves into such places in the middle of the afternoon," she'd probably say. Gwen thought she discerned a candle in the pattern overhead, a candle with a small flame, and was puzzled to find that it made her think of Gerald.

She wondered which of her predicaments was worse — this one, lying like the reluctant bait in a trap, fully dressed in a modest pullover and tights, or that night with James, naked and getting enthusiastically shafted into the bedsprings. The comparison made her even more anxious, and she bounced her bottom on the bed to hear the springs squeak again. She settled into the little hollow in the mattress they'd snuggled into between their love-makings and imagined his rough hands on her again, and his breath hissing into her neck, when James had been James and not some monster she was helping to hunt.

My secret is a hostage who's somehow broken free. Wasn't it always about the risk? The threat of his unpredictable rough desires? I loved being overwhelmed by him, consumed by him, fucked out of my skin by him, left with only the funk of his scent on the pillow and my own raw carnal hunger.

Suddenly, her cellphone rang.

Hickey was watching the door to Unit 12 like a hawk from behind the drapes in Unit 15. Four of his men were with him, silently crouched on the bed, checking their Glocks after their long wait. Three more were out back in riot gear and four officers waited in two unmarked cruisers around the corner ready to swoop in when Hickey gave the word. A thirteenth had been installed in the office and instructed to let no one else check in. All the resources Hurtubise had been able to muster. They'd taken up position one by one early that morning.

He didn't need to look at his watch to know that Tommy was late. The sickly green numbers flickering from the Elmgrove sign in the parking lot told him it was 4.38.

Why does this shit always happen?

Nobody who hasn't been a cop understands the monotonous routine of law enforcement. Cops spend a lot of time waiting. Hickey, like most cops he knew, got into policing for other reasons, mainly to help people and make the world a safer place. Rookie officers often felt invincible, as if they had a heroic role to play — as brave defenders of justice and armed enforcers of the law. Sooner or later — later in Hickey's case — they had that idealism and noble purpose crushed out of them. The long hours wore you down. Favouritism and petty office politics destroyed morale. The unpredictable danger cops faced on any shift could turn them sour and cynical about the goodness of their fellow man. Hickey called it Tightrope Walker Syndrome, and it went like this—cops took to the high wire because of the challenge of cheating gravity to thrill a crowd, but they got worn down by the sickly fear of inching across a wire and losing their balance and falling without a safety net. Cops, Hickey believed, were the safety net for a warped society, and they were all alone on that wire. Sooner or later cops reacted accordingly to their hostile environment — they started drawing their weapons more often, even on routine traffic stops. They knew that the criminals usually had the advantage. Criminals were usually pretty sure of what they were doing, whereas cops were always the reactors. They never knew what they might be walking into. The next person they stopped could be a law-abiding citizen, or a cold-blooded, drugged-up psychopath with a gun.

There were only so many risks a person was willing to take. What cops did with that, when they felt they could be reaching their quota, is try to focus on something safer — and in Hickey's case, for the last few weeks and more than a few of his hours waiting here, he realized he had been thinking more and more about retirement.

His radio squawked. It was Cleverley in Car Alpha, parked just around the corner on Westray. "Brown Kia with someone in the driver's seat parked across the street, forty-five degrees to your left," he called in.

Hickey looked but his view was blocked by another parked car. "Our blackmailer?" Hickey asked.

Cleverley replied, "Check. Car's registered to Thomas Paxton. Will watch."

So where was Wheeler?

If they were lucky, they'd get one shot at him, Hickey thought, and he knew his plan was far from perfect. For one thing, this was a public place. There were people checked into three other rooms — long-term or overnight guests, Stover had told them, and they absolutely mustn't be disturbed. Hickey decided there wasn't much point in even checking the names. No one who stayed here probably ever gave their real one.

But the bigger flaw was that Gwen Van Loon was more exposed than he wanted her to be. He and his men could be out of their room and into hers in 20 seconds, and that could be a long time, especially if Wheeler was going to barge in after Tommy with a gun, which is how Hickey figured this could go down. Hickey had vetoed Cleverley's idea of stopping him before he got to the door, figuring that might risk a gun battle in a parking lot, which was never a good idea.

But Hickey wasn't going to order anything before he knew exactly where Wheeler was.

Just then his radio squawked and it was Gainey in Car

Beta, the second cop car patrolling streets within a five-block radius. "Code twenty-seven. Honda Civic parked on Markland. License registered to a Bannerman, but it says Frieda not James. Please advise."

Chapter Twenty-Eight

Tommy Paxton, besides being way late, must have seen something he didn't like. Gwen saw his name on the phone display and nervously pressed answer.

"I'm changing your plan," he said. "Are you dressed? Undressed?" He spoke urgently, nervously, almost hyperventilating.

She said dressed.

"Good. Open the drapes and stand where I can see you."

Gwen got up from the bed and parted the heavy drapes. The late afternoon light stung her eyes. When she was able to focus, she could see nothing other than the empty, cracked tarmac of the parking lot and the yellow time sign and some cars parked along the street. If he was able to see her looking in, she certainly couldn't see any sign of him looking out.

She thought the movement at the window would alert Hickey but she realized what Tommy Paxton's instruction was intended to do. She couldn't use her phone, he'd see her doing it. Hickey would have to guess what was going on.

"What now?" she asked. "I thought you might have changed your mind."

His voice seemed to recover his control. "So where the fuck's your boyfriend, Gwen?"

So he did suspect a trap. She wondered what she could say to reassure him. "I told you he's not my boyfriend anymore."

"I think he's there with you, isn't he? Or nearby."

"No, he's not." She wasn't sure what else to say. "Are you coming in or not?"

"No," he said. "You're coming out."

"Wait," she said, not expecting this kind of change. "You want me to come out? Why?"

"Hang on a minute. Fuck."

"What's the matter?"

He didn't say anything, just kept her on the phone. She thought she heard the sound of a car starting, but maybe it was her imagination. She just stood there wondering what he wanted her to do next, and knew that if she got in a car with him, and he even suspected she might have solicited help, her life would be in danger.

"Okay," he said after a long pause. "Here's the drill, Gwenny. I'll be in a white car. Leave the room and get in as soon as I pull up. Two minutes."

Hickey hadn't thought of *this*, she realized angrily. She certainly didn't sign up for *this*.

Just then she heard a door opening and movement behind her, and another person's voice. A voice that wasn't Hickey's either.

"Make him come in," a man's voice said.

Surprised, she turned and saw James Bannerman, holding a menacing length of rope in his hand. The door to the adjoining room was open—in her nervousness she'd forgotten to check it was locked—and sidling smokily through it behind him was Frieda, whose intent was already registering on her covetous face.

CHAPTER TWENTY-NINE

"We've got movement," Cleverley's voice squawked in his ear.

"Who?" Hickey asked, barking back into the radio. He'd noticed the drapes being parted in Unit 12 and Gwen standing at the window. There was no reason for her to be standing there. She was supposed to wait for Tommy to come to her door, then let him in.

"Paxton," Cleverley reported. "Gainey says the Civic's empty."

Hickey knew what that meant. Wheeler, or Bannerman, or Sullenberger must have already been in the motel. Perhaps he'd checked in last night before they got their stakeout organized. He kicked himself for yielding to Stover's arguments against disturbing guests. *Christ, wasn't one of the occupied rooms Unit 13?*

When he turned his attention back to Number 12, she wasn't at the window anymore. *What the fuck was going on?*

"Follow him in," Hickey ordered Cleverley and Gainey. He grabbed his service Glock and shouted, "Let's go" to his men, wrenching open the door.

Everything seemed to happen at once—the frantic dash by armed men along 20 feet of walkway to get to the other room, the white car pulling up off to the side followed by the squeal of tires as Cleverley and Gainey rushed in to sandwich it off, the crash through the door with the police battering ram and, when Hickey managed to stumble into the room, four cops with their Glocks drawn and their quarry standing on the other side of the bed with a ligature wound around Gwen Van Loon's neck.

Okay then. There are only two ways this can go.

CHAPTER THIRTY

H is breath was short and his heart was pounding. *Jesus Christ!* Wheeler knew the symptoms of high adrenaline. He'd experienced them often enough, whenever he placed his gun at someone's head intending to pull the trigger. But he'd learned to anticipate and handle that kind of adrenaline shock. *Fuck!* It wasn't anything like this.

There'd been no warning, absolutely no sign they were onto him. All he'd had time to do when he heard the squealing of tires and people running outside was grab Gwen and use her as a shield. He didn't like his chances, confronted by all these cops, but he tightened the rope around her neck and felt her press back against him, gagging and gasping for air.

He saw Hickey enter the room. The detective stopped on the other side of the bed and took stock of the situation. Unlike the other cops, he didn't have his gun out and he looked calm.

"You hurt her and we'll kill you on the spot," Hickey said in a low, even voice. "Is that how you want this to end, Mr. Sullenberger?"

Shit he knows my real name. How did the little bastard manage to figure it all out?

Wheeler knew that, if a shooter was good, he could pull off a head shot on a silhouette target at this distance maybe 90 percent of the time. He'd spent lots of time on the range. But silhouette targets didn't move and hostages did. And there was only a small area of the face that was the kill zone — what trainers called the T-box, middle of the eyes, eyebrows to top of mouth. You gotta be good to hit that, and most cops probably weren't that good. They didn't put in the time. So there was a one or two out of ten chance they'd miss or the shot wouldn't be fatal. He didn't think Hickey would want to take that chance.

Wheeler's mind was racing. *What's the best I can hope for? What's the worst? What's the price for Malvolio's wish – life without pain?*

He was going to go to prison for a long time, he knew that. And he was certain the cops weren't going to let him leave with someone whose life was in danger. Not a lot of options.

Hickey seemed to be reading his mind. "I can think of a better way," he said. "Do you want to talk about it, son?"

He eased up on the rope to let Gwen breathe. He didn't want to choke her to death. Perhaps she had something to do with them finding him, perhaps not, it was not a point to get hung up on anymore. It wouldn't help his situation to have her thrashing around or passing out. Her standing still in front of him was the only protection he had.

"So talk," Wheeler said.

Instead, Hickey seemed to notice who was lying on the bed in front of him, her blouse hanging out and her short skirt askew. Frieda Bannerman didn't look like her real estate photo anymore. Her eyes were locked open, like she'd just been caught in a searchlight on a dark night. Suddenly her play room was filled up with cops.

"I'm Detective-Sergeant Hickey, Mrs. Bannerman. We mean you no harm. We're here for your husband."

All she managed to ask in a croak was a weak, "Why?" She looked petrified.

Hickey glanced back at Wheeler. "Do you want me to tell her, or will you?"

Wheeler said nothing.

"We believe he murdered twelve people, ma'am," he said to her. "He was paid a lot of money to do it."

That was clever of him, Wheeler thought. Telling her she married a monster was bad enough, but also gave her a good reason to resent all the times he'd tried to sponge off her income, not contributing a cent to running the household. There was venom in the look she directed his way.

The room was still bristling with Glocks but Hickey chose that moment to do something disarming. He shoved his hands in his pockets and slowly moved to his right behind his officers, then back the other way in front of them—not coming around the bed or anything threatening, just showing him that maybe it was time to discuss this calmly like reasonable people.

"You know what I wondered? I wondered why you were still hanging around," Hickey said. He stopped and looked his way, perhaps to check that Gwen Van Loon was breathing properly. "All I could figure was that it was to follow the trial, am I right?"

"Right enough," Wheeler said. *Why not?* "I never knew why they were doing what they were doing. We never even met."

"So tell me, what do you think? Is that a defence that's gonna work for you?"

"Why is that important, what I think?"

"Oh, because you're a professional," Hickey said. "And they're not."

Wheeler didn't think that was a bad card to play under the circumstances. Flattering someone—even if it was for pulling off a dozen murders—was probably right there in the police handbook for how to handle hostage situations. There was probably also other stuff like widening the suspect's options, making him think, making him feel understood, that sort of thing. As a matter of fact, as he'd followed the trial, he'd formed quite a negative opinion about the people who hired him. They were amateurs, entitled and arrogant elitist amateurs, and it seemed to him they had a good chance at getting away with it. He, on the other hand, was now a lock to pay for their sins.

"Listen son," Hickey said, taking his hands out of his pockets and placing them on his hips. "You won't get out of here alive the way this is going. Why don't you just release the lady?"

Wheeler managed a tight smile. "I don't think I'm going to get points for good behavior, am I?"

Hickey shook his head. "No, but then we can talk about letting you maybe have something else."

Wheeler felt he had to think about that. He didn't want to go back to prison but he didn't want to die either. He didn't think Toronto police would get much blowback if they decided to just open fire when he released Gwen. The only neutral witness was F and he didn't think she'd be sympathetic anymore.

"Okay," he said finally. "What guarantees?"

"What? Guarantees that we won't shoot you down?"

"Something like that, yeah."

Hickey shrugged. "Why would we? You haven't heard what I want to say yet."

"About?" he asked. "Why don't you give me a hint?"

"Oh, let's say about how it might be in your interest to help us nail these clowns for good, son."

CHAPTER THIRTY-ONE

Courtroom 4-2 was an entirely different kind of place on verdict day, especially since it marked the end of an important trial that had gripped the city's interest and shaken it to its moral core. Toronto the Good, they once called it. This trial had far more sinister themes — vigilante justice in defence of order, criminality to protect the law, piousness in the service of evil, entitlement as an excuse for getting away with serial murder.

First to arrive were the committed and the curious — reporters, most of whom had been there every day, and a brace of lawyers who happened to be around and not arguing cases themselves. It was the second day of deliberation and word had gone out at 10.30 that the jury had reached its verdicts. Hickey, who guessed it would be quick, had used his police privileges to slip Stephanie in. She could have claimed one of the seats in front with relatives of the victims but chose to abide with Hickey at the back. There were still empty seats around them but Hickey figured they'd be claimed soon by curious members of the public who'd been hooked by the high stakes at the trial and wanted to witness its conclusion. They'd drift in as the line-ups cleared through security downstairs. A lot of people besides Stephanie would be skipping work this morning to see this.

A quick verdict is usually a guilty one, Maddow always said. Hickey knew conviction statistics would surprise anyone who believed the justice system was more balanced. Nearly 65 percent of criminal cases in the province of Ontario ended in guilty verdicts. Acquitted—a mere 3 percent. The rest were dismissed, stayed or the charges were withdrawn, usually as the result of plea bargains. Still, the verdicts in this one had so much riding on them that Hickey felt uncharacteristically nervous.

Stephanie squeezed his arm reassuringly. "Be still, my heart," she whispered and pressed close.

They were getting along better since she moved out. She said that was because they'd been forced to come to terms with what they most required from each other. For her, it was respect for her independence. For him, respect for the relationships he had to forego in order to do his job. "We were pushing too far into each other's private spaces," she'd told him on one of their dates. Once this case was disposed of—one way or the other—Hickey knew he'd have to deal with the feelings he had for her.

When she said she wanted to be in court when the verdict came down, he was mildly surprised, until she told him it wasn't because of her involvement, but his.

"I know how important this is to you, Hickey—three years of your life."

It was now almost a month since he'd arrested Wheeler at the Elmgrove. The next day Maddow, instead of delivering his closing arguments, filed for an adjournment on grounds that new evidence *that goes to the heart of the case* had surfaced and it would be impossible for the jury to decide guilt or innocence without hearing it. Juris and the other defence attorneys, of course, reacted with surprise and objections but because the arrest of Wheeler was obviously relevant, ended up petitioning for a delay to prepare for cross-examination. Judge Foley noted how unusual it was to be asked to adjourn a criminal trial that was about to wrap up, but allowed it on grounds of fairness and the public's interest in the efficient administration of justice. A telling argument used by

Maddow was that the evidence already heard could very well be influenced by the new testimony. The fact that both sides had requested the continuance was not a factor, Judge Foley archly explained, since a judge is always master of his own proceeding.

Wheeler's riveting testimony two days ago, of course, drew international attention—one of the few times a serial killer-for-hire has ever taken the witness stand. He told how he got his orders, produced as evidence the cheques he was paid with, and described the role laid out for him by Judge Leishman and Morgan Cathcart. He also confessed to a twelfth killing—Cathcart at his wife's grave.

Many of the outside media, including the *New York Times* and CNN, were staying for the verdict and another courtroom had been set aside with a video feed so everyone could be accommodated.

Courtroom 4-2 was filling up around them, and Hickey took the time to explain to Stephanie what would happen. The defendants would be brought in over there and be ushered to their boxes, then the judge would enter back there and call things to order, then he would wait for the jurors to troop in from that door there. He pointed out Maddow, who he thought looked brightly confident, and Juris, who was as inscrutable as ever, and some of the media he thought she might recognize, including Christie Blatchford of the *National Post* and Rosie DiManno of the *Star*, the city's two most popular columnists who usually agreed on things but had come down on different sides this time—Blatchford predicting convictions all around, DiManno writing several times and at length of the very real possibility that the Mandamus Six could walk free.

Of course, since Stephanie hadn't attended any part of the trial, he pointed out Sheridan Barrie, who'd been there every day in the front row, and how he had to endure the brutal cross-examination of the pompous Desmond Burnside, and learn that the powerful man he'd turned to in his hour of need had played a role in ordering his son's death.

He also drew her attention to Blanche Burnside, the stunning wife, who today was turned out in a purple off-the-shoulder number with stiletto heels. She seemed to be dripping with jewelry. She'd been there most every day, too, playing the role of her life — steadfast beautiful younger spouse of a wrongly charged exemplar of society.

"Now that," Stephanie whispered cattily, "probably set her back fifteen thousand dollars at Holt's."

"So tell me, I'm curious," Hickey said. "What did you notice coming in, the way other people dress when they go to court?"

"Notice? How do you mean?"

"In the halls. The people who look like they're waiting for their cases to be called."

She squeezed his arm again. "If you've got a point, Hickey, why don't you just spit it out?"

"Lots of people in hoodies and jeans, right?"

"Meaning?"

"People in nice tailored suits and Holt's dresses are very rare here, wouldn't you say?"

They'd talked about it often enough. Hickey confessed that he'd started out as an idealistic cop but bitter experience taught him the truth — that the so-called rule of law had begat a vast and impenetrable bureaucracy designed to criminalize poverty and weakness and immunize wealth and success.

"Since when have you turned into such a cynic?" she'd asked.

No, he said, he knew it was possible for the wealthy to literally buy justice. Early in his career he'd charged the son of a rich real estate developer with manslaughter for getting drunk and running down a mother and child with his Porsche. He was just a pampered, spoiled and reckless twenty-one-year-old brat but he never served a day in jail or prison because everyone accepted that he was someone of promise who could learn from his mistake. His parents hired the best lawyers, paid for the best experts, had the highest-profile friends who could vouch for the boy's character and potential, and it worked. It was the same formula that usually spared the few well-heeled businessmen who got caught committing white-collar crimes. They escaped with fines instead of prison terms because, after all, they had businesses to run and employees to pay. Some rich people were too important to punish, just as some banks were too big to fail.

"So guess who gets convicted?" he'd asked Stephanie. "Roughly sixty percent of people in prison are racial and ethnic minorities, many who lack the resources rich people enjoy."

"So you're saying racial discrimination is to blame? That's it?"

"No, it's not as simple as that. These are people whose neighbourhoods are more likely to be policed, who are more likely to be stopped for no reason, who are more likely to be charged rather than warned, who are more likely to be incarcerated instead of released pending trial and who are less likely to be able to afford adequate counsel. They are more likely to be locked up for actions that are linked to poverty, lack of education, lack of a job, mental health concerns and histories of sexual abuse and trauma."

"So unfairness is engrained in the system. Is that what you're saying?"

"Look," he said. "Prisons have become the new residential schools. Twenty-seven percent of the prison population is aboriginal."

"And your point is?"

"Aboriginals make up only four percent of the population."

Maddow had touched on these themes in his summation. "For whatever reason this case has not become simply a media sensation, but something of a liminal moment, a chance for us to take stock of what we and our society have become," he'd said. "Above all, the rule of law should guide us but here we have its opposite. These defendants, with moralistic and self-righteous zeal, resolved to take the law in their own hands. Self-appointed vigilantes, they set out to do on their own what they felt the laws of the land could not accomplish. You are here to decide whether the idea of equal justice under the law for all people is a reality, or is but an empty dream."

Stephanie had drawn him out of his funk with her usual ironic sense of humour. "Listen, Hickey," she'd said over chicken marbella and wine at her condo last night. "You need to stop this. You're starting to think like the people you're trying to put behind bars."

That stopped him short. Christ, and what was he thinking of doing about it? The Mandamus Six had taken the law into their own hands in a misguided attempt to right the justice system. He'd caught them at it and was determined to see them do time. With any justice, that would happen. The systemic abuses he was concerned about — unequal justice, entitlement, racism, elitism — defied such easy solutions. They required much harder work. Perhaps his growing cynicism was blinding him to that truth. Perhaps, as part of that system, he was even part of the problem—

Stephanie squeezed his arm, bringing him out of his thoughts, and Hickey saw the court clerk rise and the large room fell into a hush.

"All rise."

Hickey had been in court for moments like this many times, and he knew that twelve strangers, from many walks of life, had been compelled to reach a life-changing verdict based on a common-sense consideration of the evidence presented to them, and they could surprise even the finest legal minds. Their job was to decide this case beyond reasonable doubt, which Judge Foley had stressed to them was a very high bar to clear, especially in a murder conspiracy case. If there were two sets of facts and each one seemed plausible, they had to acquit. Most legal authorities agreed that *beyond a reasonable doubt* required jurors to be at least 98 percent certain that the evidence proved the defendants to be guilty.

Judge Ezra Foley managed to delay his entrance just long enough to ratchet up the suspense and drama in the courtroom even more, and he took up his position without his usual pile of evidence and notes. He nodded sternly to counsel who took their seats followed by the media and spectators in court. And instead of instructing the clerk to do what everyone was waiting for, he took a moment to address his courtroom.

"Before the court calls in the jury and receives the verdicts, I need to remind all of you present that this is a court of law. The court recognizes the emotional nature of this case and its importance to all parties involved. However, verbal outbursts or displays of emotion will not be tolerated. Any violation of this rule will result in your removal from my courtroom."

A small man with prominent eyebrows and thin, wispy gray hair, Foley looked around like an owl to determine that he was understood. Then he turned to his clerk and asked, "I'm told the jury has reached a verdict?"

"It has, your honour."

"Then you may call them in."

The clerk instructed everyone to rise and a door opened and the jurors shuffled slowly into the room and took their seats. Hickey scanned each face, looking for clues to what they'd decided. He noticed that the foreman, a bespectacled, fortyish Toronto transit driver who'd paid rapt attention during all testimony, avoided looking at any of the defendants or their lawyers. Maddow had told him jurors about to acquit usually looked at the accused.

Judge Foley asked everyone to be seated. There was almost complete silence in the courtroom.

"Ladies and gentlemen of the jury," Judge Foley said. "Have you reached your verdicts?"

The foreman stood. "We have, your honour."

Foley nodded to the clerk, who called on the first defendant to rise and face the jury. "Do you find the defendant Arthur Bailey Terwilliger guilty or not guilty of the charge of conspiracy to commit murder?"

The foreman cleared his throat and said, "We find the defendant . . . guilty."

The courtroom reacted, but almost in disbelief rather than with loud cries of triumph or dismay. The only sounds were the rustle of reporters tweeting out the stunning news and people in the crowd—presumably family and friends of the defendants—gasping and embracing each other because the unthinkable had actually happened. Hickey, who'd squeezed his eyes closed until he heard the foreman say guilty, opened them to see Stephanie's smiling face.

"Hickey! Wow! Will that happen to all of them?" she asked in a whisper, and Hickey nodded.

One by one the other defendants were asked to stand and receive their verdicts. Selwyn Forbes Balfour, guilty. Nathaniel Tarnes Hodge, guilty. Gabriel Carson-White, guilty. Gregory Carl Jaccobs, guilty. When, finally, Desmond Scott Eaton Burnside, QC, rose in his plexiglass dock and faced the jury, every juror looked back at him. Hickey knew he could be wrong but chose to interpret that as a hopeful sign—of civil society registering its contempt for someone whose sworn duty had been to uphold and strengthen the law, but whose

murderous actions had undermined it. Burnside refused to
flinch when he heard his guilty verdict, gamely wearing his
privilege to the end. But in the gallery, his coiffed young wife
fell into the arms of friends, quietly sobbing, playing her part
out as perhaps it had been scripted for her.

Judge Foley thanked the jurors for their deliberations and
ordered the defendants held until sentencing in two weeks —
a small gesture but, Hickey thought, a significant one, since
that usually only happened to people of lesser means. The
rich usually were able to put up their multi-million-dollar
homes as surety and be given time to put their affairs in order.

Before he ushered Stephanie out of the courtroom into the
crowded corridors, Hickey received a handwritten note
passed back from Maddow by a constable that said, "That's
another one for common justice, my friend."

"You know," he said to Stephanie, after they managed to
avoid the press by finding their way out the back door of the
courthouse, "there are friends of those men who will see this
as a great miscarriage of justice, a sign that the barbarians
have been allowed inside the gate."

"Then here's to more barbarians," she said, squeezing his
hand and pressing close.

They took their time walking slowly across Nathan Phillips
Square, in front of Mies van der Rowe's iconic City Hall,
which looked like a giant clam opening to embrace the sun to
the south over Lake Ontario. There was a band playing music
from a stage near the large reflecting pool and groups of tourists taking pictures — ordinary people doing ordinary things,
and taking their time doing it.

"So what now, Detective Hickey?" Stephanie asked.

She may just have been asking him where he wanted to go
for dinner or a drink.

But he turned to her and said, "You know, I think I've decided you might find me more agreeable as a retired person.

You willing to take that on, Miss Lord?"

You may also enjoy the following from eXtasy Books Inc:

In Extremis
V.V. Drummond
Released July 2018
The prequel to Clueless

Excerpt

First thing Jason Oosterhuis did when he got out was take the bus to Toronto and check into the Chelsea. It would be one of the last things he'd ever do. Slightly upscale honky-tonk suited his frame of mind—a big, anonymous hotel that had seen better days, just steps away from the centre of action. He strolled around downtown to stretch his legs, stopping only to look at the provocative pictures of dancing girls in the window of the Zanzibar Tavern, then came back to his room to enjoy a long, hot, soapy shower. Getting ready for a little trouble tonight, and wasn't he way overdue for that. Two hundred a night for the room, shit. Hell of a better deal than the three hundred and fifty a day it had cost to keep him in a Canadian prison.

Not that he minded it. Managed to keep himself out of trouble, which took a little doing on account of wife beaters didn't exactly rank highly on the social scale there, even though actually doing it was perfectly understandable to many men he met doing time. Sentence was six years, but he got out after thirty-nine months for good behaviour—and wasn't that a fucking joke.

Now Jason was soaking up his freedom, thinking of Stephanie and her Lhasa Apso she called Jill. The dog that wouldn't stop barking. Lively, playful, devoted, obedient, fearless, intelligent, she said when they got her, Stephanie reading from the brochure. The dog was really only good for one thing, though, which was barking every time he was beating Stephanie up.

She sent him the divorce papers soon after he got in. Well, let's see how much in demand she is now on the open market, with that jaw he broke one time, and that badly bent nose.

Jason—Candy to his friends when he had some—was thinking of maybe heading south somewhere, Cuba or Costa Rica, although Costa Rica was starting to crack down on guys like him, sex tourists no longer *simpatico con la pura vida*. There was Thailand, but he didn't think the little nest egg he'd put away would take him that far with enough left over to have any fun. He'd managed to squirrel away a bit of money working those three years legit after his first conviction, the one for sexual assault. Could have been for a hell of a lot more, too, that one. Got four, out in two. Fuck, how about beating the system twice like that?

First time's always the best, no? That little bunny Sara Jane McGoohey. Remembering her, just eighteen and a half, Bimbo Barbie, proud of everything and always showing it off, only not so foxy with it when he kept her in his basement for nine hours, having his fun and finishing with the duct tape when she made too much noise. At least he didn't bust up her pretty face. Oh, they could have got him for forcible confinement, too, but his lawyer plea-bargained that one away, raising reasonable doubt about whether Sara Jane was there against her will or by consent. To the Candy Man, it was always a bit of both. *See*—and he's thinking of the lawyer now, not Sara

Jane — *the whole secret to life is just knowing someone who understands the system you have to deal with.*

The parole board held up his release a few months because a psychologist called him a remorseless psychopath whose violence toward women was likely to escalate to serious bodily harm or death. He just waited them out. Shit, they were right about that, though, weren't they?

Maybe he'd just phone Stephanie up before he skipped bail, tell her what she could do with the divorce. Yeah, and even how that might go, them talking together after so long . . .

"Why are you calling me?" she'd probably ask. "I'm finished with you, Jason."

"Well, I sure ain't finished with you, you try asking for support."

"You never supported me when we were together. Why would I bother now, you bastard."

Stephanie could be quick like that. He liked it at first but it got old fast, like her complaining, and that fucking dog.

Or maybe he'd tell her she'd better go into hiding, knowing how he was. Make her go live with her pilot brother and his wife, give him a chance to do something to them, too, maybe make them watch through the drapes for him a lot. Stephanie, who married him on parole the first time, didn't even ask what he was on parole for, the stupid bitch.

Maybe she'd be dumb enough to ask how he got out so soon. That would be good, too. Give him a chance to tell her what the system looked like from inside, prisons crowded to overflowing so they had to let some out early so they could let all the rest in. Or about the bloodsucking lawyers, like his guy, good at fucking over the system, knowing which rules they could bend, getting rich on all the poor bastards careless enough to get caught. Imagine the holiday he could have had with the ten grand or so he had to fork out?

Or maybe he'd want to leave Stephanie with some of the thoughts he'd had that time in solitary. Like why women make up more than half of all crime victims but are a minority of offenders. Because most of their violence is caused by their mouths, and that hasn't been made illegal yet, although it sure as fuck should be. Or why they're mostly attacked by people they know? Don't have to strain yourself to figure that one out either.

All lathered up now and enjoying the luxury of lingering under hot water without the fear of getting something shoved up his ass, thinking maybe the best thing might be to not call her at all, just let her hear the usual way, the parole board telling her she might want to take precautions despite the restraining order against him. Let her think he may be coming to finish the job when he was really sunning his ass, sipping a margarita on a beach somewhere, his mind on other little things.

Wheeler learned about Jason Oosterhuis that morning, the usual way. Call from the same man as always. Just, "Oosterhuis, Chelsea Hotel, room one one four nine," nothing about the guy or what he'd done or what was supposed to happen. That was the arrangement. After so many times, there was a level of trust.

The hotel was familiar to Wheeler. He knew every room had its own balcony. That's where he was hiding when the guy came back to his room and headed for the shower, Wheeler having sneaked into the suite when he saw the maid's laundry cart parked in the hallway, the door wide open.

ABOUT THE AUTHOR

V.V. Drummond is the fiction pen name of John Miller. His first novel, In Extremis, was published in 2018 by eXtasy Books. Clueless is the sequel. Miller, a journalist and academic, won critical acclaim for Yesterday's News, a non-fiction warning about the future of newspapers, which he published with Fernwood Books in 1998. That book was chosen for the Globe and Mail's prestigious Hundred Notable Books list.